STRANGE PREY

AND

OTHER TALES OF THE HUNT

short fiction

by

George C. Chesbro

Published by
Apache Beach Publications
New Baltimore, New York
September/2004

ISBN: 1-930253-17-6

These stories originally appeared in the following publications:

"Strange Prey"
   Alfred Hitchcock's Mystery Magazine, Aug. 1970
"Broken Pattern"
   Alfred Hitchcock's Mystery Magazine, May 1972
"Snake In The Tower"
   Alfred Hitchcock's Mystery Magazine, March 1969
"Wotzel"
   Nugget, Oct. 1974
"Four Knights Game"
   Ellery Queen Mystery Magazine, Sept. 1974
"The Club of Venice"
   Mike Shayne Mystery Magazine, March 1974
"Tourist Trap"
   Alfred Hitchcock's Mystery Magazine, Oct. 1970
"Firefight of the Mind"
   Alfred Hitchcock's Mystery Magazine, Nov. 1970
"The Tower"
   Syracuse University Magazine, June 1989
"Dreams"
   Mike Shayne Mystery Magazine, April 1975
"The Dragon Variation"
   Alfred Hitchcock's Mystery Magazine, August 1975

For Rachael and Leah

STRANGE PREY

"It is most difficult to know to whom we are speaking; in this troubled world the Civilized and the Savage wear identical trappings." Sentor Thaag, speaking before the U.N. General Assembly.

It was starting again; someone was near.

Victor Rafferty looked up from the milky-blue water in time to see a squat, balding man with a limp emerge from the locker room at the opposite end of the pool. The man knelt clumsily in the gutter and grunted as he splashed handfuls of the cold water into his armpits and across his hairy chest.

Rafferty frowned with displeasure and stared down into the water at his own legs with their large, jagged patches of fish-white scar tissue that registered neither heat nor cold. He knew, of course, that the athletic club was open to any of its members at any time; yet this man had chosen a piece of the afternoon that Victor had come to think of as his own. The pool was usually deserted at this hour, enabling Victor to swim endlessly back and forth rebuilding his damaged body, savoring the silence in his mind that came only when he was alone and at peace. There wasn't any pain yet. The man was still too far away. Now there was only the familiar pressure in Victor's ears as if he were ascending in a plane, an agonizing buzzing sound that seemed to emanate from a vast, dark abyss somewhere behind his eyes.

The man was swimming in Victor's direction, struggling through the water with a ragged crawl. He drew closer, and Victor pressed his fingers hard against the chlorine-bleached tiles as the noise and pressure were suddenly transformed into a needle-strewn veil that seemed to float beneath his skull, lancing his brain as it closed around his mind. *It is so much worse with strangers,* he thought as he waited for knowledge of the man, which he knew would come next.

"Swimming," the man said, spewing water and blowing hard. He was hanging onto the edge of the pool, a few inches away from Victor. "Best all-'round conditioner there is. A man can't do enough of it."

Victor smiled and nodded through a haze of pain. The man pushed off the side and began to swim back toward the shallow end. Immediately the pain began to recede until finally there was only the residue of pressure and buzzing.

Rafferty knew the man was an accountant, suffered from hypertension, and had a headache that had been with him since early in the morning. He was also worried about his wife.

Madness, Victor thought grimly, rising and reaching for his towels.

He paused inside the locker room and stared at his naked image in one of the full-length mirrors that lined the walls. At forty, he was neither exceptionally handsome nor vain. It was not narcissism that held him motionless before the glass but rather fascination with the structure reflected there, the structure that housed his being; a body that should have been, by all the laws of probability, destroyed in the automobile accident four months ago. His hair was grayer now, and he was still too thin, but the swimming should remedy that; Roger had said so. At least he was alive.

But was he *well?*

2

Rafferty stepped forward so that his face was only a few inches from the glass. He reached up with his hand and slowly separated the hairs on the right side of his scalp to reveal a long, thread-thin scar that began an inch above the hairline and snaked down and along the side of his head and around to the base of his skull. He touched the wound, pressing on it with the tips of his fingers, first gently and then with increased pressure. There was no pain; there was hardly any sensation at all. Roger and his team had done a beautiful job inserting the steel plate.

No, it was not the wound or the piece of metal that was causing the agony. He was fairly certain of that now. Other people; *they* were the source of his pain. In which case, Victor mused, he must indeed be going mad.

He stepped back but continued to gaze at his flat, scarred reflection. Perhaps it would have been better to die; better that than to suffer this ruptured consciousness that warped his senses and made even the close physical presence of his wife a fount of unbearable discomfort. Too, it was getting worse; his *awareness* of the man in the pool had been sharper, more distinct than ever before.

He knew now he should have told Roger about the pain and the images from the beginning. Why hadn't he? Victor wondered. Was it possible that he was so afraid of discovering the truth that he would wrap himself in his own silence before allowing himself to be told that his brain was permanently damaged . . . or that he was dying? Or was it a different fear, this ten-fingered hand that clawed at the inside of his stomach every time he even considered describing to anyone his symptoms?

Victor forced himself to walk away from the mirror. Then he dressed quickly. He lighted a cigarette and was not surprised to see that his hand was trembling. He was due in Roger's office in half an hour and he had decided to tell Roger everything, ignoring the possible consequences.

3

Victor wondered how the neurosurgeon would react when he was told his famous patient thought he could read minds.

It came as always; tongues of molten metal licking the scorched, exhausted sands of his mind; dagger thrusts that bled into a psychic pool of images and sounds that he could *feel* as well as hear as he approached the woman behind the desk.

"Dr. Burns will see you in a few moments," the receptionist said in her most professional tone. She'd spoken those words to him at least forty times in the last four months and her tone never changed. "If you'll be kind enough to go in and sit down . . ."

Victor thanked her and walked the few paces down the corridor into the large waiting room with its magenta walls and overstuffed, red leather chairs. He selected a magazine from a mahogany rack and tried to focus his attention on the lead article while waiting for the man who could hold the key to his sanity—or his life. He had barely enough time to finish the first paragraph before there was the soft click of a door opening and Victor looked up at the tall, lean frame of the man who had put his body back together after the accident. Roger was studying him through large, steel-rimmed eyeglasses that made his thin face seem all out of proportion.

"Come in, Vic," the doctor said at last, motioning Victor into a huge, book-lined office. "It's good to see you; first interesting case I've had all day."

Victor strode quickly into the office, avoiding the other man's eyes. He automatically stripped to his shorts and sat down on the long, leather examination table. He studied Roger as the doctor glanced through the reams of charts and other papers that were the record of Victor's recovery.

4

He'd known Roger Burns for some time, even before the accident. In fact, he had designed the award-winning house in which Roger and his wife lived. He knew Roger to be—like many great men—lonely and estranged, the victim as well as possessor of prodigious skills. Victor could understand that. Still, he resented the cold, clinical detachment that Roger brought to this new doctor-patient relationship, an attitude that he knew was prompted by Roger's concern about his condition. Victor would have discerned this even without the flood of anxiety that flowed from the other man's mind; it was written in his eyes. He'd probably been talking to Pat.

"How was your walk?" Roger had risen from the desk and strode across the room to a huge bank of filing cabinets. He drew a bulging file from one of the sliding drawers and began clipping X-ray negatives along the sides of a huge fluoroscope suspended from the ceiling.

"I didn't walk."

Roger's eyes flicked sideward like a stroke from one of his scalpels. "You should walk. The exercise is good for you."

"I've been swimming."

Roger nodded his approval and walked toward Victor, who lay back on the table and closed his eyes against the sudden onrush of pain.

"Elizabeth is giving a cocktail party Friday evening for one of the new congressmen," Roger said, glancing back over his shoulder at one of the X rays. "You and Pat be sure to be there. I'll need someone to talk to."

Victor grunted as the surgeon's long, deft fingers probed and pulled at the muscle and bone beneath the fresh scar tissue on his arms and legs. Roger was bent over him, following the path of the thin, bright beam of light that was lighting the interior of his eyes.

5

Victor reached out and touched a thought. "Why are you thinking that my intelligence may be impaired?"

There was a sudden wave of anxiety that flowed across his mind like a cold wave as Roger shut off the light and straightened up.

"What makes you think I consider that a possibility?" Roger's voice was too tight and controlled.

Victor stared hard into the other man's eyes, very conscious of the beads of sweat that were lining up like soldiers across his forehead. There would never be a better time. "Just guessing," Victor said at last. The words tasted bitter on his tongue and he felt empty inside. "What *do* you think?"

The light came back on and the examination continued. Victor fought to keep his mind away from the pain and the noises.

"You're a walking miracle," Roger said, resuming his probing, and Victor swallowed a bubble of hysterical laughter that had suddenly formed in his throat. "I don't have to tell you how lucky you are to be alive. How many men do you know who've had half their skull crushed and lived to worry about their intelligence?" He paused and seemed to be waiting for some reply. Victor said nothing.

"Your most serious injury was the damage to your brain," Roger continued matter-of-factly. "You're obviously aware of that."

"And?"

"I don't know. Really. There's so little that we actually know for certain about this kind of injury. It's still much too early to know for sure how any of your functions are going to be affected." Roger hesitated, trying to read the expression on Victor's face. "I'm not putting you off," he continued very quietly. "I really don't know. Every rule in the book says that you should be dead or in the terminal stage of coma."

6

"I owe my life to you," Victor said evenly, noticing the slight flush that appeared high on the cheeks of the other man. In a moment it was gone. "I think there's something you're not telling me."

"Pat tells me that you seem . . . *distracted* lately." Roger had returned to his desk and was writing something on one of the charts in his folder. "She says you've become very absentminded. I understand you haven't even been . . . close with her since the accident."

"You need a record of my love life?"

"No," Roger said, suddenly slapping the folder shut. "I need information. That is, I need information if I'm ever going to answer your questions. Have you lost the desire to make love?"

"No," Victor said, searching for the right words. How could he explain how it hurt his *mind* to be so close? "I've been . . . upset . . . worried. You can understand that." He hurried on, conscious of the rising note of impatience in his voice, eager to leave the subject of his relationship with his wife. "You must know what parts of my brain have been damaged. And you must know what happened to others with the same kind of injury."

Roger was preparing to take X rays. Victor rose from the couch and walked to the machine.

"Much of the left cortex has been destroyed," Roger said. His voice was low, muffled by the lead shield and punctuated by the intermittent buzzing of the machine at Victor's head. "Usually, the patient dies. If not, there is almost always a loss of coordination and speech. For some reason that I don't pretend to understand, you don't seem to have suffered any appreciable loss of any kind. Of course there's no way of knowing what damage has been done farther down in the brain tissue."

7

"You mean I could drop dead at any moment. Or I could be losing my mind."

The machine continued to click, recording its invisible notes. "I can tell you this: neurosurgeons all over the world are following your case. You may or may not be the world's greatest architect but you're certainly the leading medical phenomenon."

Victor swallowed hard. "I—I wasn't aware that many people knew anything about it."

Roger came out from behind the shield and repositioned the machine. "I haven't published anything yet, although, eventually, I'd like to if you'll give your consent. I need your permission, of course. I'll need more time to run tests and chart your progress."

"How did it get so much publicity?"

Roger looked surprised. "Victor, there isn't a major city in the world that doesn't have one of your buildings. You're like public property. Then there was the fantastic way you recovered from the injuries. Didn't you suppose people would be interested?"

"It never occurred to me . . ." Victor's voice trailed off, stifled by the thought of a world watching his disintegration; cold, dispassionate men and women examining him like a worm wriggling beneath a microscope. The machine had stopped. "Roger," he continued quietly, "I think I can read people's minds."

His voice seemed swallowed up by the large room. There was the sharp click of a match as Roger lighted a cigarette. The surgeon's face was expressionless.

"I tell you I can *hear* people *thinking"* Victor said too loudly. He took a deep breath and tried to fight the panic he felt pounding at his senses like some gigantic fist. He searched Roger's face for some kind of emotion, but there was nothing; the other man was staring intently at a thin stream of smoke that flowed from his mouth. "It's true.

I know it sounds crazy—maybe it *is* crazy—but I can feel you inside my mind right now."

"Can you tell me what I'm thinking?" Roger's tone was flat. He had not raised his eyes.

"It's not always like *that,*" Victor said quietly. He knew . . . and then he didn't know, not for certain. He knew it seemed as if he had been challenged and was coming up empty. Still, he felt more relaxed and at peace than he had for months; at last he had invited someone else to peer into his private hell. "It's not always definite words or sounds. Sometimes it's just a jumble of sensations. But they're not a part of *me.* Can you understand that? It's like I'm listening in on other people's conversations with themselves!" Victor paused and waited until Roger's eyes were locked with his. His voice gathered strength. "Right now you're fascinated; you'd like to pinpoint the damaged area of my brain that's causing me to hallucinate. You don't believe a word I'm saying."

There was the slightest flicker of surprise and consternation in the doctor's eyes. It was quickly masked. "Let's not worry about whether or not I believe you," Roger said. "At least not right now. It's obvious that *you* believe you're reading other people's thoughts, and that's all that's important. Why don't you describe these sensations?"

"I'm not sure exactly when it started," Victor said slowly, taking a cigarette from the pack on Roger's desk and carefully lighting it. His hand was steady. "A week, maybe two weeks after I got out of the hospital. I began getting these headaches; but they *weren't* headaches, not in the usual sense, and God knows I'd had enough real headaches to know the difference. And there were noises that would suddenly spring up from nowhere. Sometimes there were words, but mostly it was just noise, almost like . . . static. And it hurt.

9

"It took me a while to realize that I experienced the pain and the noises only when I was near other people. I'd walk up to people and immediately there'd be pressure in my ears and behind my eyes. I'd walk away and it would stop. Lately, I've *seen* whole strings of words in my mind, words and sounds all floating around in my head. And pain that I can't describe to you. And I *feel* things— emotions—that I know come from somebody else."

"Has there been any change in the *way* you feel these things?" Roger's voice was even.

"Yes. The impressions are stronger, and the pain is worse. The more I know, the more I hurt."

"And you think these sensations have something to do with the thought patterns of other people?"

"I don't know what else to think," Victor said hesitantly. He was conscious now, more than ever, of how sick and foolish he must sound. The words were coming harder; he was pushing them out of his throat. "A few minutes ago, while you were leaning over me on the table, I thought my head would split. I kept *feeling* the word, *intelligence.* Over and over again: *intelligence, intelligence.* In some way that I can't explain, I knew that was *your* thought. You were wondering how much my intellectual capacity had been impaired by the accident."

Victor watched Roger light another cigarette. Now it was the neurosurgeon's hands that trembled. "Go on."

"It's like the words have teeth. There's just no other way I can think of to describe it; they sit in my mind and they *bite*. And just before they come there's a kind of pressure, a buzzing . . . a *numb* feeling." Victor hesitated. "All right," he continued at last, "you still don't think it's possible. For a moment there, you were almost convinced; you were thinking about the Russian claim that they have a woman who can read colors with her fingertips."

Again Roger's eyes registered surprise but he spoke without hesitation. "Let's be realistic," Roger said, leaning close, inundating Victor with his thoughts. "It's *most* important that we be realistic. You've survived a terrible injury and it's to be expected that there's going to be some residual pain. You must understand that the mind plays tricks, even in a healthy individual, and you're still far from well. You're going to have to give your body, and your mind, time to *heal*. That's what you have to think about, Victor; that and only that."

"Test me!" Victor was surprised at the vehemence in his voice. It had cost him a great deal to come to Roger with his fears. He would not now be denied; one way or the other he would know the truth. "If you're so sure I'm imagining this, test me!"

"Victor, as your doctor, I—"

"Do it as my friend! Roger, I *need* this! Have you ever read anything about ESP?"

"Well, naturally, I've read the literature. But I don't think—"

"Good! Then you know the tests are fairly simple as well as statistically reliable. There isn't that much work involved."

"It's not the work that I'm thinking about," Roger said. He was wavering now, torn by uncertainty that was clearly communicated to Victor. "Maybe next week."

"Tonight!" Victor had to struggle to keep from shouting. He was intoxicated with the vision of an end to his nightmare. "You won't help me to relax by forcing me to wait a week," Victor said quietly. "It won't be difficult to get the materials or set up the equipment. If I fail, well, I'll have all the time in the world to relax. Isn't that right, Roger?"

11

Victor gazed steadily back into the eyes of the tall man. "All right," Roger said, picking up Victor's folder and tucking it under his arm. "Tonight."

Victor paused in the lobby of the medical center and studied the knots of people moving past, crowding the sidewalk on the other side of the thick, glass doors. All his anger had been drained. In a few hours he would do battle with his fears in the neutral territory of a laboratory before the disinterested eyes of a man who believed he was hallucinating. It was all he asked. The tension and anxiety that had been steadily building over the long months was suddenly gone and in their place was an insatiable curiosity. Talking to Roger had brought him out of himself; his words had lanced the psychic wound that had festered in his silence. He was sure now that the sounds and images were real. Since he was not hallucinating, there was only one other possibility; he was telepathic.

Telepath. Victor rolled the word around in his mind, speaking it softly with equal parts fear and fascination. What if he could learn to control and interpret these sensations?

Victor pushed open the doors and strode out into the auburn glow of the late afternoon, plunging without hesitation into a small crowd of pedestrians who were waiting on the corner for the traffic light to change. Quickly, like a man pitching his body into an icy lake, Victor opened his mind and extended it out toward the man standing next to him. He remembered the time as a child when he had sought to prove his courage to a group of older boys by holding his arm over a campfire, holding it there until the soft down on his flesh had shriveled and fallen to the ground. It was like that now; his mind was suspended in the consciousness of another and he was burning.

Still he hung on, struggling to stretch the words into sentences and trace the images and sounds to their source. A shaft of pain tore through him, erupting like a geyser.

Victor staggered back against a building, ignoring the frightened stares of the people at the crossing. The man whose mind he had touched was holding his head in his hands; he had dropped the briefcase he had been holding and was looking about him with a dazed expression. Victor pushed away from the stone facade and forced himself to walk the few paces to a phone booth that stood empty across the street. He half-stumbled into the glass enclosure and slammed the door shut behind him.

Icy sweat had pasted his clothes to his body. Victor rested his head against the cold metal of the telephone and peered out from his sanctuary as he waited for the scream inside his head to subside. He had seen something inside the man's mind, something cold and dark that he did not understand and which frightened him; this time he had seen what before he had only felt.

I must practice, Victor thought; *I must delve even deeper into this mysterious awareness which 1 now possess. Perhaps, in time, I could even learn to control the pain.*

He hunted in his pockets for change, having decided to call Pat and tell her he would not be home for dinner, not until after he had seen Roger. Right now there was no time to waste; there was too much to learn.

Roger hesitated with his hand on the telephone as he tried to dispel a lingering uneasiness about the call he had decided to make. He finally picked up the receiver, dialed a number and spoke in quiet earnestness for some minutes. When he had finished he poured himself a tall drink from a bottle that had been a Christmas present and which had been around the office, unopened, for the past two years. He

13

ground his knuckles into his eyes and groaned as pools of electric, liquid light darted and swam behind his eyelids.

Acting on an impulse, he had gone ahead and developed the latest series of X rays, the set he had taken of Victor's skull earlier in the afternoon. He had not expected to find any significant change. He had been wrong. Now the entire surface of the large fluoroscope in his office was covered with negatives arranged in chronological order so as to provide, at a glance, a complete visual record of X-ray exposures taken over the past four months. Viewed in this manner, the effect was astounding.

On the left were the plates taken soon after Rafferty had been rushed to the hospital, more dead than alive. The carnage on the right side of the skull was indicated most vividly by small dots of light in a sea of gray, bits of bone imbedded deep in the tissue of the brain.

The next series of plates had been exposed three days later, after the marathon operation had been completed. The splinters of bone had been removed from the brain tissue and a metal plate inserted into the area where the skull had been pulverized. The rest of the exposures had been taken at two to three week intervals.

Now that he knew what he was looking for, Roger realized that the effect was evident, even in the early exposures: a tiny discoloration a few millimeters to the left of the injured area. Placed side by side, the plates offered conclusive evidence that the discolored region was rapidly increasing in size. It was almost as if the machine were not recording this area, but Roger had checked and rechecked the equipment and there was nothing wrong with it.

In the set of plates taken that afternoon the normal skull and brain tissue patterns were virtually nonexistent; the entire plate exploded in rays of light and dark emanating from that same tiny region just below the steel plate. It was as if the architect's brain had somehow been transformed

14

into a power source strong enough to interfere with the X rays—but that was impossible.

Roger licked his lips and swallowed hard but there was no moisture left in his mouth. He turned off the fluoroscope and reached back for the wall switch before pouring himself another drink. In a few minutes there was the soft ring of chimes in the outer office. Roger glanced at his watch and rose to greet the first of the evening's two visitors.

Victor knew immediately that something had happened in the past few hours that had made Roger change his mind; he could sense the excitement radiating from the consciousness of the neurosurgeon in great, undulating waves.

"Tell me again how you feel when you experience these sensations." Roger's voice was impassive but his eyes glowed.

"Something like a second-grader trying to read Ulysses," Victor said easily. "You can recognize a few words but most of the time you haven't any idea what they mean."

His gaze swept the small anteroom where Roger had brought him. Shipping cartons, boxes of records, and obsolete equipment had been pushed back against the walls to make room for the two wooden tables that had been placed in the middle of the floor. Wedged between the tables and extending about four feet above their surfaces was a thin, plywood partition. On one table was what appeared to be a large stack of oversized playing cards, a pad and a pencil. The other table was bare.

"I want you to sit here," Roger said, indicating a chair at one end of the empty table. He waited until Victor had seated himself. "I believe you may have been telling

15

the truth this afternoon. Now I think we can find out for sure."

Victor felt as if he had been hit in the stomach. A few hours ago he would have given almost anything to hear Roger speak those words; now they stirred a reservoir of fear. He might have risen and left if it were not for the knowledge that, by doing so, he would be cutting himself off from the one person who might be able to return him to the world of normal sights and sounds.

"Let me show you what we're going to do," Roger said, fanning the cards out, face up, in front of Victor. They were pictures of farm animals. "I'm going to try to duplicate some of Duke University's experiments in parapsychology. There are figures on my pad that correspond to the pictures on the cards. Each time I turn over a card I'll signal with this." Roger produced a small, toy noisemaker from his pocket and pressed it several times. It emitted a series of distinct clicking noises. "You'll tell me whatever it is you see or feel: dog, horse, cat or cow. At the end, we'll compute the number of correct responses. Any significant difference between your score and what is considered *chance* must be attributed to telepathy. It's as simple, or complex, as that."

"Fine. Just as long as it helps you to treat me."

"Victor," Roger said, shooting him a quick glance, "do you realize what it would mean for you to be proved telepathic?"

"Right now it means that I have a constant headache, occasional severe pain, and that I continually find myself knowing things about other people that I neither want, nor have the right, to know."

"Yes." Roger's voice was noncommittal. He disappeared behind the partition and Victor could hear him shuffling the cards.

It suddenly occurred to Victor that the other man was trying to hide something from him, concentrating hard on a set of words in what seemed an effort to mask an idea; the thought of *hiding* was floating in the other man's consciousness, soaring above and hovering over the other things on which he was concentrating. Why should Roger want to hide anything from him? Victor attempted to break through the curtain but Roger's will, and the pain, were too great. Victor let go and leaned back in the chair.

"Are you ready?"

"Ready."

Click.

". . . Dog." He said it with far more certainty than he felt.

Click.

"You're waiting too long."

"I can't . . ."

"Your first reaction!"

Click.

Victor said nothing. There were no animal words in Roger's thoughts. The words that were there were scrambled and totally unrelated to one another. Why would Roger want to ruin his own experiment? Unless there were no words except those that sprang from his own shattered imagination; unless he had been right in the beginning to suspect he was on the verge of madness.

Clickclickclick.

"You're not responding, Victor! Tell me what animal you see! Tell me!"

Nerves shrieking, Victor sprang from his chair and stepped around the partition, slapping at the cards, strewing them over the table and floor. Sweat dripped from his forehead and splattered on the wooden surface, their sound clearly audible in the sudden silence. Victor stepped back

17

quickly, profoundly embarrassed. Roger was studying him quietly.

"I—I can't see anything," Victor said, his voice shaking. "For God's sake, Roger, I ... I'm very sorry."

"Let's try it once more."

Victor reached for his handkerchief and then stopped, his hand in mid-air; there was a new emotion in the other man, almost a sense of elation. He waited for Roger to look up, but the doctor seemed intent on rearranging the stack of cards, pointedly ignoring Victor's questioning gaze. Victor returned to his chair and sat down.

"Ready?"

"Ready," Victor said weakly, cupping his head in his hands. He Suddenly felt very tired.

Click.

Victor slowly dropped his hands away from his head; his heart hammered. "Dog," he whispered.

Click.

"Cat."

Now the clicks came faster and faster, and each one was accompanied by a clear, startling, naked impression. It was *there!* Roger's mind was open and Victor barked out the words as the images came to him.

Click.

"Cow."

Click.

"Dog."

Clickclickclick.

"Cowcatdog."

Clickclickclickclick.

Finally the clicking stopped. Victor could feel Roger's mind begin to relax and he knew it was over. He sat very still, extremely conscious of his own breathing and the rising excitement in Roger as the results were tabulated. In a few moments the excitement had risen to

18

a sharp peak of unrelieved tension. Victor looked up to find Roger standing over him, his facial muscles forming a mask of undisguised astonishment.

"One hundred percent," Roger said breathlessly, repeating the figure over and over as if unable to accept his own calculations. "Victor, you *can* read minds. You're telepathic to an almost unbelievable degree. Here, look at this!"

Victor glanced at the pad on which his responses had been recorded. On the first test he had scored about one correct answer in every four. *Chance.* On the second test all of the answers were circled in red; the marks grew darker and more unsteady as they proceeded down the page.

He looked up and was startled to find the neurosurgeon still staring at him. It was unnerving; the man's pupils were slightly dilated and his mouth worked back and forth. His thought patterns were strange and somehow unpleasant.

"Let me guess," Victor said tightly. "You're looking for antennae."

"I'm sorry," Roger said, stepping back a pace. "I was staring, wasn't I?"

"Yes."

"Well, you're a little hard to get used to. If you have any idea what this means . . ."

"I'd rather not get into that."

Roger flushed and Victor immediately felt ashamed. Were their situations reversed, he felt certain he would be the one staring.

"You were blocking me on the first test," Victor said easily. "Why?"

"Control." Roger's fingers were tracing a pattern up and down the columns of red circles. "I had the cards face down on the first run. I didn't know what they were myself. The second time . . . Well, you saw what happened the second time."

"Where do we go from here?" Victor shifted uneasily in his chair. He had the distinct impression that Roger was already thinking in terms of *application.*

"I wish I knew," Roger said. "I wish I knew."

Victor's head was splitting and the nervous sweat in his armpits was clammy. He concentrated on shutting out Roger's thoughts; he wanted nothing more than to go home and sleep, but first he needed some answers. "How?" Victor asked at last.

"How what?"

"How does all this happen? What's going on inside my brain?"

Roger tugged at his lip. "If I knew that, I'd be famous."

"You already are famous."

Roger grunted and continued to tug at his lip. When he finally spoke, his tone was flat, his gaze fixed on some point at the far end of the room. "It's been estimated that during our entire lives we only use fifteen to twenty percent of our total brain capacity. Nobody really knows what happens with the other eighty. For all we know, there may be a great source of power there, power that we never use. We never have need to tap that power and so it atrophies like an unused muscle. Maybe that power is there in reserve, to be used by some future generation; or maybe it's simply the difference between the ordinary man and the genius. It's just possible that in your case the energy, or whatever you want to call what's happened to you, was released as a result of the accident."

Now Roger rose to his feet and began to pace, lost in thought, his voice a beacon beckoning Victor to follow him through this thicket of ideas into which he had wandered. He fumbled for a cigarette, finally found one in a crumpled pack and lighted it. He couldn't sit down. "We've always assumed brain damage to be disabling," Roger continued, dragging heavily on his cigarette. "The brain controls everything; coordination, thinking, reflexes. Different areas control different functions and when one area has been damaged, its function is almost always lost.

"We always assume that our present condition is the best. It never occurred to us that brain damage could be *beneficial* in any way." Roger stopped and looked at Victor. "You've shown us how wrong we were. Your injury somehow altered the function of your brain cells, releasing a power like nothing that's ever been recorded." He crushed out the cigarette. "I think evolution may have something to do with it."

"Evolution?"

"Yes!"

"I'm not a superman," Victor said cautiously. "I'm all of the things everyone else is; no more and no less."

"That's not true," Roger said, his excitement undiminished. "You were gifted—apart from other men— even before the accident. Now you're telepathic." He paused for emphasis. "The Cro-Magnons' forebears were not obviously different from their fellows; they lived, ate, drank, fornicated, and died just like the others. The differences were too small to be seen, at least in their own lifetime. It must be the same with us; to generations of men a thousand years from now, *we* will seem like Neanderthals. And some of us— you, for instance—are their genetic forebears. If I'm right, a freak accident triggered a mechanism inside your brain that most men will not know for dozens of generations!"

"But how does it happen?" Victor lighted a cigarette, his moves slow and deliberate, his voice completely noncommittal.

21

"All *thinking* involves a release of energy. Electrical impulses are triggered by certain chemical reactions within the cells that we don't yet fully understand; it's precisely those impulses that we measure in an EEG." Roger sat down suddenly and began drumming his fingers on the tabletop. "In your case, the cells have been altered to a degree where the nerve endings not only pick up your own impulses but other people's as well. We've always suspected that there was a certain amount of electrical radiation or *leakage* from the brain, just as there is from any power source. Besides, there are quite a few recorded instances of telepathic communication—but never anything like this. It's just *fantastic,* Victor! I wonder if you realize just how unique you are?"

Victor was gently probing now, looking for the meaning behind the words, trying to determine just what Roger planned to do with his newly acquired knowledge. He gave up when he realized that the neurosurgeon was effectively, if unconsciously, blocking him.

"All right," Victor said, concentrating his attention on a water stain just over Roger's shoulder. "How do we stop it?"

Roger blinked rapidly as if just startled by a loud noise or awakened from a deep sleep. "Stop it?"

"That's what I said, stop it! Do you think I want to *stay* like this?" Aware that he was almost yelling, Victor dug his fingernails into the palms of his hands and took a deep breath. "I'm an architect," he continued more calmly. "I used to build things and that was all I ever asked out of life; it's all I ask now. If you had any idea . . . but you don't. There must be something you can do, an operation of some sort; I want it."

"That's impossible at this point," Roger replied, passing his hand over his eyes. His voice was now blurred with weariness. "To attempt any kind of operation

22

now is out of the question; I wouldn't even know what I was supposed to be operating *on.* Besides, another operation now would probably kill you."

"There may not be *time,*" Victor said, tapping his clenched fist gently but insistently on the table. "I tell you it's getting worse; each day I know more about people I've never met, strangers I pass on the street. And my head hurts. For God's sake, Roger, sometimes I wake up in the morning and I don't—"

"Have you considered the *implications* of this thing?" Roger seemed unaware of the fact that he had interrupted Victor. "You can read men's minds, know their innermost feelings! There are all sorts of—"

"I've thought about the implications and I don't like any of them."

"Police work. Imagine, Victor! You would know beyond any doubt who was guilty and who was innocent.. ."

"Some sort of mental Gestapo?"

". . . International relations, psychiatry . . ."

"Forget it, Doctor," Victor murmured, half-rising. His voice was very soft. "If you won't help me, I'll find somebody else who will."

"I didn't say I wouldn't help you," Roger said, sobered by the intensity of Victor's tone. "I said I didn't think I *could* help you; at least, not yet, not until I know more. We'll have to conduct tests and *those* will be mostly guesswork. Even if I do operate, there's no way of knowing for sure whether it will do any good. That is, if it doesn't kill you."

"I'll take that chance. You can administer any test you want. The only thing I ask is that you do it quickly and that you keep this matter completely confidential."

"I'm afraid it's already too late for that, Mr. Rafferty."

23

Startled, Victor leaped to his feet, knocking over the chair. He turned in the direction of the voice and was stunned to see a well-dressed woman standing behind him at an open door that he had assumed was a closet; now he could see the adjoining room beyond the door. The woman had been there all the time. She had seen and heard everything, and now Victor knew what Roger had been trying to hide.

Visual and mental images came at him in a rush: young and attractive but cold, high self-esteem, exaggerated sense of self-importance, fiercely competitive, slightly paranoid, and habitually condescending. She concealed her nervousness well.

"Tell me, Mr. Rafferty," the woman continued, "don't you think the scientific community— your country— has a *right* to know about you?"

Victor turned slowly to Roger. "Who is she?" he asked very deliberately.

Roger's face was crimson. "Victor—Mr. Rafferty—I'd like you to meet Dr. Lewellyn, one of my colleagues."

"What the hell is she doing here?"

"Victor, I ... I asked Dr. Lewellyn to observe. I value her opinion. I thought perhaps—"

"You had no right." Victor turned to face the woman. "The answer to your question is *no,*" he said tightly. "Neither you nor anyone else has any right to my life or my personal problems."

"Mr. Rafferty, I don't think you understand—"

"I mean it, Roger," Victor said, cutting her off, turning his back on her once again. "I expect this case to be handled with the utmost confidence. And I hold you responsible for this woman!" He hesitated, wondering why he suddenly felt so afraid. "If any word of this gets out, I'll deny the whole thing," Victor continued softly. "I'll

24

make both of you look very foolish. Roger, I'll call you tomorrow. You can experiment with me all you want, but my condition *must* be kept secret. Is that clear?" He did not wait for an answer. Glancing once at Dr. Lewellyn, he walked quickly from the room.

"You've made a fantastic discovery, Doctor," the woman said.

"Yes," Roger agreed, but there was no trace of his former enthusiasm.

"But he's terribly naive, don't you think? He must realize that we have certain obligations."

"I suppose so," the doctor said, crumpling the cards in his hands and studying their motions as they drifted lazily to the floor.

Pat Rafferty glanced up as her husband came through the door. She watched him for a moment, and her eyes clouded. "Victor," she said gently, "you smell like a brewery."

"I should." he said evenly. "I just drank a fifth of Scotch." He went quickly into the bathroom and splashed water over his face and neck. When he came back into the living room he was startled to find his wife standing in the same spot staring at him, her pale blue eyes rimmed with tears of hurt and confusion. Six years of marriage to the slight, blonde-haired woman had not dulled his love for her; if anything, the years had magnified his desire and need. It had been three days since the tests in Roger's laboratory and still he had not told Pat about them. It would have been hard enough, at the beginning, to tell her he feared for his sanity. Confirmation of his ability had only compounded his problem. *How,* he thought, *does a man tell his wife she's married to a monster?* "I'm not drunk," he said, turning away from her eyes. "I'm not even sure if it's possible for me to get drunk anymore."

25

Pat continued to stare, dumbfounded at the words of this man who had, seemingly by intent, become a stranger to her. There was something in his eyes and voice that terrified her, robbed her of speech.

"You see," Victor continued, "I've made a remarkable discovery. If I drink enough, I can't hear other people thinking. I'm left *alone.* I ..." Victor stopped, aware that his need had spoken the words his intellect would not. He turned away to hide his own tears of anguish. He did not flinch when he felt Pat's soft, cool fingers caressing the back of his neck. "I need your help," he murmured, turning and burying his face in his wife's hair.

Victor talked for hours, pausing only once when night fell and Pat rose to turn on the kitchen lights. He told her everything: the pain, his fear, and the experiments in Roger's office. When he had finished he drew himself up very straight and stared into her eyes. "Do you believe me?"

"I don't *know,* Victor. You've been acting so strangely for the past few months. I want to believe you, but. . ."

"The alcohol's worn off. Would you like me to demonstrate what I'm talking about?"

"I. . ."

"Think of a number. Go ahead; do as I say."

Victor held Pat's gaze and waited, probing, hunting for the numbers that he knew must eventually merge with the doubt and confusion he felt in her mind. When they came, he called them off with machine-gun rapidity in a voice that never wavered. One by one he exposed every thought, every fleeting impression. He did not stop even when he felt the doubt replaced by panic. He could not escape the conviction that something terrible was about to happen. He needed Pat. Therefore, she must be convinced beyond any doubt that—

26

"Stop!" Pat clapped her hands over her eyes in a vain attempt to stem the tide of thick, heavy tears that streamed in great rivulets down her cheeks. "Stop it, Victor! Stop it! *Stop it!"*

Pat leaped from her chair and ran into the living room. Victor waited a few minutes and then followed. She was huddled on a far end of the sofa. He reached out to touch her but immediately stepped back as he felt her flesh quiver beneath his touch. In that moment he had felt what she felt and the knowledge seared him. He stepped farther into the darkness to hide his own tears.

"I'm not a freak," he said quietly, and he turned away and headed back into the kitchen in an attempt to escape the sound of Pat's sobbing.

Her voice stopped him. "Forgive me, darling."

Victor stood silently, unwilling to trust his voice. He watched through the doorway as his wife sat up and brushed away the tears from her face.

"I'm so ashamed," Pat continued in a voice that was steady. "I don't know what to say to you. All that time you were hurting so much ... I *love* you so much, so very much . . ."

He went to her, folded her into his arms. They stayed that way for several minutes, each enjoying the renewed warmth and security in the touch of the other's body.

"You're afraid," Pat said at last.

"Yes."

"Why?"

Victor told her about Dr. Lewellyn.

"I still don't understand why you're so afraid."

"They'll try to use me."

Pat pulled away just far enough to look up into Victor's eyes. "There's so much you could contribute, darling. Imagine what you could do in psychiatry, helping

27

to diagnose patients. Think how much more scientists could learn from you about the human mind."

"They won't use me for those things," Victor said, surprised at the conviction in his voice. He had found the elusive source of his fear. "They'll use me as a weapon."

Pat was silent for long moments, her head buried once again in his neck. "We'll move away," she said at last.

"They'll follow."

"We'll change our names, start all over again."

"We'll see," Victor said, but he sensed that it was already too late.

Later, Victor lay back in the darkness and listened to Pat's troubled dreams. The orange-yellow glow of dawn trickled through the blinds of the bedroom window. He had not slept. If Roger was right, if his mind was, indeed, a window on Man's future, what right *did* he have to keep that portal shuttered?

Pat was beginning to stir and Victor recognized the sharpening thought patterns that he had learned to identify as the bridge between sleep and consciousness. He slipped on his robe and went to the kitchen to make coffee. Pat joined him a few minutes later, kissed Victor lightly on the cheek and began preparing breakfast.

They ate in silence. Victor had poured a second cup of coffee and lighted a cigarette when the doorbell rang. He rose and kissed Pat full on the mouth, holding her close to him. He sensed, even before he had opened the door and looked into the man's mind that the waiting was over.

He was a small man. His short arms and thin, frail body were in direct contrast to the strength Victor found in his mind. His face was pale and pockmarked, punctuated with a large nose that sloped at an angle as if it had been broken once and never properly set. He wore a thick topcoat and even now, in the gathering warmth of the morning, drew it around him and shivered as if he were cold.

"I'm Mr. Lippitt," the man said to Victor. "I think you know why I'm here."

"Come in," Victor said, surprised at the steadiness of his own voice. The man entered but politely refused Victor's invitation to sit. Victor glanced over his shoulder at Pat and waited until she had returned to the kitchen. "What do you want, Mr. Lippitt?"

The man suddenly thrust his hands into his pockets in a quick motion. The dark eyes in the pale face riveted on Victor, measuring his reaction as he allowed his thoughts and knowledge to rush forth.

He's too strong, Victor thought; *too strong.* But he didn't react.

"If my information is correct," Mr. Lippitt said slowly, "you know what I'm thinking right now."

Victor returned the other man's gaze. He sensed pain, chronic discomfort that Mr. Lippitt went to great lengths to conceal. "Are you sure you have the right house?" For the briefest moment there was a flicker of amusement in Mr. Lippitt's eyes and Victor found that, in spite of himself, he liked the man.

"The people I represent believe you have a rather remarkable talent, Mr. Rafferty. Obviously, I'm not referring to your abilities as an architect. We know all about your interviews with Dr. Burns. We'd like to test and interview you ourselves. We would pay well for the privilege."

"No," Victor said evenly. "I don't wish to be tested or interviewed by anyone."

Mr. Lippitt's gaze was cold and steady. He hunched his shoulders deeper into his coat. "You understand that we could force you. We don't want that. Surely, you can see the necessity—"

29

"Well, I *can't* see the necessity!" Victor exploded. "What do you want from me?"

Lippitt's face registered genuine surprise. He drew his hand out from his pocket and gestured toward his head. "Don't you see?"

"I know who you work for," Victor said impatiently. "I can tell that you're not quite sure what to do with me and that I'm considered some kind of potential threat. The rest is very vague. Your training was very thorough; you're subconsciously blocking all sorts of information that you don't think I should have."

"You scored perfectly on a telepathic indicator test," Lippitt said, eyeing Victor curiously. "You can read thoughts like the rest of us read newspapers."

"It's not quite that simple."

"But it could be! I've heard the tapes of your conversations with Burns! You can control—" Mr. Lippitt paused and again Victor sensed his physical discomfort. When Lippitt spoke again his voice was softer and his breath whistled in his lungs. "We live in an age of technological terror. Both sides spend millions of dollars gathering information to assure themselves that they're not going to come out second best in any nuclear war."

"I'm not a spy, and I don't have the training or inclination to become one."

"Your mind makes conventional methods of espionage obsolete," Mr. Lippitt said, his eyes blazing. "Don't you see, Mr. Rafferty? You could gather more information in one hour spent at an embassy cocktail party than a team of experts could gather in a year! One drink with a foreign ambassador or general and you'd have the most valuable diplomatic and military information! There'd be no way for them to stop you. You'd know who was lying, what military moves were being considered, information that other men must risk their lives to get! In a

30

way, you'd be the ultimate weapon. We would always be assured of having the most up-to-date and reliable—"

"Have I done anything wrong? Committed any crime?"

"No," Mr. Lippitt said, taken aback.

"Do you have the authority to arrest me?"

"No."

"Then my answer is still *no*" Victor said firmly. "I have a right as a citizen of this nation to be left alone."

"Have you considered your *duty* to this nation?"

"How would you know I was always telling the truth?"

"Ah, well . . . I don't have an answer for that; not now. I suppose, eventually, we would have to consider that."

"I don't want to work for you. I *won't* work for you."

Mr. Lippitt lighted a cigarette. Victor handed him an ashtray. Their eyes held steady.

"It's not that simple, Mr. Rafferty," Lippitt said. "It's just not that simple. No matter what you decided, you'd still need our protection."

"Protection?" The idea was there in Lippitt's mind but it was hazy and undefined.

"Our informant—"

"Dr.Lewellyn?"

"Dr. Lewellyn was more fervent than discreet," Mr. Lippitt said in a matter-of-fact tone that failed to conceal his embarrassment. "The channels she used to inform us of your existence were not, as we say, *secure*"

"You mean that in the spy business nothing stays a secret for very long."

"Not always," Mr. Lippitt said evenly, ignoring the other man's sarcasm. "But in this case we must assume that there's a possibility other powers may already

31

know about you. If so, well, I think they'd go to great lengths to prevent you from working for us."

"They'd kill me?"

"Without a second thought. Unless, of course, they felt they could force you to work for them."

Victor was conscious of his wife moving about in the kitchen. "You'd have to eliminate every trace of my existence," he said. "Otherwise, I'd be useless to you. And what are you going to do with Pat? Maybe she wouldn't care to undergo plastic surgery. Certainly, I'd have to."

"We'd handle everything. Would you rather risk having her see you killed? Or they might torture her if they thought it would do them any good. You know, their methods can be quite effective. You might have a more difficult time explaining to them that you simply choose not to use your skills for a dirty business like spying."

Victor's head hurt from the prolonged contact with Lippitt. His entire body ached and throbbed with exhaustion. "What if I decide to take my chances?" He no longer made any effort to mask his anxiety.

"I'm afraid that would put *us* in a difficult position," Mr. Lippitt said slowly, for the first time looking away from Victor. "You see, if you weren't working for us, we'd have no way of being certain you weren't working for *them*. They wouldn't hesitate to kill your wife or anybody else if it would force you over to their side." Lippitt's eyes hardened, "Or they simply might offer you a million dollars. Sometimes it's as easy as that."

Victor flushed. "Either way, then *you'd* have to stop me."

"Yes."

"Then I'm trapped."

"I'm afraid so, Mr. Rafferty. I'm sorry that it has to be this way."

32

Victor rubbed his sweating palms against his shirt. He was seized with a sudden, almost overwhelming desire to strike out, to smash his fist into the white face that looked as if it would tear like paper. He clenched his fists, but his arms dropped back to his sides in a gesture of resignation. Lippitt was right; on a planet covered with nations strangling on their own words of deceit and treachery, he was the ultimate weapon. He could determine truth, and he sensed that absolute truth and certainty would be a most dangerous possession in the hands of the wrong men. Had Hitler known the frailties of the men he fought, he would have ruled the world. On the other hand, a telepath could have prevented Pearl Harbor.

"Can I have some time to think about it?"

"What is there to think about?"

"Dignity. Allow me the dignity of believing I still have some freedom of choice."

Mr. Lippitt looked at Victor strangely for a moment before drawing a card from his pocket and handing it to him. "You can reach me at this number, any time of the day or night. Call me when you've . . . reached your decision." He paused at the door, turned and looked at Victor in the same odd manner. "I meant what I said, Mr. Rafferty. I am sorry that it has to be this way."

"So am I."

The door clicked shut behind Victor with a terrible certainty, muffling Pat's sobs, punctuating a decision Victor knew could not be reversed. There was no turning back once he had begun running. Never again could he be trusted, but he would be free.

Somewhere in the United States there had to be a place where he and Pat could lose their identities and start over, perhaps a small town in the south or the west. Victor knew he must find that place and find it quickly. Then he

33

would send for Pat. Perhaps it was, as he suspected, a futile gesture, but it was something he had to attempt, the only alternative to imprisonment in a world of uniforms, security checks and identity cards. He knew, too, that he must conserve his strength; already his arm ached from the weight of his single suitcase.

He knew there was something wrong the moment he stepped down from the porch. Victor felt the man's presence even before he spoke.

"Please stop right there, Mr. Rafferty."

Victor froze; he knew there was no sense in trying to run. Even without the suitcase, which he needed because it contained his bankbook and credit cards, he realized that his physical condition would never enable him to outrun the guard. He turned and stared into a pair of cold, gray eyes. The man was short and stocky, very well dressed, with close-cropped blond hair. Victor felt the man's mind coiled like a steel spring.

"Who the hell are you?" Victor snapped, his frustration forming meaningless words. He already knew the answer: Lippitt's man.

"I'm sorry, sir. I must ask you to come with me."

"Your boss told me I'd have time to think things over."

"I'm sorry, sir, but I have my instructions. I was told to bring you with me if it looked like you were trying to leave. Will you follow me, please?"

Victor shifted his weight back on one foot and then lurched forward, sending the suitcase swinging in an arc toward the man's head. The guard stepped easily aside, allowing the weight of the suitcase to carry Victor around until he was off balance. He moved with the grace of a dancer, stepping behind Victor, knocking the suitcase to the ground and twisting Victor's arm up behind his back gently

34

but firmly, so that the responsibility for any pain would be Victor's if he attempted to struggle.

Victor acted instinctively, throwing back his head and closing his eyes in fierce concentration. He probed, ignoring the blinding pain, searching for some fear or anxiety in the guard's mind that he could touch and *grab hold of* with his own. There was something there, dark and shapeless, rough and rattling with death. Victor strained, probing harder and deeper, obsessed with the need to escape. Now the guard was making strange, guttural sounds deep in his throat. Victor felt steel-hard fingers at his neck, pressing, searching for the nerve centers at the base of his skull. He was inside the guard's mind and there was pain there that he was causing; still the man would not let go. Victor probed still deeper, wrenching the sensations, magnifying the pain.

Then the fingers were no longer around his neck. Victor turned in time to see the man sink to the ground. The guard was moaning softly, writhing on the ground and gripping his head in his hands. The moaning stopped. The guard twitched and then lay still.

Victor knelt down beside the guard and was immediately aware of yet another presence. He threw himself to one side and missed the full force of a blow delivered by a second, larger man who must have been positioned at the rear of the house. The second man tripped over the first and sprawled on the flagstone walk.

This time it was Victor who attacked, swinging around and stepping close to the second guard who was just springing to his feet. There was already pain in the other man as a result of his fall, fear and uncertainty at the sight of his prostrate partner. Victor seized on both thoughts and concentrated, thrusting deep. The man slumped to the sidewalk without a sound.

35

Victor reached for his suitcase and looked up into the face of Pat, who had run out onto the porch at the sounds of the struggle. Her eyes wide with fear, the woman had jammed her knuckles into her mouth so that only her mind screamed in terror and ripped at Victor's consciousness. Victor threw aside the suitcase, turned and ran, away from the fallen men, away from the horror in his wife's mind.

Roger Burns was certain he'd turned off the lights in his office and laboratory. Even if he'd forgotten, the cleaning woman would have remembered. He'd had no way of knowing that sleeplessness and excitement over the Rafferty file would bring him back here to his office in the middle of the night. Now, someone had broken into the building. There was no other explanation for the shaft of light that leaked out from beneath his office door into the darkness.

Roger's hand rested on the doorknob. He knew he should call the police, yet the only phone was the one on the other side of the door. He could not wake up a neighbor at three o'clock in the morning, the nearest pay booth was three blocks away, and he did not want the intruder to escape. He was outraged at the thought of someone rifling through his highly confidential files, if that was it.

Anger triumphed over reason. Roger burst into the room and then stopped short, frozen into immobility by the sudden realization that the two men in the office were no ordinary burglars and that he had stumbled into a situation he was totally incapable of handling.

The light came from the fluoroscope. One man, an individual Roger had seen a few times at Washington cocktail parties, was taking photographs of Victor Rafferty's X rays. The other had been microfilming files that Roger knew must also be Victor's. This man now had a revolver

36

in his hand. The long, thick silencer made it seem ridiculously out of proportion, like a toy rifle.

Roger raised one arm and the gun kicked. There was a soft, chugging sound and a small, round, white hole opened in Roger's forehead, then quickly filled with blood.

Victor sat in a booth at the rear of the coffee shop, toying nervously with a cup of muddy-brown coffee and staring at the front page of the newspaper he had spread out before him. He felt numb, dazed with guilt; the stories seemed to leap from the page, stabbing at his senses with twin fingers of accusation. *So,* Victor thought, *I am responsible for the deaths of two men.*

He was sure Roger had been murdered because of him; the guard, a man who had merely been doing his job, he had killed himself.

Some enterprising reporter had outwitted the dozen policemen outside his home with a telephoto lens. The picture showed the dead man on the walk. The second guard was just rising to his feet. Mr. Lippitt was standing off to one side, obviously unaware that the photograph was being taken. The picture had been captioned with a single, large question mark.

The waiter, an elderly man with dirty fingernails and a soiled apron, kept glancing in his direction. Victor wearily signaled for another cup. The waiter came to the table and wiped his hands on his shirt.

"Coffee," Victor said, not looking up.

The waiter pointed to the unfinished cup on the table. "You don't look so good, pal," he said. "Maybe you oughta' get some food in your stomach."

"I'm all right," Victor said, aware that he sounded defensive. "You can get me some bacon and eggs. And orange juice."

37

The waiter swiped at the table with a damp rag and then shuffled off, mumbling to himself. Victor reached out for the sugar bowl and began rolling it back and forth between his hands. With the suitcase gone, he had little money and no place to go. In any case, Mr. Lippitt would have all the airports and bus terminals watched. It was too late to do anything and so it didn't bother him that he was too tired to think clearly; there was nothing left to think about. He wondered if they'd shoot him on sight.

He could still feel the *texture* of the guards' minds as he had entered them to twist and hurt; he could see their bodies lying on the ground. Most of all, he remembered the expression of sheer horror on Pat's face.

Victor stopped spinning the sugar bowl. He had been staring at it and it had suddenly come to him that he was seeing the object in an entirely different way, with more than his vision. He *saw* the glass he was touching with his hands; at the same time he could *feel* the mirror image of the bowl somewhere in his brain, elusive, ephemeral, and yet seemingly real enough to be grasped.

Victor slowly took his hands away from the bowl and touched the image in his mind.

The pain was greater than any he had ever known. Victor immediately released the image and gripped the edges of the table in an effort not to lose consciousness. The pain passed in a few moments, gradually ebbing away. He opened his eyes but did not have enough time to evaluate what had happened. The waiter, approaching his table with a tray of food, tripped over a loose linoleum tile. The tray and its contents came hurtling through the air. Victor reacted instinctively in an effort to protect his only set of clothes; he reached out and pushed at the tray with his mind. At that instant Victor felt his body bathed in searing fire. The walls and ceiling tilted at an odd angle and the floor rushed up to smash into his face.

The waiter stared, dumbfounded. His startled gaze shifted rapidly back and forth between the unconscious man on the floor and the egg stains on his apron. Something was wrong, he thought, something besides the man on the floor; there was something out of place. The old man's slow mind struggled with the problem of the flying tray and food as he hurried to call the police and an ambulance.

Now only the memory of the pain remained, like the lingering, fuzzy morning taste of too many cigarettes. Victor's mind and senses were clear at last, cleansed of their blinding crust of panic by the shock of coma. The sour, antiseptic smell in his nostrils told him he was in a hospital; the dull throb in his skull told him he was not alone. Victor kept his eyes closed and lay very still.

He recalled the incident in the coffee shop very clearly and he knew what had happened. He had seen the word in the textbooks: *telekinesis,* the theoretical ability to move objects by the intense focusing of thought energy. Except that telekinesis was no longer theoretical; he could do it. No matter that the crippling pain made it highly improbable that he could ever use it effectively; the very fact that he had exhibited the power made him that much more desirable, or dangerous, in the eyes of Mr. Lippitt and whoever had killed Roger Burns. Perhaps they had already decided that the risks of using him were too great. He had run. He had killed a man. He was a criminal. They could easily shut him away in some prison for the rest of his life to make sure, if he didn't work for them, he wouldn't work for anyone else.

In the meantime, Pat was in terrible danger. Whoever had killed Roger would be after her next; Mr.

Lippitt had said as much. They would torture her; kill her, if they thought it could lead them to him. Victor was sure Mr. Lippitt had assigned men to guard her but that couldn't last forever. No, Victor reflected, he was endangering Pat by the very fact that he was alive.

The guard testified to the fact that he was caught. Probably the police or the hospital had called his home, and Mr. Lippitt would certainly have the phone tapped. Victor was surprised the thin man in the overcoat wasn't already at his bedside.

His was a prison with no doors and windows, a killing trap that was sucking his wife in to die with him, a problem with no solution—except one; only one. It was, as yet, only the embryo of an idea. First, he must escape the hospital.

"I'm feeling very well now," Victor said loudly, sitting up quickly and swinging his legs over the side of the bed. "Maybe you can tell me where my clothes are."

The policeman sat up as if stabbed with a pin. Startled, he fumbled for his gun and finally managed to point it in Victor's direction, but the asking of the question had been enough to implant the answer in the policeman's mind. Victor probed gently; the policeman was very tired; and his clothes were in the white closet at the far end of the room.

"You might as well just lay back there, mister," the policeman said, releasing the safety on his pistol as an afterthought. "I'm not even supposed to let you go to the head without keeping an eye on you."

Victor crossed his legs on the bed. His lungs ached from the tension but he managed to feign innocence. "Well, do you mind telling me why?" He must put the policeman off guard and there wasn't much time.

The policeman eyed Victor suspiciously. "I'm not supposed to talk about it."

40

Victor began to probe deeper and then stopped, sickened by the memory of the man he had killed outside his home. In that moment he knew he would not kill another innocent man, even if it meant his own death. Then, how?

". . . damned silly," the policeman mumbled.

"What's that?" The policeman hesitated, and Victor probed, gently magnifying the frustration he found in the other man's mind. He smiled disarmingly. "I didn't hear what you said."

"I didn't say . . . Oh, hell, this whole thing is silly. Some little guy claims you turned a plate of eggs around in the air without touching them. Before you know it, I'm pulling this extra baby-sitting duty."

"That does sound pretty silly."

Then he knows for certain, Victor thought; *Mr. Lippitt knows I am telekinetic.*

"Mind you, I was just on my way out the door when I pull this duty. As if that wasn't enough, I'm catching a few winks and this creep comes in and belts me in the mouth! He *hits* me, mind you! Weird little guy in an overcoat. Must be eighty degrees in here and this guy's wearing an overcoat! I'd have killed any other guy did that and this creep's a *little* guy. But his eyes; I never seen eyes like that. Crazy, if you know what I mean. Man, you don't mess with a guy that's got eyes like that." The policeman sneezed and Victor sat very still. "Anyway, this guy says he'll have my job *and* my pension if I fall asleep again. Just like that! No, sir! You don't mess with a guy like that. And get this, he takes the key and locks me *in* here! He's got to be some kind of big shot or he wouldn't dare do something like that. Says he's got to go someplace and he'll be right back." The man rubbed his nose and lips with an oversize, red handkerchief, then blew hard into it and repeated the process. "I think he's some kind of spy," the

41

policeman continued, studying Victor through narrowed eyelids. "I think maybe you're a spy too. Spies are always making up screwy stories. Call 'em *cover* stories. See it all the time in the movies."

Victor choked back the strained, hollow laughter in his throat. "Did this man say where he was going?"

The hand holding the gun had relaxed. Now it tightened again and the gun barrel leveled on Victor's stomach. "You ask too many questions," the policeman snapped. "I ain't even supposed to talk to you. Maybe you're a spy. Yeah, for all I know you're some kind of terrorist."

"It's all a mistake," Victor said very quietly, eyeing the gun. "I asked where the man went because I'm anxious for him to get back. I'm sure everything will be straightened out when he gets here. It's just too bad you had to get dragged into it, particularly when you didn't sleep much last night."

"Hey, how'd you know I didn't get much sack time?"

"Your eyes look tired. You were probably out playing poker with some of your friends."

"Son of a bitch, you know you're right? Dropped twenty bucks and my wife's going be screaming at me for a week!"

Victor began to concentrate on a single strand of thought. "You must be very tired," he said, accenting each word, caressing the other man's weariness. "You should sleep." The policeman yawned and stretched, and Victor glanced toward the door. Mr. Lippitt could enter the room at any time, and he'd have other men with him. "It's all a mistake. You're free to go to sleep, to rest."

"I . . . can't do that." The man was fighting to keep his head up. The gun had fallen on the floor and he looked at it with a dazed expression.

"It's all right. You can sleep. Go to sleep."

The policeman looked at Victor with a mixture of bewilderment and fear and then slumped in his chair. Victor quickly eased him onto the floor before going to the cabinet and taking out his clothes. He dressed quickly and stepped close to the locked door. He bent down and looked at the lock, breathing a sigh of relief; it was a relatively simple, interlocking bolt type with which he was quite familiar.

Victor knew he must not think of his fear or the pain that was to come, but only of the consequences of failure. He sat on the floor and closed his eyes. He rested his head against the door, summoning up in his mind an image of the moving parts of the lock, each spring, each separate component. He knew he must duplicate his feat in the coffee shop; he must control the image in his mind so as to move the tiny metal bars in the door. Pat's life, and probably his own, depended on it.

The pain came in great, sweeping, hot waves, as it had in the coffee shop, and Victor recognized the wet, dark patches behind his eyes as the face of death. He could feel his fingernails breaking and bleeding as he pushed them into the wood, defying the agony. The lock *must* turn. His blood surged through his body, bloating the veins and arteries in his face and neck to the point where Victor knew, in a few seconds at most, they must burst.

The lock clicked.

Physically exhausted, Victor slumped to the floor. He sucked greedily at the cool draughts of air wafting in beneath the door as he waited for the fire in his head to cool. At last he rose and opened the door far enough to look out into the corridor. Empty; Mr. Lippitt had thought the locked door would be enough.

The policeman was beginning to stir. Victor hurriedly found the man's wallet and took out the money he needed.

43

Then, summoning up his last reserves of strength, he stepped out into the hallway and headed for the emergency exit.

Pat Rafferty opened her eyes and stared into the darkness. She did not have to look at the luminous dial on the alarm clock to know it was the middle of the night; and there was someone in the room with her.

"Victor?" She said it like a prayer.

"Yes," came the whispered reply. "Don't be frightened and don't turn on the light. I want to make love to you."

Pat felt a shiver run through her body. The voice was Victor's but it was different, somehow. flat and sad. Resigned. His hand was on her body.

"Victor, I can't—"

"Don't think that, darling. Please love me. I need you now."

She felt her desire mount as Victor pressed his mouth against hers; his closeness and the need of her own body swept away her fears and she reached out to pull him down alongside her. In a few minutes they lay, spent and exhausted, in each other's arms; but Victor rose almost immediately and began dressing.

"Victor, please come and lie down again."

"I can't, darling. There isn't much time. I have to go."

Pat rubbed her eyes. Everything seemed so unreal. "How did you get in? There are men all around the house."

"I have my own built-in radar system," Victor said. "I can tell where they are." He moved closer to the bed so that Pat could just make out his shape in the darkness. She raised her arms but Victor moved back out of her reach. "I had to take the chance," he continued. "I had to see you to tell you I've always loved you. You see, I have to do something . . . terrible. There's no way to make you understand. I had to see you this one last time to say good-bye."

"Good-bye? Victor, I don't understand. Why . . .?" She was suddenly aware of a numb, thick sensation in her forehead. Her ears were buzzing. "Victor," Pat murmured, "I feel so strange . . ."

"I know, darling," Victor said. His voice was halting as if he were choking on tears. "I know. Good-bye."

He stood in the darkness for a long moment, staring at the still figure on the bed. Once he started to walk toward her and then stopped. Finally he turned and went back the way he had come.

Mr. Lippitt sat at his desk in the specially heated office. His feet were propped up on his desk and he held a steaming glass of tea in his hand. His frail body was enclosed in a thick, bulky sweater buttoned to the mid-point of his chest. He sipped at his tea and stared off into space. He regretted the fact that the order had gone out to kill Victor Rafferty.

But what else could one do with such a man save kill him? Lippitt thought. Rafferty could read thoughts, move objects and he could kill, all without lifting a finger. The military potential of such a man was too great ever to risk its possible use by a foreign power. Unlike the atom, there was only one Victor Rafferty, and whoever commanded his allegiance possessed a terrible weapon, a deadly skill that was silent and could be used over and over again undetected, with virtually no risk to its user. He had always prided myself as a good judge of character. He would have sworn to Rafferty's decency and patriotism. Then why had the man run?

Mr. Lippitt was interrupted in his thoughts by the buzz of the intercom. "Yes?"

"There's a message on an outside line, sir. I've already scrambled the circuit. Should I put him through?"

45

Mr. Lippitt's feet came down hard on the floor, jarring the desk and its contents, spilling the tea over a stack of multicolored, cross-indexed documents Lippitt had spent the day ignoring. He waited until he was sure he had regained control of himself and then picked up the receiver. "All right," Mr. Lippitt said, "patch him through."

There was a soft, whirring sound in the line, an automatic signaling device signifying that the scrambling device had been activated. "Lippitt here."

"He's in New York City," said the voice on the other end of the line. "He has a research lab in the Mason Foundry. He's hiding there. What are your instructions?"

Mr. Lippitt bent over and picked up the overturned glass. "What's your code name?"

"Vector Three," came the easy reply.

"Of course," Mr. Lippitt said, fingering the glass. "And I suppose that's where you are? The Mason Foundry?"

"Of course."

"All right, now you listen carefully," Lippitt said, opening a drawer and removing a small, snub-nosed revolver. He opened a box of shells and carefully loaded each chamber as he spoke. "I'll be in New York in an hour. Mason Foundry. You'll wait for me, of course."

"Of course."

Mr. Lippitt hung up and shoved the revolver beneath his sweater, inside his waistband along the hard ridge of his spine. He jabbed at the intercom.

"Yes, sir?" came the quick reply.

"I want a jet to New York, *now*" Mr. Lippitt barked at the startled secretary. "Arrange for helicopter and limousine connections. All top priority."

46

Mr. Lippitt was not surprised to find no agent waiting for him outside the building; neither was he surprised to find Victor Rafferty waiting for him inside.

"Come in," Victor said, leveling a pistol at Mr. Lippitt's forehead and motioning him to a chair across the book-lined executive office. "You look as if you expected me."

Mr. Lippitt shrugged. "You picked the wrong man's brain. Vector Three left for France two days ago."

"Then why did you come?"

"May I have a cigarette?" Victor threw a pack of cigarettes across the room and Mr. Lippitt purposely let them fall to the carpet. He bent over, freeing the revolver. He was certain his speed was sufficient to draw and kill Rafferty before the other man could even pull the trigger. He sat back up in the chair and lighted the cigarette. "I was curious," Mr. Lippitt continued casually. "I don't think you meant to kill that man. If I did, I'd have had this place surrounded with troops. Why did you run?"

"I don't think I could make you understand."

"That's too bad. You see, having you around is like living with an H-bomb; whether it's ticking or not, it still makes you uncomfortable."

"Now you're beginning to understand."

Mr. Lippitt glanced around the room, fascinated by the many models of buildings Victor had designed, relying on the properties of the high-tension steel alloy developed by the foundry. *Strange,* he thought, *how buildings had never interested me before.* He rose and walked across the room to examine one of the models more closely; he could feel the gun aimed at the back of his neck.

"So, what are you going to do?" Mr. Lippitt asked.

"I've already been contacted and all the arrangements have been made. I leave for another country tonight."

"That means you'll have to kill me."

47

"Yes."

Mr. Lippitt turned to face Victor. "Why? I mean, why defect?" He no longer made any effort to hide the emotion in his voice. "I wouldn't have thought you were a traitor."

Anger flickered in Victor's eyes, and then quickly faded. "You forced me to do what I'm doing," Victor said. "An H-bomb! That's what you compared me to, right? To you and your people—"

"They're your people, too."

"All right, *people!* To people, I'm nothing more than a weapon! Did it ever occur to you I might want to lead my own life?"

"We've already been over that. Without us, you and your wife would either be killed or kidnapped. We wouldn't want you to be killed; we couldn't allow you to be kidnapped."

"Exactly. So it boils down to this: since my life is no longer my own anyway, the only thing I can do is choose the side which can best provide protection for Pat and myself. By definition, a police state can provide more protection than a non-police state. Since I wouldn't be *free* in either country, I have to pick the country where I would be *safe*. Their very lack of freedom guarantees my life and Pat's."

"Very logical."

"Oh, there's money, too. I won't deny that. As long as I have to live out my life in virtual captivity, I may as well be comfortable. I've been assured of ... many things. You don't operate that way, do you?"

Mr. Lippitt ground out his cigarette and immediately lighted another. He regretted not killing Rafferty when he'd had the chance. "No, we don't. Unfortunately, our budget forces us to rely on patriotism."

48

Victor said nothing. Mr. Lippitt watched the other man rise and walk toward him. He tensed, waiting for exactly the right moment to drop to the floor and grab for his gun. He knew it would be very difficult now, for Rafferty was close and the element of surprise was gone. Yet, he knew he must not fail; he was the only remaining barrier between Rafferty and a foreign power or terrorists.

"Out the door," Victor said, prodding Mr. Lippitt with the gun. "Left and up the stairs. Walk slowly."

"Don't be melodramatic. Why not just shoot me here?"

"I want to show you something. If you prefer, I'll shoot you now."

There was something strange in the other man's voice, Mr. Lippitt noted, an element that he could not identify. In any event, he realized he would stand little chance if he made his move now. He walked ahead and through the door. The barrel of Rafferty's pistol was pressed against his spine, no more than an inch above the stock of Lippitt's revolver.

The stairway led to a long, narrow corridor. Mr. Lippitt walked slowly, the echo of his footsteps out of phase with those of the man behind him. He said, "It's quiet. Where is everybody?"

"There's no shift on Saturday," Victor said tightly. "There's only the watchman. I put him to sleep."

"You can do that?"

"You know I can."

"Just making conversation." Mr. Lippitt hesitated. "There is such a thing as *lesser evil* in the world, Rafferty. We need you on our side. Think about it."

"I'm sorry," Victor said. He reached out and grabbed Mr. Lippitt's shoulder. "In there."

Mr. Lippitt pushed through the door on his left marked *Restricted.* He found himself on a very narrow

49

catwalk overlooking a row of smelting furnaces. The cover hatches of the furnaces were open and Mr. Lippitt looked down into a liquid, metal sea that moved with a life of its own, its silver-brown crust buckling and bursting, belching huge bubbles of hot, acrid gas. The air was thick, heavy with its burden of heat.

"You wanted to show me where you were going to dump my body," Mr. Lippitt said.

"Yes."

Mr. Lippitt watched Victor's eyes. He could not understand why the other man had not been able to probe his thoughts and discover the existence of the gun. Perhaps he had not felt the need; the reports had mentioned the pain linked with the act. In any case, Mr. Lippitt thought, Rafferty would be dead the moment he blinked or looked away for even a fraction of a second. "You're going to do very well in your chosen profession," Mr. Lippitt said, steeling himself for the move he knew he would have only one chance to make. "People tend to trust you, give you the benefit of the doubt. You have a very disarming air about you."

"That's not all I wanted to show you," Victor said.

Lippitt's muscles tensed but his hand remained perfectly still. When he did go for the gun it would be in one fluid, incredibly explosive motion.

"I want to show you what might have been if things were different," Victor said.

Mr. Lippitt said nothing. It seemed to him that Rafferty was relaxing, letting down his guard. Also, he judged that the angle of the gun would allow him to get off at least one shot, even if he were hit, and one shot was all he needed. Still, he waited.

"You're cold," Victor said suddenly. "You can't even feel the heat from those furnaces."

"What?"

50

"I said, you're cold. You're always cold. You've been cold for the past twenty years. That's why your mind is so strong. You can't block out the memories so you control and discipline yourself to the point where they no longer make any difference, but still you can't feel any warmth."

"Don't," Mr. Lippitt said, his voice scarcely a whisper.

"You can't forget your torturers and their ice baths. They put you in the water and they left you there for hours. You shook so much you thought your bones would break. You remember how they laughed at you when you cried; you remember how they laughed at you when you begged them to kill you."

"You stay out of my mind! Stop it!" Mr. Lippitt's voice was quivering with rage.

"It takes enormous courage to keep going in the face of memories like that," Victor continued easily. "All those coats, all those overheated rooms; none of it does any good. We're alike, you and I. Both of us suffer agony others can't begin to understand. That's why you broke all the rules and came here alone, even when you knew I'd be waiting for you; you were reluctant to see them kill me."

"You devil," Mr. Lippitt said in a hoarse whisper. "You play with people, don't you?"

"There's nothing wrong with your body, you know. That healed long ago. The torturers are gone. You don't have to be cold anymore."

There was something soothing and hypnotic about Rafferty's voice. Mr. Lippitt struggled to clear his mind as he fought against the pervading warmth spreading through his body, fought it and yet embraced it as a father his dead child returned to life.

"It's a trick," the thin man said, startled to find his eyes brimming with tears.

"No," Victor said quietly, insistently. "I'm not putting the warmth in your body; it was always there. I'm simply helping you to feel it. Forget the water. All that happened a long time ago. You can be warm. Let yourself be warm."

"No!"

"Yes! Let me into your mind, Lippitt. Trust me. Let me convince you."

Mr. Lippitt closed his eyes, surrendering to the strange, golden warmth lighting the dark, frozen recesses of his soul. He thought of all the years he had spent in the prison of his memory, immersed in the water that was sucking away his life . . .

"You don't feel cold anymore."

"No," Mr. Lippitt whispered. Now the tears were flowing freely down his cheeks. "I don't feel cold anymore."

"Why don't you test it? Take off your coat."

Mr. Lippitt slowly removed his heavy overcoat. Now the revolver was within easy reach. "I'm sorry," he said. "I'm grateful to you, but no man should have that kind of power."

"Not unless he can use it wisely," Victor replied, raising the hand with the gun. The hammer clicked back with the soft, assured sound of finely tooled metal. "The demonstration is over."

Mr. Lippitt dropped to his knees and rolled over on his side, clawing for the gun in his waistband. Years of experience and training had transformed him into a precision killing instrument, the movements of which must be measured in milliseconds. Still, inside Mr. Lippitt's mind, it was all slow motion, as in a nightmare; he drifted through the air and bounced on the concrete, the gun in his hand and aimed at Victor Rafferty's heart, but there was something pulling at the gun, an invisible force that he

52

could feel writhing like a snake in the metal. Steel bands had wrapped about his head and were squeezing, crushing his brain. He pulled the trigger twice, then peered through a mist of pain as Victor Rafferty toppled over the guard rail and plummeted through space to land with a grotesquely muffled, crackling splash in the liquid inferno below. It was the last thing Mr. Lippitt saw before sinking down into a black void laced with the smell of gun smoke.

The barrel of the revolver was still warm, leading Mr. Lippitt to conclude that he couldn't have been unconscious more than a few minutes. He lurched to his feet and, supporting himself on the guardrail, stared down into the pit where Victor had fallen; the slag continued to belch and bubble. There was no trace of the other man, not even the smell of burnt flesh. So, he reflected, he had killed the man who had cured him. No matter that there was no choice; for the rest of his life, even as he savored the warmth of the sun on his body, he would remember this day and welcome his own approaching death; he had simply traded one nightmare for another.

He paused at the foot of the stairs and, after a moment's hesitation, entered one of the offices. He picked up a telephone and dialed one of the outside lines to the agency.

"Good afternoon," came the cheery voice, "this is—"

"This is Mr. Lippitt. The fox is dead."

There was a long silence on the other end of the line. When the woman spoke again, her voice was punctuated by heavy breathing. "Sir, this is an outside line. If you'll wait for just a moment—"

"This is an emergency," Lippitt said slowly. "Fox is dead. Fox is *dead.*"

53

He hung up before the frightened woman had time to reply. He reasoned that the others would be suspicious at first, at least until they'd had time to check their sources for the code words. Besides, he'd make sure that certain information was leaked. That, he decided, should keep them away from the woman. He lighted a cigarette, and then picked up the phone again to call the Rafferty home.

I'm here to see Mr. Thaag.

The Civilized and the Savage. He'd been a guest of the United Nations the day Senior Thaag had made that speech. He'd never met the man. That should make things easier.

Some men would kill for a tattered tribal banner. Their imagination sets with the sun, their world ends at the horizon. Others travel the planet, whisper many tongues, and find only the face of their brother.

The Civilized and the Savage. How does one tell the difference? He could tell the difference.

May I have your name, sir?

Nagel. John Nagel.

Or any other name. It didn't make any difference. His real name had died with his old identity. It was all there in the two-column obituary in the *Times*. Everything in his past had died back in the foundry with the image he had planted in Mr. Lippitt's mind. Eventually, he would need a new appearance, a new manner and personality. For now, John Nagel would have to get along with tinted contact lenses, false beard and an exaggerated limp.

He'd miss Pat; he'd ache for her. But his "death" had been her only guarantee of life.

I'm sorry, sir, but your name is not on the appointment list. Are you expected?

He would lean close, make contact with her mind. She must be convinced of his *importance*. The secretary would disappear for a few minutes, then reappear, smiling.

The Secretary General will see you now.

He was not sure what would happen next; he would have to wait until he could get close to Thaag and explore his mind. Even then, he was not sure what he would be looking for; perhaps, simply, a man he could trust.

Victor Rafferty went over his plan once more in his mind. Satisfied, he began walking slowly across the United Nations Plaza toward the massive glass and stone obelisk rising up from New York's East River. He stopped and looked up into the bright, sun-splashed day; a breeze was blowing and the multitude of flags strained against their stanchions, painting a line across the sky.

BROKEN PATTERN

Emily finished grading the last of the homework papers, fastened them together with a large clip and placed them carefully in her briefcase. She closed the case, rose and walked to the window. She loved this room, with its view overlooking the school's vast athletic field. Below her, to the right, was a small stand of blue spruce. At the far end of the field the ninth-grade football team was just finishing practice. Sometimes when she was very upset, when the old feelings caught her by surprise, she would stop whatever she was doing and come to stand by this window. Usually a moment was enough, and she could turn back to her class without a scream in her throat.

Already the first month had passed, and she was happy for the first time in more years than she could remember. This time everything was going to be all right; she just knew everything was going to be all right.

"Mrs. Terrault?"

Emily wheeled and choked off a cry when she saw the two students standing by her desk. Heath Eaton stood a few inches taller than Kathy, his twin. Both children had blond hair, fair skin, and bodies that had been flattered by the onset of puberty. Their physical appearance was marred only by blue eyes that seemed too bright and did not, in Emily's opinion, blink often enough.

"You startled me," Emily said in a voice that was not as steady as she would have liked. "I didn't hear you come in." She paused and smiled. The children stared at her impassively. "What are you doing in the school so late?"

"Kathy asked her counselor for permission to come and speak to you about her grades," the boy said. "I got permission to come with her." The boy's tone was flat, a perfect cover for the strange hint of insolence that was forever peering around its edges. Emily had noticed this before, in class, but now it seemed especially pronounced. She turned her attention to the girl.

"So, speak." She had meant the words to be light and cheerful; they came out heavy and tired.

"You failed me on this paper, Mrs. Terrault," Kathy said, taking a neatly folded paper from her purse and handing it to Emily.

"Yes, Kathy, I know," Emily said, keeping her hands at her sides. She found it somewhat unnerving that the small hand with the folded paper remained stretched out toward her. "But I didn't 'fail you,' as you put it. You failed yourself. I gave you what you earned."

"I'd like you to change it please, Mrs. Terrault."

"Kathy, you know I can't do that."

"You mean you won't."

"Kathy!" Emily said, and glanced sideways at Heath. The boy was studying his hands, seemingly oblivious to the entire conversation. "I've never heard you talk like this before."

"This is the third paper I've failed this term, Mrs. Terrault. Besides that, my work in class hasn't been what it should. I know that. I'm going to fail if you don't change my marks."

Emily turned quickly to the window. Heath was already there, staring out, tapping his fingers on a desk. She turned back as the girl spoke again.

"I'm bright, Mrs. Terrault, very bright. You know that, if you've bothered to look at my record. I've been upset the past few weeks. You know very well I could get good grades if I tried, and I *am* going to try. It's not as if you were *giving* me something."

"I don't know about your other courses, Kathy, but in this subject you will get exactly what you earn. No more, and no less." Emily's tone had been very soft, masking the tension under it. Kathy's matched it.

"Both Heath and I plan on getting into good colleges," the girl said evenly. "Since we're both in a home, an institution, that means we'll have to depend on scholarships—good scholarships. And *that* means we're going to have to be at the top of our class. Either Heath or I—we haven't decided which one as yet—is going to be valedictorian. The other is going to be salutatorian. But we have to start now, in the ninth grade. You know that too. I can't afford to fail even a single subject, especially Social Studies."

"Kathy . . . Kathy, I don't know what to say to you. I do think, though, that there's someone else you should speak to. I'm going to make an appoint—"

"Hey, Kathy," Heath said loudly from his place near the window, "I've got things to do." Emily did not turn. She heard the boy's footsteps coming across the room, around the desks, and then he was standing in front of her. "Change the mark, Mrs. Terrault," the boy said. "If you don't, we'll kill you."

The room was suddenly silent, the stillness grazed only by the sound of Emily's heavy breathing. She wanted desperately to look out the window, but she was afraid to move.

"You're very impatient," Kathy said to her brother.

"I told you I've got things to do. Sister Joseph gave us permission to watch the Knicks on TV, but we have to start study period an hour earlier."

"My brother's telling the truth, Mrs. Terrault," Kathy said to Emily. "If you don't change the mark, we will kill you. We've killed people before. Just last month we killed Margie Whitehead, and—"

"Shut up, Kathy," the boy said.

"But she should know that we're not fooling, Heath."

"I think she knows, don't you, Mrs. Terrault?" The boy's eyes were steady on her. "There isn't going to be any problem. Mrs. Terrault is going to take care of you this term, and then you're going to promise to do the work you're capable of. Right, Kathy?"

"Right. Take the paper, Mrs. Terrault. Change it in the grade book too."

Emily started to run toward the open door, stumbled and fell to the floor. The two children remained where they were. She slowly pulled herself to her feet and turned to face the children. Now she was grateful she had tripped; she had almost allowed two desperately sick children to stampede her. But she couldn't panic, couldn't run, not again. Not ever again.

The problem remained as to what to do if the children actually attacked her. There was a letter opener in the desk, but that was too far away. No, she would have to rely on her authority; she was the teacher, they were the students. She took a very deep breath.

"Come with me, Heath and Kathy," Emily said, grateful that her voice did not quaver. "Did you hear me? I want you to come with me."

The children exchanged glances. "Where do you want us to go, Mrs. Terrault?" Kathy said.

"You know very well. We're all going down to see Mr. Atkins."

"You're going to do that old office number?" The boy laughed, quickly and without humor.

For one long, terrible moment Emily did not think they would obey her. Then the boy shrugged and started across the room. Kathy followed.

The custodians had already shut off the lights in the corridor and dusk seeped through the skylights, painting the lockers, the walls and the air a murky gray. Emily walked at a steady pace, shoulders back and head high. The children's footsteps echoed on the floor behind her. She would not run, and she dared not turn. She knew she must not, for a moment, show fear.

Somehow she made it down the stairway to the ground floor. Behind her, the children marched in step. She rounded the last corner, stopped and burst into tears. The office area was dark and deserted.

Kathy stepped around in front of her. Heath remained behind, very close. Emily was afraid—very afraid. She closed her eyes and put her hands to her face.

"Well, it's just as well nobody's here, Mrs. Terrault," Kathy said easily. "Believe me, it wouldn't have gone well for you."

Emily slowly took her hands away from her face. The girl was smiling up at her, supremely confident. In that moment their roles had been reversed; Emily was the child, the child was the teacher.

"What did you say?"

"Mr. Atkins would never believe you. Nobody would believe you. Heath and I came all the way back to school for extra help. You started to talk and act funny. It wouldn't be the first time, would it?"

"I don't know what you mean," Emily said in a strangled voice.

"Yes you do, Mrs. Terrault," Heath said, stepping forward to stand next to his sister. "You know how teachers sometimes talk to each other in the halls and classrooms without bothering to see who else might be listening. We know all about you. We know you used to teach in the high school and then you had some kind of breakdown. You spent the last two years in a mental institution. When you got out you asked if you could come back and teach at a junior high level. The school board hired you, but you're still on probation. I'm betting they keep a pretty close eye on you. If you start telling crazy stories, they'll get rid of you."

Emily turned to the wall, pressing her hands and her cheek against a cold metal locker. She swallowed hard, and discovered there was no moisture left in her mouth. "'Get out," she whispered, closing her eyes. "Get away from me." When she opened her eyes they were gone.

The psychologist was young, Emily thought, not yet thirty, about her own age. She had fine features that were complemented by just the right touch of expensive cosmetics and good fashion sense. Emily knew some men might find the other woman attractive despite the thin, compressed line of her mouth and the infuriating air of superiority she carried with her like the cloying aura of cheap perfume.

The seconds dragged on. The initial rush of relief Emily had experienced when she had finished her story had been short-lived, smothered by the woman's seeming indifference. The psychologist continued to avoid Emily's eyes as she drew concentric circles on a scratchpad placed on the table between them.

"Well, why don't you *say* something?"

"Quite frankly, Mrs. Terrault, I don't know what to say," the woman said. There was an edge to her voice. She dropped the pencil and looked up. "I just don't know what to make of your story."

"You think I'm lying?"

"Now, I don't say that *you* don't believe—"

"*I* believe, poppycock!" Emily said, half rising from her chair. "I know what you're trying to say!"

"It's not going to serve any purpose for you to get excited, Mrs. Terrault."

Frightened by the strength of her own emotions, Emily sat down again, clasping her hands tightly together. "Do you know what it *cost* me to come to you?" Emily's voice trembled. She could feel herself walking a high wire of words over an abyss of hysteria. She stumbled on. "Don't you suppose I knew the risk 1 was taking in telling someone that two fifteen-year-old children had threatened to kill me? But it's true. It's *true*"

"They're much more than just ordinary children, Mrs. Terrault, as I'm sure you're aware, from having them in your class. They both have I.Q.'s in the genius range, and they have already experienced severe trauma in their lives. Their father was hacked to death with an ax, and the killer was never found. The mother then proceeded to withdraw into herself to the point where she could no longer care for the children. Heath and Kathy were placed in a home for children upstate near their own home. Last year they were transferred down here to St. Catherine's. All in all, I'd say they have made a remarkable adjustment to circumstances that would crush lesser children . . . and some adults."

Emily winced under the lash of the last words. "They're monsters," she said very softly. "Monsters. They told me they killed Margie Whitehead."

63

"Really, Mrs. Terrault. At least twenty other children saw Margie fall under the wheels of that bus, not to mention the two adult bus monitors."

"I know, but even to *say* such a thing a child would have to be terribly, terribly sick. That's why I came to you, that's why I'm telling you all this. I feel they should be helped."

The psychologist sighed. "I must be frank with you, Mrs. Terrault. Heath and Kathy Eaton came in to see me last week."

Emily unconsciously put her hand over her mouth. Suddenly it was hard to breathe.

'They were very upset," the woman continued, "which is quite unusual for them. They said that for some reason they didn't understand, you didn't seem to like them. Kathy said you frightened her, and both children claimed that you picked on them. They asked me if I could help *them* change so that they could please *you,* Mrs. Terrault. In light of that conversation, I'm sure you can see the difficulty of my position."

"When did they come to see you?" Emily's voice sounded apart from herself, an alien echo inside her head.

"Last Tuesday."

"That was the day after I handed back the papers."

Their eyes met and held.

"Mrs. Terrault," the psychologist said, her smile too sweet, too bright, "may I ask you the name of your doctor?"

"Go to hell," Emily said softly, "You go straight to hell."

"Do I have to tell you about it, Mrs. Terrault?"

"No, Mary Ann, you don't. But I would like you to."

"My mother said I shouldn't talk about it. I still get nightmares sometimes."

Emily felt tears spring to her eyes. She understood nightmares, the cold sweat of the mind. She reached out and stroked the girl's thin shoulders. "Mary Ann, I know how it must hurt you to talk about it. Believe me, I wouldn't ask if it weren't very important to me."

"Well, we were all standing in our place outside B wing waiting for our bus. Margie was standing right next to the curb. Bus Eleven had picked up some students and was going around the driveway. Margie fell in front of it just as it was passing us. Her . . . her body made a real funny sound when the wheels went . . . when the wheels—"

"You don't have to tell me that part," Emily said quickly. "Were there many students there when it happened?"

"Billy Johnson was absent that day.'

"Yes, but how many other students were waiting for the bus?"

"I don't know exactly, Mrs. Terrault. Fifteen, I guess. Maybe more."

"And Mr. Johnson and Mrs. Biggs were there?"

"They were farther down the sidewalk talking to each other like they always do. Frank Mason said he saw them kissing one time."

"Mary Ann, can you remember who was standing closest to Margie?"

"It's awfully hard, Mrs. Terrault."

"I know, Mary Ann. Please try."

"Well, I was on one side of her. There was Frank Mason, Steve, Kathy and Zeke. I think Sammy was close to her too."

"Kathy Eaton?"

"Yes. Mrs. Terrault, your finger is bleeding."

Emily quickly took her hand from her mouth and wrapped the raw knuckle in the folds of her skirt. "Did . . . Margie have any trouble with anyone? You know what I mean. Did she ever fight with anybody?"

"Do I have to tell the truth, Mrs. Terrault?"

"Please, Mary Ann."

"Nobody liked Margie. She was always making fun of people, and she thought she was better than everybody else just because she was good in Gym." The girl paused. "I'm sorry to say those things about Margie, but you asked me to tell the truth."

"I know, I know, Mary Ann." Emily took the girl in her arms, as much to hide her own tears as to comfort the child. "Was there one particular person she picked on more than anybody else?"

"Margie picked on everybody."

"Did she pick on . . . Kathy Eaton?"

"Margie was always trying to pick a fight with Kathy, always bumping into her in Gym and calling her names. But Kathy never fought back. She'd just walk away. Kathy acts real grown-up. I like her a real lot."

Emily gently pushed the girl away. Mary Ann's head was bowed, her eyes cast down. Emily put her fingers under the girl's chin and pressed very softly until the girl's eyes met her own. "I just want to ask you one more thing, Mary Ann. Please try to think very hard before you answer. Did anything . . . unusual happen that day? I mean, do you remember anything strange that might have happened just before . . . the accident?"

The girl stared thoughtfully at Emily for a few moments, and then smiled, as at a happy memory. "Heath was being funny."

"How was Heath being funny, Mary Ann?"

"He came running out of the school door—"

66

"Was this just before Bus Eleven started up?"

"I guess so. Anyway, Heath came running out of the school, and he was pretending he was an opera star, you know, singing funny and clowning around. Heath didn't usually do things like that, so everybody was staring at him. Everybody was laughing at him except Mr. Johnson and Mrs. Biggs. I think they were mad. Then everybody stopped laughing when the bus ran over Margie."

The dismissal bell rang. Emily made a pretense of searching for a paper, opened her desk drawer and turned on the tape recorder. She left the drawer partially open, then glanced up at the two children who had remained behind.

"You wanted to see us, Mrs. Terrault?"

"Yes," Emily said, then hesitated. She had intended putting on an act, but now discovered that the fear she felt was not at all feigned. She suddenly pushed back her chair and stood. "I have decided to do nothing about Kathy's grades. Now, do you still intend to kill me?"

Heath and Kathy Eaton glanced at each other. They seemed confused.

"We don't know what you mean, Mrs. Terrault," Heath said quietly.

The girl reached out and touched Emily's arm. "Do you feel all right, Mrs. Terrault?"

"Maybe you didn't hear me, Kathy," Emily said, backing away. "I am not going to help you by raising your grades, no matter how much you threaten me. As I told you the other day, in my class you will get exactly what you earn."

"I don't know what you mean by 'threatening you,' Mrs. Terrault. As for my grades, I know how fair you are and I know I'm getting exactly what I deserve. I'm just going to have to work harder from now on. I know that. Isn't that right, Heath?"

"That's right, Kathy."

"Kathy," Emily whispered, "just the other day you and your brother threatened to kill me. You know you did."

Emily watched in amazement as tears began to roll down Kathy Eaton's cheeks. Heath stepped in front of his sister.

"Why are you trying to frighten us?" the boy said. "You made my sister cry."

Emily glanced helplessly back and forth between the faces of the two children. They were so *good* at what they were doing. Even Heath's tone had changed to that of a frightened boy; it was not at all the voice she had heard several days before, or the voice she would hear many hours later.

The insistent ringing tore through the early morning silence. Trembling, Emily picked up the receiver and held it to her ear.

"Mrs. Terrault? This is Heath."

"I know who it is."

"I just wanted you to know that we're not stupid. We'll never talk to you in school again, and this is the last time I'll phone. That's just in case you have a tape recorder and know how to use it."

"Heath! Listen to me, Heath! You're sick! Kathy's sick! Both of you need *help* Let me help you!"

"Look, *Emily,* we're not the ones who just got out of a nut house, so you'd better just shut up and listen. The only help we want from you is for you to change Kathy's Social Studies grades like we asked you to. You haven't so far because you don't believe we'll do what we say we will. That's a mistake."

"Where are you, Heath?"

"I'm in a phone booth across the street from my cottage. By the time you hang up and call St. Catherine's I'll be back through the window I came out of, in bed. So don't bother. In the meantime you'd better check out your car."

"My car?"

"It's shot. The tires and upholstery are slashed, and all the wiring ripped out. There's also ten pounds of sugar in your gas tank and carburetor. My opinion is that it'll be cheaper to buy a new car than to try and have that one fixed. No charge for the advice."

"Why, Heath? *Why?*"

"Because you're so *stupid,* Mrs. Terrault! *Emily*" The boy's voice was shrill now, almost hysterical. *"All* of you, you have such little minds! And you think that you have the right to *control* people like Kathy and me!"

"Heath, you're mad!"

"Tomorrow, Mrs. Terrault." The voice was calm again.

"Heath-!"

"No! No more talk! Tomorrow! That's the last day. After that we'll do the same to you as I did to your car. Then we'll go cry on that moron psychologist's shoulder about how shocked we are by your death, and how we loved you even if you did always mark Kathy unfairly. Think about it, Mrs. Terrault, and sleep well."

"Over a *grade?!*"

"It's not just a grade, Em," Sykes said, leaning back in his leather chair that always squeaked, and propping his feet up on the desk. "After all, you must

69

admit that their logic is impeccable. In four years, this quarter grade could make a difference of, say, a tenth of a point, possibly enough to alter their class ranking. After all, they want to go to Harvard, and they're too smart to underestimate their competition."

"But to *kill*"

"From what you've described to me, the Eaton children both have sociopathic personalities. To compound the difficulties, they're both extremely intelligent. You see, they've mapped out their whole lives, their goals, like a chess problem, and they're the only major pieces on the board. Everyone—everything—else is a pawn. A sociopath does not feel as you and I feel. It is quite conceivable that, given enough provocation, those children would kill you with no more thought than you might give to kicking a stone out of your path."

Emily shook her head. "I still don't understand. They're only *children.*"

"There is a definite pattern to physical and psychological growth, Em. The pattern of physical growth we can see, while we can only feel the effects of psychological growth. An infant is a raging bundle of *need,* pure id, the center of the universe. Gradually, the pattern grows as the ego—the "I"—develops, and the ego is perceived in terms of others. In other words, a child knows that he exists as a human being because he sees *other* human beings. But this does not make him civilized. The child will not be truly civilized until he can empathize, to a degree, with other people's pain and wants. Contrary to the public image, a small child is a veritable savage who would gladly kill another in a moment of rage if that other child somehow stood in the way of something the first child wanted very badly. Of course, he doesn't have the strength, and his goals—and his rage—are very short-lived. This allows time for the child to develop a superego, a con-

70

science, if you will, which will modify his behavior toward other people. In a sociopathic personality, the pattern has been broken. How, we can only guess. In this case, the 'how and why' isn't important. If what you say is true, you're probably in a great deal of danger. You may have become a special challenge to them."

Emily closed her eyes, and then slowly spoke the words, as if exorcising the demons that had plagued her the past week. "Do you think I've imagined all this?"

"I don't know, Em," Sykes said easily. "What are your thoughts on the subject?"

Emily reached into her pocketbook, took out a neatly folded piece of paper and handed it to the psychiatrist. Sykes opened it, studied it, and then glanced up quickly. "This is-?"

"Mrs. Elizabeth Eaton. Heath and Kathy's mother."

"You've seen her?"

"Yesterday. I took a day off from work, rented a car and drove upstate to see her. I got her address from records at the home. I told them I was calling on school business. She's a strange woman, broken, living alone. She was very happy to have someone to talk to. We talked all day."

"What did you talk about?"

"Her children." Emily paused, trying to think of some easy way to phrase what she had to say next. There was none. "Mrs. Eaton thinks that Heath and Kathy killed her husband; their father."

Sykes rose, walked to a window and drew back a curtain. "Did she say so?"

"Not in so many words," Emily said, rushing now, once again feeling panic whispering in her ear. "But I knew that was what she was telling me, in her own way. What woman in her right mind would accuse two children— *young* children— of hacking their father to death?"

71

"Exactly."

The word was spoken softly, but it came at her like a cannon shot. Emily whimpered and put her hand to her mouth, but she would not be denied. She *knew* what she had heard. "There's my car! It's still sitting in the parking lot."

"Along with three others wrecked in the same way, if I remember your story correctly. If Heath did do it, he went to the trouble of making it look like a random act."

Emily slumped in her chair, exhausted, beaten. "What do I do, Doctor?"

"Change the mark, of course."

Emily looked up. Sykes had turned from the window and was gazing steadily at her. "I didn't say I didn't believe you, Em. It really doesn't make any difference, at least not at this point. Maybe we'll find out more about that in therapy. For the time being, we must assume that one of two things is true: either you are imagining this business with the Eatons, or you are not. If you are imagining it, then no harm will come in any case from changing Kathy 's grade. If you're *not* imagining it, well . . ."

Sykes left the sentence unfinished.

"What then?" Emily whispered.

"Then I suggest that you take a leave of absence for the rest of the year, until Heath and Kathy Eaton are transferred to the high school."

Emily was astonished to find herself shaking her head. "I can't. They killed a little girl. Maybe they've killed more. Maybe they'll kill again."

"If so, there's nothing you can do about it, Em. They not only won't believe you, they'll destroy you."

"You're talking about other people."

"Yes, Em. I would have thought that two years of therapy would have taught you that evil doesn't wear a sign around its neck. Just because *you* see evil doesn't mean that others will; sometimes they can't, sometimes they choose not to. In this case I'd say it's a lot of both."

"I can't just leave them free to kill again."

"I'm sorry, Em, but I can't think of any other option. Can you?"

The snow was gone, chased by spring's laughter. Outside the window, down on the athletic field, a lone runner bobbed along the border of trees, nimbly skirting the puddles. Emily turned from the open window. The twins were waiting beside her desk.

"Thank you for coming in after school to see me," Emily said. "Heath, I know you have track practice. I won't keep you long." She smiled. "First, I'd like to compliment both of you on your work the past two quarters. You're by far the best of my students."

It was true. Since Emily had changed Kathy's disastrous first-quarter grades, both children had been model students, earning straight A's. Since then, aside from the stiff formality that was a part of the uneasy truce of silence they maintained, it was as if the incidents earlier in the year had never happened. Emily decided to probe.

"Kathy, you never did tell me why you were so upset at the beginning of the year."

"That's right, Mrs. Terrault, I didn't." The girl was making an effort to sound unruffled, but there was an edge to her voice. There had been no warning that she would be forced to play the role of belligerent, and she was having trouble shifting emotional gears.

"Was it Margie Whitehead, Kathy? Was it because you might have felt just a little bit of guilt at killing another human being?"

73

The girl started to whimper, but her eyes remained dry.

Heath was more convincing. "Why are you trying to scare us, Mrs. Terrault? You're starting to say funny things again."

"It doesn't really matter, you know," Emily said matter-of-factly. She went to her desk and sat down behind it, folding her hands in front of her.

"Mrs. Terrault," Heath said, "I have to go to track practice, and Kathy has to be home early. May we go, please?"

"Did I ever tell you why I was confined to a mental institution?" Emily said softly. The two children stared back at her, and she smiled again. The Hunter and the Hunted, with the roles continually shifting. But the children did not move. Emily had known they wouldn't, for a new factor had been added to an equation they had thought solved, and they would need time to evaluate it to their complete satisfaction.

"I could not tolerate evil," Emily continued quietly. "More precisely, I could not tolerate the idea that there was so little I could do about the evil I saw. I was really quite pathetic. When I read of a starving child, I could not eat my meals. If I heard a news report of families without heat in their homes, I couldn't face my own blankets. I won't dwell on my past, because I'm not proud of it. I was a very sick woman. Eventually it got to the point where I couldn't function at all. When I wasn't crying, I was breaking things in a blind rage. I lost my husband because of my sickness, and eventually I was hospitalized, as you know. Finally I learned— accepted would be a better term—that the best most people like myself can do is to function *themselves* as good men and women."

"Why are you telling us all this, Mrs. Terrault?"

74

"I'd like to show you two something," Emily said, opening her purse. She took out a packet of photographs and spread them across the desk. "These are some pictures of the institution where I stayed. Look at them."

The children remained where they were. Kathy had begun to cast anxious glances at her brother, who continued to stare at Emily. A smile tugged at the edges of his lips but never quite materialized.

"You should look at them," Emily said. "You'll see that it's really quite a nice place. Then you'll understand why I won't mind going back there. You see, Heath and Kathy, I'm going to have to kill you."

"Boy, *Emily,*" Heath said, "you really have flipped out."

"Yes, Heath, I'm sure that's what everyone will think. I'm counting on it." Emily opened her drawer, took out the pistol and pointed it at them. She needed both thumbs to pull back the hammer, but the hand holding the gun was steady. "You have no idea how much trouble I had getting this thing," she said casually. "But then, practicing was fun." She raised the gun. "I hope it won't hurt. I truly do."

Heath seemed frozen, his mouth half open. His hands trembled. The tears in Kathy's eyes were real.

"They'll kill you if you do this, Mrs. Terrault. You know they will." Heath's voice cracked and he too began to cry. "No woman in her right mind . . ."

"Precisely, Heath. No woman in her right mind would kill two children. But I'm not in my right mind, am I? Certainly that 'moron psychologist' friend of yours doesn't think so. No, only you and I will know how sane an act this really is, killing the two of you. It's simply something that must be done, precisely because there is no alternative. I would gladly die, if need be, but even

75

that isn't necessary, not with my background. I'll be committed. I have a good psychiatrist, and with a little luck I might even be sent back to the same place. Of course, I won't have as much freedom, and it may take me longer to be 'cured' this time, but at least I'll have the satisfaction of knowing that for once in my life I was able to *do* something about a particular evil."

Heath opened his mouth to yell.

"Don't bother," Emily said easily. "Everyone's gone to the middle school for a faculty meeting, and the janitor's half deaf."

"Mrs. Terrault?" The girl's voice was barely audible. Emily swung the gun around until it was pointed at the small, white forehead. "Please, Mrs. Terrault, I don't want to die."

"Neither did Margie Whitehead, Kathy. Neither will God knows how many other victims, people the two of you will kill or maim unless I kill you first. You see, Kathy, your tears mean nothing to me . . . because I have seen your true face. Besides, even if I decided not to kill you, you'd find a way to kill me."

"No, Mrs. Terrault." Heath had come forward and placed both hands on her desk. Emily swung the gun around and he backed away. "We wouldn't, Mrs. Terrault. I promise we wouldn't. We'd confess, and they could send us to a hospital."

Emily laughed. "Who would believe you, Heath?"

"We'll *make* them believe us! I'll tell them about your car! I'll tell them about how we planned it so that Margie's death would look like an accident! I'll—"

"Be quiet, Heath," the girl said suddenly. "She doesn't believe you. She knows better." Emily let the girl come closer. "I know you're not going to believe me, either, Mrs. Terrault, but . . . I'm . . . I think I'm sorry we killed Margie. And I'm sorry we . . . killed . . . our father."

"Did you kill your father, Kathy?"

"Yes," the girl said after a long pause, "but he wasn't our real father. I know he wasn't—and he hated us. When we killed him it was like . . . playing a game."

Emily pointed the gun squarely between the girl's eyes. Kathy's face was completely drained of blood, something carved from marble. Heath sat down hard and retched.

Emily laid down the gun, which was unloaded, reached into her drawer and turned off the tape recorder. She was filled suddenly with a dissonant harmony of laughter and tears. But hysteria was an old friend, and she knew it would pass.

She rose and walked to the window. Outside, a light rain was falling, washing down the afternoon. "I don't know how successful your therapy is going to be," she said, "but I hope this experience will get you off to a good start. Terror isn't a nice feeling, but it's better than nothing."

She heard the door close softly, and then the easy click of a large man's footsteps. Emily smiled. Suddenly the room was filled with a warm, comforting presence. The terrible tension had almost made her forget that she wasn't alone, and had not been.

"I think Dr. Sykes will want to talk to you now," she said softly.

THE SNAKE IN THE TOWER

The glass door opened hard and Burt Abele shivered as he passed into the steamy heat that kept at bay the winter cold on 8th Avenue, The sudden warmth flushed his face and stirred the alcohol in his stomach. There was a heavy odor of cooking hamburger and onion.

It was always the same, day after night after day. Go to work on that cursed elevator; up down, up down. Leave work, drink, eat, go home and sleep, wake up furry-mouthed, go to work; MOVE DIRECTLY TO JAIL DO NOT PASS GO; up, down, up, down.

Only the weekends were different. Then Burt would drink all the time to kill the feeling, slow the hours leading relentlessly forward to Monday when the mechanical jaws of the elevator would fold him back into his own personal hell.

At thirty-one, he was too young to be caught in this vise, Burt believed. Always there was the taste of stale beer in his mouth. Life must be *more*. But what to do? Of course he could always "pull a muscle" and go on welfare or live off workmen's compensation but then there'd be nothing else to do anyway and he'd only drink more; and more. Burt was not stupid; he was better off working.

"Two with onions," Burt muttered thickly, raising his fingers. "Black coffee and a side of potatoes." That'd fix him up. Go to sleep on a full stomach so he could go up-down in the morning and not be sick.

Abele folded his napkin into intricate patterns and looked about him at the other patrons. What did they do? Were they, too, dying inside? Of course they'd never tell, even if they were; people don't talk about such things.

The White Tower was fairly crowded and there was but one man, a boy really, behind the counter that Burt judged to be no older than eighteen or nineteen. Freckled, with flaming red hair, the boy moved easily and casually from customer to grill and then back to customer, obviously in no hurry.

Maybe he should get a job like that, Burt considered; no up or down, just back and forth. But where was the difference? The boy's pale face and dull, clouded eyes told him there was none; it was all deadly monotony, eating bit by bit, day by day, into the sharp edges of a man's soul. He wished he had the guts right now to get up and walk out to the street. He could hitch a ride, flag a bus, ride a train, keep going for a long, long time, but somehow Burt knew it would make no difference. Life's a disease of lengthy duration but a disease nonetheless; first the mind goes, then the body.

A distraught mother on his right struggled to cope with her two excited children. A large collection of badges, balloons and peanut shells indicated there had been a visit to the circus holding forth in Madison Square Garden, a few blocks away. Burt stared, remembering times long past when he too had been pushed to the heights of ecstasy by leaping men and painted clowns and he too, like these children, had spun and spun on his stool and demanded more candy. Now it was just up down drink sleep up ...

How does a person change his life?

He was a prisoner of the city, the great mirror that reflected and magnified his own boredom and frustration. But what does one do? The day of the covered wagons is past and neon light blasts into both oceans.

80

Next to Burt, also on his right, was a small, bookish man with a crumpled brown suit and glasses with very thick lenses. The man had just finished a large piece of pie and was now rounding up all the flakes and crumbs, pressing them into the tines of his fork and transferring them to his mouth.

The coffee came, hot on his tongue, acid in his stomach. Where were the hamburgers? The red-haired boy was very slow; back and forth, back and forth.

The young couple on Burt's left got up and left amidst a spatter of giggles. Their fingers groped and intertwined. How long had it been since he had had a woman ? A *nice* woman? Updown, backforth.

Farther down, near the door, Burt spotted a young woman, good-looking but heavily made up, with garish black net stockings showing beneath the hem of her very long, wool coat. Probably a go-go girl from one of the bars nearby. Burt smiled to himself. Here was a girl with an even worse problem; up and down, back and forth, around and around with a bunch of lushes watching her to boot, all wanting the same thing as if she were some kind of object or piece of merchandise. At least he didn't have anybody watching him. He was left alone to do his dying each day.

The hamburgers came and they tasted good. Maybe the red-haired kid had a little book explaining in detail just how to prepare each item of food. Except the coffee; that was still acid.

A man entered, carrying a large, closed basket under his arm. Burt stared hard. Another one from the circus, he decided; this one, a performer of some kind. The man sat two seats away from Burt, placing the basket on the empty stool between them. The man was dark-skinned, with very thin, compressed lips, complemented by a thin, angular nose. There was strength in the man's face. He wore a well fitted, neatly pressed suit and yet he looked slightly uncomfortable, as if he were used to another form of dress. His hands were folded in front of him as he waited patiently for the red-haired boy to take notice of him.

Burt's gaze swept down past the wooden basket and then shot back again. His eyes stayed riveted on the dark cane and the white letters on the crimson label. He felt a little chill along his spine.

"Hey," Burt said, waving his fingers at the dark-skinned man, "you really got a snake in there?"

The snake-man turned slowly and smiled. In a voice very soft and deep, like the lead in a movie, he said, "Yes, but it can't hurt you."

"A king cobra?"

The snake-man smiled again. "The basket is secured very tightly," he said, lightly shaking the container. "You see? You have nothing to fear."

"I wasn't afraid," Burt said, somewhat surprised to find it was the truth. "It's just that it gives a person a pretty weird feeling sitting next to something like that."

The man nodded, and Burt pushed away the remains of his hamburgers and lit a cigarette to smoke while drinking the rest of his coffee. The go-go girl brushed past him, apparently on her way to make a call in one of the booths at the rear near the mother and her children. Burt wondered how the girl would react if she knew she had just passed within a few inches of a cobra—of death. People never considered things like that; just up and down, back and forth, around and around, hurrying toward nothing.

Funny, Burt realized, how that snake made him feel more alive. He dragged heavily on his cigarette and thought about that; weird. The coffee was cold and normally he would have left by now, but this sensation was too new, too heady, to walk away from so quickly. He was completely sober and had not felt so *aware* in days,

82

weeks . . . months. There was no longer any thought of up and down. His cigarette tasted sharp and exhilarating; the lights were lighter and he heard things more clearly. There was a snake a few inches away from his thigh and that snake could end all updown, backforth, forever. Funny how he should need the presence of death to make him feel more alive.

"How come that thing isn't locked up someplace?" Burt asked, immediately feeling foolish. He was *glad* the man had brought the snake.

The snake-man turned and smiled as before. Everything about this man was graceful, hinting at speed and power; perhaps like his snakes. "I am with the circus," he said. "Our contract stipulates that poisonous snakes must be with a handler at all time. There is no danger, I can assure you."

"Oh, I don't mind," Burt said quickly. "I was just curious."

What happened next blended instantly with time and space, crippling the normal process of careful reasoning, throwing each person back on the ancient reserves of instinct. As sometimes happens with the best of mothers, the woman in the back had reached the end of her patience. There was a sharp crack of flesh against flesh as the young boy screamed and leaped back, crashing into Burt, who was unable to avoid brushing the wooden basket which fell to the floor with a startling, fearsome crash.

Burt shot back hard off his stool, backing into the go-go girl who had finished her call and was returning to her seat. She was yelling something in his ear but Burt remained standing, his arms held out to his sides, blocking her passage, his eyes riveted to the spot on the floor where the basket had landed.

"Wait!" Burt commanded, tensing the muscles in his arms.

The snake-man had risen. "It is nothing," he said, reaching down for the basket.

"Wait!" Burt said again, this time extending one arm out toward the snake-man and consequently saving his life.

From where he was standing, the snake-man might never have seen the flat, green-brown head, the flicking tongue or the cold, lidless eyes that slowly emerged from the hole in the basket that had smashed on impact with the floor. Slowly— inch-by-inch, foot-by-foot—the king cobra slid out into the middle of the tile floor. People scattered in all directions; those in the front crushed through the single glass door, while those behind Burt squeezed back, in and around the phone booths.

"What the—" came from the red-haired back-and-forth boy from behind the counter. His face was even paler than before but there was more teen-age incredulity in his voice than fear. Nothing like this had ever happened in a White Tower before.

"Why, that's a king cobra!" the bookish man was saying, dropping his fork and sending the light crumbs and flakes floating to the floor. "A *cobra!*"

The go-go girl was clutching at Burt's coat and shouting a hysterical torrent of obscenities. He felt himself being pushed forward and braced hard on his front foot, all the time keeping his arms extended wide, never taking his eyes from the thick, eight-foot ribbon of death a few feet away.

"Please be quiet," the snake-man said. "It's very important that all of you be quiet."

The snake-man had frozen when he had seen the snake emerge from the basket, only inches from his outstretched hand. Now he slowly straightened and backed against the counter, shallow breathing the only sign of his agitation; his face was expressionless. One man near the

84

front who had stood rooted to the spot, paralyzed by fear, now uttered a cry and bolted for the door.

"Get help," the snake-man said, raising an arm in the man's direction but not taking his eyes from the snake. "Call the police and tell them what happened. They'll know who to call."

Burt could hear the mother's sobbing in the rear, sharp and crackling in the heavy air. The snake swayed and began to rise, the back of its head and neck swelling like a thick rubber bag.

"Please stop that crying," the snake-man said, his voice a soft but urgent demand. "And do not move, any of you. Frieda is extremely dangerous and will attack if you make her nervous. Please stay very still." The snake-man started slowly making his way toward the cobra, removing his jacket as he did so and holding it out in front of him, waving it slowly back and forth, circling around, never taking his eyes from those of the snake.

"You can put your arms down now, buster," the go-go girl said, her voice a whisper. "I'm sure as hell not going anywhere near that monster."

Burt lowered his arms and breathed easier. At least the snake-man looked like he knew what he was doing as he continued to circle the reptile, never varying his easy, rhythmic motion. The cobra was still raised up but there was no longer any swelling at the back of the head. The snake seemed mesmerized by the man's actions. Now, if the snake-man could only keep it that way until some kind of help arrived. Why was it taking so long for someone to get here? Was it possible the man, once free of danger, had simply gone home, dismissing the matter as someone else's bad luck? Impossible! But the thought kept coming back, and Burt felt cold.

"How—how dangerous is it?" the mother asked in a quivering voice.

"Very," the bookish man said. "The venom of a cobra acts directly upon the nervous system. Death comes in seconds. There's almost nothing one can do ..."

"Can't you *do something'?"* the go-go girl said to the red-haired boy, who had stopped going back and forth and was half-crouched behind the counter. "We're trapped here, and that thing could *kill* us."

The red-haired boy ducked down behind the counter and resurfaced with a heavy, bone-handled meat cleaver in his hand. The voice of the snake-man came at them again, soft but very strained.

"I asked you not to *move.*"

"What's the matter with you!" the go-go girl screamed. "Is that thing more important to you than our lives? Kill it!"

The spell over the snake had been broken. The movement and the sharp static of voices had distracted the reptile from the carefully planned, rhythmic movements of the snake-man. The flat head soared high as the hood swelled and there was a sharp hiss.

"That's how they strike!" the bookish man said, his voice muffled by the hand over his mouth.

Burt stared wide-eyed and remembered something he had read about cobras lunging forward, rather than striking from a coiled position like a rattlesnake. That made them a bit slower, which was an advantage, however slight.

The snake hissed again just before the head sailed through the air toward the snake-man, who stepped nimbly aside. The snake reared back again, but now the snake-man was weaving slowly and the reptile began rocking back and forth as the fangs retracted and the hood relaxed. The snake-man's shirt and slacks were spotted with cobra venom as the mother stifled a scream deep in her throat and the go-go girl shrieked nervously. It seemed to Burt that they were in a glass sphere whirling through space a thousand miles an hour, yet everything was very, very *real.*

"It is most important that you follow my instructions," the snake-man said, his voice betraying no more than a slight annoyance at the mistake that had almost cost him his life. "Cobras have been known to stalk and attack. If Frieda decides to come toward you I know no way of stopping her. As far as killing her is concerned, it is true that Frieda is a valuable animal. However, that is not the question here. The slightest scratch from her fangs means death. If she is to be killed before she bites her attacker, the head must be sliced off. Who is willing to come that close? No one? In that case, please remain still."

This is insane, Burt thought. Death crawled only a few feet from them, ready to strike; and a few feet further away stood at least a hundred people, their noses pressed to the protective barrier of glass, watching the drama within. He and the snake-man and the bookish man and the mother and the children and the go-go girl might have been no more than a Christmas display on Fifth Avenue. But they were *not;* they were *people* and they were in very real danger. Outside, children were jumping up and down, back and forth, pushing around and around trying to get a better look. *Insane!* This was New York City and not some jungle in India...

What was it he had read about ten thousand Indians dying each year from snakebite? That had never meant much to him; a statistic buried in the newspaper amidst a hundred other statistics whirred and lighted and coughed by some chromed computer somewhere. *Now* it meant something. Now ... Burt could see a small, frail, brown-skinned man clad, perhaps, only in a loin cloth, hurrying along some jungle path or traversing the outskirts of a city, hurrying to get home where his wife and children would be waiting with love and something cool to drink. There is a sudden, stabbing pain in the soft calf of his leg and the man looks down, terror already clawing at his stomach, to see a cobra glide away through the tall grass. The man sits alone in the middle of the path and waits for death that he knows will be soon and is inevitable; already he is having trouble drawing breath and he wishes his life had not had to end so soon but it has ...

There they are with their noses pressed against the glass and children jumping ... Those idiots!

The snake-man was circling closer and closer. Why hadn't help come? The presence of death; everything is magnified, amplified, salted, sautéed in the life juices of the man who wants desperately to see once again the warmth of the sun on his face and knows he may not. Burt wanted to go home that night and smoke the cigarettes, curse the traffic lights...

"Jamie!" The mother's scream pierced through the glass windows, and the children stopped jumping as a hundred pairs of eyes stared in terror and there were answering screams. Too late Burt caught a glimpse of the boy rushing past. The snake's head jerked back; venom dripped from the exposed fangs and the sound of hissing filled the Tower.

What Burt did next was instinctive and, in the years ahead, years filled with a new sense of life and awareness, he would look back upon that one instant in time and reflect and be proud that he had never really stopped to think about what he had done. He had acted, and in that acceptance of death he had found the key to life.

Burt left his feet and flew through the air, his arm extended full length, his hand reaching for the head of the snake that was already arcing through the air toward the fear-paralyzed body of the boy. There was but an instant of pain and a swelling, numbing sensation in his hand as the snake's fangs sliced through the flesh of his hand, and Burt

Abele fell unconscious on the cold tile of the Tower, the snake pinned beneath him.

It was instinct, too, and the reserves of courage that propelled the red-haired boy through the air, over the counter, the meat-cleaver held high over his head.

Instantly, the snake-man clutched the gushing stump of Burt's wrist in a vise-like grip and pushed the thrashing, headless carcass of the cobra aside. Then, to be heard above the screaming, milling, up-down throng of people running back and forth, around and around on the stained concrete of the sidewalk outside, he yelled, "He will live! He will *live!*"

WOTZEL

"By the winds your limbs are treed..."

"It's not *treed,* Harry!" Tom Spanik whispered urgently. *"It's freed!"*

"Sorry," Harry Hodges said disconsolately. "Limbs, you know, made me think of trees."

"Never mind, Harry! Get it right!"

"I don't know, Tom. Maybe we're wasting our time. We've been working on this stuff for a year. Nobody-nothing seems to be listening."

"This spell will work. I just feel it. Try it again."

Harry blinked and stole a glance at the ancient, tattered book beside him on the Black Altar. The ceremonial robe he was wearing was hot and uncomfortable, and the black, acrid smoke from the thurible on the altar was making his eyes water. He still wasn't sure that the man at the Witch's Wagon had sold them the right herbs; the man hadn't seemed to be able to stop laughing. The magic broth he had sold them smelled suspiciously like burning rubber.

"What do you think, Tom? Should I start over?"

"I think you'd better, Harry."

Harry screwed his eyes shut and tried to remember the words.

"By the winds your limbs are freed,
by the sound your ears are opened,
by the book your mouth is opened,
by the dark of the sun your eyes are lightened,
San ...
What's his name again, Tom?"

91

"Sancrittle, Tanscrittle . .. something like that. C'mon, Harry!"

"Sancridoodle, I conquer..."

"Conjure, Harry!"

"Conjure thee! A wake and arise!"

Nothing rose, except the stench from the thurible.

"Nothing happened, Harry."

"I can see that, Tom!" Harry said, ripping off his robe in disgust. He staggered through the blinding smoke and opened a window, then turned back toward Tom. "I'm telling you, we are two of life's biggest losers. We can't even sell our souls to the devil!"

Tom absently pulled at his moustache, and then ran his hand through his thinning blond hair. "Maybe he doesn't make house calls."

"Not for us, he doesn't!"

"I need a drink."

"Good idea."

They opened the bedroom door and almost choked on the sulphur fumes in the living room. It took the men a few moments to see the figure sitting in Harry's best armchair. Its tail was draped decorously over the arm of the chair, and its scaly, webbed feet were propped up on an antique divan. In its right hand was a bottle of liquor. As Tom and Harry watched it lifted the bottle and drained off the contents in one swallow.

"Hey!" Harry yelled. "That's my best Scotch!"

"Harry," Tom whispered, tugging at his friend's sleeve, "I don't think this is the time. We've got ourselves a demon."

The figure in the chair belched and turned toward them. It smiled. "Hi," it said. It lifted the bottle. "Great stuff. *Great* stuff! Booze is only a legend where I come from."

"A drunken demon," Harry whispered.

92

As one, the two men turned and rushed back into the bedroom, slamming shut and locking the door behind them.

"Hurry, Harry!" Tom yelled as Harry struggled to get back into his robe.

"How do we send it back?"

"How do I know? Try saying the spell backwards!"

"Backwards? I can't even remember it forwards!"

"Do something!"

"Don't yell, Tom! You're making me nervous!"

The demon ended the conversation by coming through the wall, "Excuse me," it said, extricating a piece of plaster from one of its horns. It waved one of its hands; the Black Altar, books and thurible disappeared. "I know you're a little upset by all this," it continued pleasantly, "but there's no way I'm going back to where I came from. No way. Life in hell is, well, hellish. I want to change my life-style."

"You talk in stereo," Tom whispered haltingly. "That's a pretty good trick."

"Yes," it said with a touch of pride. Something flickered in the holes where its eyes should have been. "I have a pretty good singing voice, too. Do you have any favorites?"

"Well, I like ..."

"Shut up, Harry!" Tom said sharply. Then, to the demon: "Who are you?"

"My name is Wotzel," Wotzel said. "You're Tom and Harry. I'm really happy to meet you. And I want you to know that I appreciate ..."

"We've never heard of you," Tom said shortly.

Wotzel's scales and horns turned a deeper shade of red. "It doesn't surprise me," he said with a trace of sadness. "I'm not written up much. As a matter of fact, I'm not written up at all. I'm afraid that I'm considered rather ... incompetent. I was just starting to tell you how much I appreciate your efforts on my behalf. In the entire history of mankind nobody else has ever figured out a spell to conjure me up."

Tom turned to Harry. "It figures," he said dryly.

"Listen, I'm really sorry about all this," Wotzel said, gesturing around the room. "Let me see what I can do to tidy things up."

Wotzel wiggled a horn. The wall materialized back into place; original editions *of Alice In Wonderland, Moby Dick,* and *Superman* appeared on the bed.

Tom whistled softly. "I thought you said you were incompetent."

Wotzel shrugged. "I can't handle the heavy stuff."

"What heavy stuff?"

"Evil. I get migraine headaches if I try to do anything evil." Wotzel shuddered and his scales rustled. "Which brings us to the question of why you summoned me. I'll be happy to work some spells, as long as you don't want to hurt anybody."

"I need a drink," Tom said woodenly.

"He drank it all," Harry replied with a touch of petulance.

Wotzel wiggled his left horn and produced a case of Chivas Regal and two glasses.

Harry looked at Wotzel suspiciously. "Who's not drinking?"

"I'll take mine right from the bottle, if you don't mind," Wotzel said."

Tom poured Harry a drink, then said: "You want to tell him?"

Harry lifted his glass to Wotzel who had already drained off three-fourths of a bottle. The black holes that were Wotzel's eyes were developing a cloudy appearance, and the demon's tail was beginning to flop uncontrollably on the floor.

"You'd better tell him quick, Harry," Tom whispered. "I think he's getting sloshed."

"Basically," Harry said, "the problem is simply that Tom and I are *losers.*"

"Gotcha," Wotzel said, breaking wind. "I can understand that: I'm a loser too."

"I mean," Harry continued, "we're such losers that our wives have left us. That's why we're living together in my house. Understand, it's not that our wives don't love us; it's just that they've forgotten."

Wotzel belched and broke wind at the same time. "I dig it," he mumbled. His left channel of stereo sound was beginning to fade.

"Take our boss, Mr. Notbaum," Harry continued. "Both Tom and I work in an advertising agency, and we're good. But Notbaum waits until we finish a project, then he takes the credit for it. He steals all our best stuff!"

"And it's the little things that are so annoying," Tom interjected. "Harry and I go to Rome for a vacation and we get pinched by fat Italian women!"

"Traffic jams!" Harry cried. "For some reason, Tom and I are always getting stuck in traffic jams. Three o'clock in the morning on a country road and we find ourselves in a traffic jam! It's gotten to the point where we always leave for work three hours early!"

"We don't want to do anything evil," Tom said plaintively. "We just want a little luck for a change. We think we're entitled to it."

"I'll see what I can do," Wotzel mumbled, and then passed out.

"I'm a failure," Wotzel blubbered.

Mary Spanik knelt down beside Wotzel while Virginia Hodges caressed his forehead. Harry and Tom anchored his tail; they were used to Wotzel's fits of depression after drinking bouts and they were sure he would get over it.

"You're not a failure," Virginia said, her large brown eyes flashing with indignation. "You've brought us all back together again."

95

"A simple love spell," Wotzel moaned. "Kindergarten demon stuff. It doesn't even work unless the people love each other to begin with."

"C'mon Wotzel," Tom said, obviously embarrassed. "I can't stand to see a grown demon cry."

Wotzel shook his head and reached for the bottle Mary had taken away from him. Mary pulled it away from him again.

"What about the traffic jams?" Mary said, pulling back her shoulders and ignoring Tom's warning gesture. "You got Harry and Tom out of a traffic jam."

Wotzel moaned loudly, his stereo carrying and reverberating around the house until the walls shook. "I stopped the whole world!" he cried. "For half an hour I stopped the whole world, and I was too drunk to remember how to get it started again! If it hadn't been for Harry and Tom and their magic potion . . ."

"It was a gallon of black coffee, Wotzel," Harry said wryly.

"A mere trifle." Virginia sniffed.

"Don't cry. Wotzel," Mary murmured. "We love you and you know we love you."

"The race track." Wotzel wailed.

"The army had no business sending four battalions of troops to guard one little race track. They were overreacting."

Harry coughed. "The troops are still there. And the army has twenty thousand people who swear they saw a horse sprout wings and fly across the finish line. Not only that, they've got the horse, wings and all."

"I shouldn't have bet on him," Tom sighed.

"Don't blame yourself, Tom," Mary said. "You couldn't have known that horse had never won a race. There was a misprint in the program; it read 'Secretariat' when it should have read 'Caesarian.' The important thing is that Wotzel *tried* to help."

96

"How's the jockey?" Virginia asked.

"They've got a dozen Army psychiatrists working on him." Harry said. "He'll be all right." Suddenly he snapped his fingers. "Notbaum! That was a success! Wotzel certainly got Notbaum off our backs!"

Tom laughed. "Right. That was ingenious, Wotzel, making Notbaum forget to zipper up his fly every time he went to the toilet. It gave him something else to think about besides stealing our work."

Wotzel's tail twitched. "I don't want to go back!" he cried. "I don't want to go back!"

"You don't have to go back," Virginia said. "We're all going to stay together for the time being, and, if anyone asks, remember that you're our butler."

As if on cue, the doorbell rang. Harry and Tom pulled Wotzel to his feet while Mary and Virginia straightened his wig, gloves and dark glasses.

"C'mon, buddy," Tom said, slapping Wotzel on the back, "shape up. You've got to answer the door."

Wotzel weaved toward the door while Harry performed the finishing touches on his appearance by tucking the demon's tail into his trousers.

Wotzel opened the door and promptly fainted. The man standing in the doorway was tall and wore dark glasses and gloves, as well as what appeared to be an ill-fitting wig. Mary and Virginia exchanged glances; they recognized the man as the one who had moved into the house next door the previous day while Tom, Harry and Wotzel were at the racetrack.

Harry and Tom dragged Wotzel over into a corner as the man, unbidden, stepped through the doorway.

"Uh, pardon our butler," Mary said. "He hasn't been well lately."

"No need to apologize," the man said in a voice that sounded suspiciously stereophonic. "Allow me to introduce myself: I am Mr. Amodeus. I've come to discuss a matter of mutual concern."

Virginia stepped forward. "What matter would that be?"

"Your butler."

Wotzel was awake now, moaning. "Amodeus," he cried. "Don't hurt them! Please don't hurt them!"

"Look, pal," Harry said in what he hoped was a threatening tone, "are you a friend of Wotzel's?"

"'Friend' is not the word I would use," Amodeus said in a deep, rich stereo. "'Guardian' would be more accurate. Wotzel is, well, *backwards*. He's a retarded demon."

"Well," Virginia said archly. "I don't think you have any right to talk that way about our butler!"

"Now, Mrs. Hodges, do you really want a butler who breaks wind all the time?"

"He doesn't do that anymore!" Virginia said defensively. "He's a perfectly capable butler!"

"Well, I'm afraid he's going to have to come back with me now."

Wotzel began to cry.

Harry stepped forward and grabbed Amodeus by the front of the shirt. Amodeus wrinkled his brow and Harry turned to stone. Virginia screamed.

"Please leave them alone!" Wotzel cried. "I'll come back with you!"

Amodeus almost smiled. "You'll come voluntarily?"

Wotzel nodded his head, dislodging his wig and exposing one trembling horn.

"Now wait just a minute!" Mary said sternly. "Wotzel, you don't want to go back to that nasty place, do you?"

Wotzel hung his head. Something that sounded like electronic feedback issued from his lips.

"Uh, Mary," Virginia said, tugging at her friend's sleeve, "what about Harry?"

Mary shook her head obstinately. "We'll pray!"

"Now wait just a minute!" Amodeus said. But he was already backing away as Mary fell to her knees. "You shouldn't be too hasty! Let's talk this over!"

Mary continued to pray. Virginia and Tom dropped to their knees and joined Mary in prayer. Amodeus suddenly turned and sprinted across the lawn, leaping a hedge and rushing into his house, slamming the door behind him.

"Amen," Mary said, rising and turning to Wotzel.

Wotzel was clutching his stomach, and his red scales had taken on a sickly greenish-orange hue. "All that praying," he mumbled. "I think I'm going to throw up."

Tom and Virginia had risen to their feet. "Don't throw up now!" Virginia said. "Can't you do something about Harry?"

Wotzel glanced at the statue that had been Harry. "Xrcmslpm," he said.

The flesh tones came back into Harry's limbs and he crumpled to the floor. Virginia brought him a drink, which he downed quickly.

"Damn," Harry said. "I mean, *damn!*"

Wotzel beamed with pleasure. "It isn't true what Amodeus said about me being backwards," he said with more than a touch of pride. "They're all the same down there: they think anyone who can't do evil is backwards."

"Wotzel," Mary said thoughtfully, "if you're so good, why does praying make you sick?"

"I don't know," Wotzel said distantly. "I suppose a demon is judged by the company he's kept." He paused, then added: "I suppose I have to go."

"That might not be a bad idea," Harry said weakly.

"That is *not* a good idea," Virginia said quickly. "Harry, where's your gratitude? Wotzel has every right to stay here if he wants to! We all love him and we want him to stay. We'll just tell that Amodeus where he can go!"

Wotzel coughed. "Harry's right," he said. "Amodeus is much more powerful than I am. He'll try to hurt you, and I won't be able to stop him. That stone thing with Harry was just a warning, a minor spelling exercise. He doesn't want you; he wants me. I don't know what he'll do now."

"Well, whatever he does, we'll just fight!" Mary said determinedly.

"Right on!" Tom yelled. "Wotzel, the only thing you lack is self-confidence. If we stick together we can lick this Amodeus creep!"

The four humans began boarding up the windows while Wotzel sat on the floor, holding his head in his hands.

The attack began an hour later. It was a double-flank operation, with a horde of Black Widow spiders descending from the second floor and dozens of King Cobras crawling up from the cellar. Wotzel took up a position in the middle of the floor and began a series of disappearing spells while Tom, Harry, Virginia and Mary took cover behind a chair in the corner of the living room. The snakes and spiders seemed to come in a never-ending stream. Still, Wotzel seemed to be holding his own.

It was Harry who first noticed that the corner of the living room in which they were hiding had turned into a quicksand bog. Within a matter of seconds the four of them had sunk into the mud up to their hips.

"Wotzel!" Harry screamed. "We've got a problem over here!"

Wotzel turned in their direction and blanched a deep purple. His hands and horns seemed to be moving in all directions at once, "I ... I can't," he stammered. "Amodeus is too strong!"

"Things don't look too good, do they?" Tom said wistfully. The quicksand was now up to their armpits.

Virginia was staring off into space. "See if you can reach the telephone," she said to Tom.

100

"The telephone?" Harry cried in exasperation. "Virginia, this is no time to be calling your friends!"

"I need a telephone," Virginia repeated calmly. "Tom, the stand is on the other side of the chair. Can you reach it?"

Tom reached out and jerked the telephone stand. The phone and directory fell toward them and Virginia plucked them out of the mud.

"Virginia," Harry said, struggling to keep his chin above the mud, "just who do you plan to call?"

"Not who, what. Churches, synagogues and mosques."

"Churches, synagogues and mosques?"

But Virginia had already found the listings she wanted in the Yellow Pages and was dialing a number.

"Hello?" The voice at the other end of the line was soft and well modulated.

"Hello," Virginia said. "Are you a priest?"

"Father McCarey."

"I'd like to report a miracle."

There was a long silence at the other end of the line, then: "A miracle?"

"Yes. A big one."

"Well, Madam, uh, just what kind of a miracle is this?"

"It's not the kind of thing you want to discuss over the telephone." She gave Amodeus' address. "You'd better get over there right away. And bring any assistants you may have. This is going to need some documentation."

"Wotzel!" Tom shouted. "You're going to have to give us a boost!"

Wotzel half-turned and wiggled his right horn. That brought the four humans back up to waist level, but then Wotzel was forced to turn his attention back to the snakes and spiders. Virginia continued making her calls, repeating the same message. When she had finished she had completed calls to ten churches, seven synagogues and a mosque. But the army of spiders and snakes was advancing, and Wotzel had been forced back almost to the brink of the quicksand bog.

"What do we do now?" Tom said.

"Pray again, I suppose," Mary said wistfully.

"Don't pray!" Wotzel said. "You'll make me throw up! I've got all the problems I can handle!"

Mary squirmed around in the bog until she could see out the half-open door to her right. There was the sound of police and fire sirens in the distance. "Hey!" Mary said. "I can see across the way. There are a couple of priests wandering around Amodeus' yard."

"Priests?" Wotzel cried in a strangled voice. A pair of cobras slithered between his legs and sniffed at Tom's face.

"Just keep your mind on your work, Wotzel!" Harry shouted. "We're not going to let them come over here!"

Reassured, Wotzel managed a powerful horn wiggle. The two snakes that had been threatening Tom vanished.

"I see a rabbi," Mary whispered so as not to upset Wotzel. "Three ministers ... they're getting together now ... I think they're holding some kind of conference."

"Hey!" Harry yelped. "The snakes and spiders are disappearing!"

It was true. The snakes and spiders were popping all around the living room, going up in tiny wisps of smoke. The four humans were rising, and the quicksand was evaporating, being replaced by the reassuring hardness and color of wood flooring.

"There he goes!" Mary screamed with delight. "Amodeus is climbing out his bedroom window ... the crowd's chasing him . .. he's gone!"

Everything in the living room was as before; the quicksand, snakes and spiders were gone.

Wotzel was hanging out a window, retching. It took a while to quiet him, but Mary and Virginia finally forced some chicken soup down him, and that settled his stomach.

The battle with Amodeus had been won, and they decided to celebrate by going out to a movie.

It was a mistake.

"She's *beautiful,*" Wotzel sighed, staring at the image on the screen in the darkened theater. "I'd never dreamed that any human could be so beautiful."

Virginia shook her head. "She's also a ..."

"She's not your type, Wotzel," Harry said. "Lottie Lobo's a cold-blooded, vicious woman who cares about nothing and nobody other than herself. She's the only movie star who admits to all the bad stories printed about her. She's proud of them."

Wotzel said nothing, and it was obvious to the four humans that the demon had fallen in love. Suddenly Wotzel rose, adjusted his wig, and started down the aisle.

"Wotzel!" Mary said, grabbing his hand. "Where are you going?"

"Hollywood," Wotzel said without hesitation. "I've got to meet her. She's the most *beautiful* thing."

"She'll bring you nothing, but trouble," Tom warned.

Wotzel shook his head stubbornly. "It would be worth it."

Harry decided to try a different tack. "What about Amodeus?"

Wotzel crossed and uncrossed his horns in thought. "I think you scared him away," he said at last. "It doesn't really make any difference. I must meet Lottie Lobo."

The four humans glanced at one another, then rose together and went after Wotzel. Wotzel looked at them quizzically.

"We're going with you," Mary said to Wotzel. "Tom and Harry can get a week off from work. You'll need somebody to pray for you if Amodeus turns up."

103

Wotzel considered it, then nodded his head. In the next instant they found themselves ensconced in the Presidential Suite of the Beverly Hills Hilton.

It was the fifth evening of their stay in Hollywood, and the four humans could not remember ever seeing Wotzel so depressed. The demon was sitting in a corner of the suite, starting on his second case of Chivas Regal. His tail was twitching, occasionally flopping out of control; the tail had already broken a lamp and a chair. He had tried every love spell he knew and had finally come to the belated conclusion that no love spell would work on a woman who, as described, had never loved anyone but herself. That love, Wotzel realized, was far more powerful than any spell he could conjure up.

"Forget her, Wotzel," Mary moaned. "You've been at it almost a week; Lottie Lobo's insulted you, humiliated you, and called you backwards. You still haven't gotten over that."

"She wants things I can't give her!" Wotzel wailed. "She wants to hurt other people, get even. I try that and I get migraines so bad I can't work spells anyway."

"How's your migraine now?" Virginia asked.

"A little better," Wotzel slurred.

"I think the fact that you fogged every inch of film within a fifteen mile radius might have something to do with your headache," Harry said quietly.

"I didn't know," Wotzel said, beating his chest. "It was an accident."

"Wotzel," Tom said quietly, "I think we should pack up and go home."

Wotzel dragged himself to his feet and balanced unsteadily on his tail. "I suppose you're right," he said in a scratchy mono. "But we'd better wait until I sober up some. In the state I'm in, there's no telling where we'd end up."

"For heaven's sake .. ."

Wotzel clutched his stomach. "Virginia, *please!*"

104

"Sorry," Virginia said. "I was about to suggest that we simply take a plane back home."

Wotzel nodded his assent. Mary was just about to pick up the phone when it rang. She answered it, listened for a few moments, and then handed it to Wotzel with a gesture of disgust. "I think it's your heartthrob," she said.

Wotzel staggered across the room and put the phone to his ear. A few moments later his face lit up. He replaced the receiver on the hook, clicked his heels and snapped his tail.

"Whoopee!" Wotzel said in full stereo.

"Wotzel," Mary said, "don't be taken in by her."

But Wotzel wasn't listening. "Lottie wants to make up," he gibbered. "She's going to meet me on Lot Seven right now!"

"It's a trick, Wotzel," Harry warned. "Let us come with you."

"Uh-uh. She says she wants to meet me alone."

There was a wink of light and Wotzel was gone.

The four humans raced out the door, successfully evading a squad of hotel detectives who had been sent to throw them out. They took the elevator downstairs, out-sped the manager, and jumped into a taxi outside the hotel. It took a half hour to get to Lottie Lobo's studio, and another twenty minutes to find a hole under the fence. Once through that, they raced along a roadway, following the signs indicating the direction to Lot Seven. They turned a corner and Harry, in the lead, held up a hand for them to stop.

There was a full moon, and Lottie Lobo could clearly be seen standing at the top of a great pile of scaffolding. She was tapping her foot impatiently.

Wotzel suddenly emerged from the shadows to the right. "Lottie," he said in a voice that sounded suspiciously like an impression of John Wayne. "My darling!"

Lottie Lobo's deep, throaty voice drifted down from where she was standing. "Where have you been, big boy?"

"I was excited and a little drunk, I admit," Wotzel said, imitating Steve McQueen. "I wound up in a Tibetan monastery."

Lottie held out her arms invitingly. "Well, dumpling," she purred, "the important thing is that you're here now. Come to me."

"He must be awfully tired," Virginia whispered. "He's climbing."

Wotzel was laboriously making his way up the maze of scaffolding. At one point he got a webbed foot stuck on a nail and it took him a few moments to work it loose.

"Do you really love me, Lottie?"

Lottie Lobo laughed. "I loathe you, stupid."

"Huh?" Wotzel had stopped climbing. His magnificent stereo voice had been reduced to a barely audible hi-fidelity.

"I said that I loathe you, you retarded, good-for-nothing excuse for a demon! You promised me a rose garden. Amodeus has promised me the world!"

"Time to start praying," Harry whispered.

"There'll be no prayer meeting tonight, folks," a voice said.

The four humans started to turn toward the source of the voice and found they couldn't move. Or speak. They were completely paralyzed.

"You've betrayed me!" Wotzel cried out.

"The *world!* The *world!* I'll get all the best parts, pick my own leading men!"

A cold shadow passed overhead, and Amodeus suddenly materialized on Wotzel's back. Virginia, Mary, Tom and Harry watched in horror as a huge pit opened in the earth beneath the struggling demons. Flames and smoke shot into the night sky. The scaffolding shook and Lottie

106

Lobo tottered, and then plummeted to the ground. She landed on her head. She twitched, and then lay still. Amodeus lunged off the platform, carrying a squealing Wotzel with him down into the fiery pit. Then the earth closed and the night was still.

"Are you people okay?"

The words sounded strange, coming as they did from the mouth of a gorilla that was about to crush a "White Hunter" who had foolishly defied a restriction on "Taboo Territory" in the "Heart of Darkest Africa." And the gorilla spoke with Wotzel's voice.

Harry looked at Tom, Virginia and Mary. They were all tapping their earphones or changing channels. None of the other passengers on the flight seemed to sense anything out of the ordinary; they were still watching the in-flight movie.

"Look out the window."

The four humans crowded in front of the nearest window while Tom lifted the shade. Wotzel was sitting out on the wing, his tail blowing in the jet stream, his nose pressed against the window.

"Wotzel!"

Wotzel pressed a webbed finger to his lips as the other passengers *shushed* angrily. "Are you okay?"

"We're fine," Virginia said softly. "The spell passed after .. . Hey, you escaped! We thought . . .."

Wotzel grinned. "I didn't escape. But I did get a special dispensation to come back and say goodbye to you."

"You have to go back?"

Wotzel nodded. He didn't seem at all displeased at the prospect. He pointed one finger downward. "I've got to go now," he said. "Lottie's waiting for me. She needs someone to show her the ropes." And then he was gone.

"Ouch," said the gorilla as the White Hunter kicked him in the shins.

107

FOUR KNIGHTS GAME

Giving a simultaneous chess exhibition against 50 players was nothing new for Douglas Franklin. A prodigy as a child, an International Grandmaster at 18, Douglas had spent the last 10 of his 29 years wringing out a living doing what he loved best: playing chess. He had been around the world a half dozen times. He had little money, a small walk-up flat in New York City, an unbroken string of invitations to all the major international tournaments, and he called that freedom.

Like most Grandmasters, Douglas was accustomed to playing simultaneous exhibitions in a kind of trance. Not that he didn't know what was happening on the boards, but he relied on his prodigious skills, natural instincts and vast experience to sustain him through the long hours as he moved around the inner circle formed by the players' tables, working to obtain an advantage in the openings, then allowing each game to take its course, to play *him*.

This exhibition was different. The girl was a distraction.

She was good, Douglas now realized, too good to be a casual weekend player like the majority of participants on the "Chess Cruise' he had been hired to host. He had underestimated her and chosen a line of attack that was quick and powerful, but ultimately inferior. She had withstood the attack, and Douglas now found himself in *zugzwang,* where all the moves available to him were bad ones.

Sensing a game of unusual interest, a number of spectators had crowded around the girl's board. Armand Zoltan, the ship's owner, had positioned his huge bulk directly behind the girl's chair and was staring over her shoulder at the score sheet she had been keeping. Zoltan's eyes were large and black, like two pieces of coal shoved into the puffy dough of his face. His gaze momentarily flicked upward as Douglas approached. Then he turned his attention back to the score sheet.

There was one other man who appeared more interested in the record of moves than in the actual position on the board. He had slipped between two of the tables and was standing inside the circle, studying the piece of paper by the girl's hand. He was tall and thin, with pale, almost yellow eyes that seemed to blink in spasms. A bald pate was sparsely covered with a few strands of hair combed from one side to the other and plastered down with hair lotion. His suit was obviously well tailored but failed to disguise the fact that he needed a bath. He smelled of spicy after-shave and sweat.

Douglas touched the man on the shoulder. "Excuse me, I need some room." The man stared hard at Douglas for a few moments, then moved quickly back.

Douglas lighted a cigarette and pretended to study the position on the board in front of him. He knew the position was hopeless; what he was really interested in was the girl. If she were nervous, she didn't show it. She was cool and poised, despite the crush of onlookers and Zoltan breathing down her neck. She had a high forehead framed by silky, raven-black hair; cold, penetrating green eyes that seemed to reveal little were contradicted by a full, sensual mouth.

The score sheet had no name on it.

Douglas tipped over his king in the traditional gesture of defeat. "I resign," he said easily.

There was scattered applause, quickly stilled by the angry shushing of the other players.

"Thank you," the girl said quietly. She rose and began to fold her score sheet.

Douglas gently touched her arm. "May I ask who just beat me?"

The girl smiled and extended her hand. "My name is Anne Pickford." Her grip was firm, like her game. She spoke with a pronounced British accent.

"You play a fine game, Anne. Do you mind if I borrow your score sheet? I'd like to look it over."

Anne laughed as she handed him the paper. "If you like. But my guess is that you know every move that was made. The line you used was refuted three years ago in Copenhagen. You were the one who refuted it, against Barslov."

Douglas grinned and slipped the sheet into his pocket. Many of the spectators had moved on to the other boards, but Douglas was aware that the man with the yellow eyes was standing close by, watching them. Douglas leaned closer. "Actually, I was looking for an excuse to ask you to have a drink with me."

"Why must you have an excuse, Mr. Franklin? Where's your natural Grandmaster egomania?"

"It's badly bruised at the moment. Eight o'clock in the upper lounge?"

"Fine."

111

The girl nodded curtly, then turned and walked away. Douglas waited until she had disappeared from sight out on the deck, and then moved on to the next board. He studied it for a moment, then reached down and moved a bishop. "Checkmate," he said cheerfully.

"Pickford," Douglas said. "There was an English Grand-master, Samuel Pickford."

Anne smiled and sipped her drink. "My father. He taught me how to play."

Douglas tapped the score sheet in his pocket. "Of course. It really was a beautifully played Sicilian."

Anne shrugged. "We both know you'd beat me easily in a match."

Douglas' glass was empty. He looked inquiringly at the girl, who shook her head. He ordered another Scotch for himself, then leaned back and studied her.

"Why haven't I heard of you? Judging from the way you play, I'd say you were at least an expert. Considering the state of women's chess, I'd think you'd be in international competition."

Something moved deep in the girl's eyes, a dark, silent laughter that Douglas found disconcerting.

"I find my own game more interesting," Anne said quietly.

"Really? What game would that be?"

"I'm a journalist." Her eyes were veiled again. "Actually, this is a working trip for me."

"You're not here as a player?"

"No. I'm afraid I sneaked into the exhibition."

"I'm glad you did."

"I was in Barcelona when I heard about this junket to Glasgow for the Interzonal elimination. Obviously, chess is very chic now and I thought there might be a good story in the cruise. I was right. Here I am in the middle of the ocean, having drinks with the infamous Douglas Franklin."

Douglas laughed. "Infamous?"

"Well, perhaps that's overstating the case. But it's true that most serious players resent you, and non-chess players admire or envy you. For the same reasons."

"What reasons?"

"Take the Glasgow Interzonal. You won't be playing in it because you never bothered to try to qualify. Instead, you're hosting a boatload of *patzers* on their way to sit in the audience. Who else but Douglas Franklin would win his share of major tournaments every year, then turn his back on the chance to play for the world championship? The chess Establishment thinks you're irresponsible."

"What do you think?"

"I think you're having a lot of fun. You're waiting for your wanderlust to burn itself out. When you want the world championship enough, you'll go after it."

Douglas shrugged. He felt it was time to change the subject.

A steward arrived with his drink. As Douglas pushed back his chair to give the man room he noticed two men watching them from a table in a far corner of the lounge. One was Zoltan, and the other was the man with the yellow eyes.

Douglas waited for the steward to leave, then pulled his chair back close to the table. "Let's see how good a journalist you are," he said quietly. "The two men at the corner table—the fat one's Armand Zoltan, right?"

Again, something moved in Anne's eyes. She glanced quickly over his shoulder, then back into his face. She seemed puzzled. "Yes. He owns this ship. But didn't he hire you?"

113

Douglas shook his head. "I was hired by the travel agency booking the cruise. Who's the guy with him?"

"I don't know:" Her voice cracked almost imperceptibly and she quickly swallowed some water. "Why do you ask?"

"Just curious. They seemed to take a special interest in our game this afternoon. Maybe they think it's still going on."

Anne paled and her eyes shifted slightly out of focus, as if she were looking at something ugly and menacing far in the distance, beyond the confines of the ship.

Douglas tried to bring her back. "Does Zoltan play chess?"

"A Four Knights Game," Anne said absently.

"I must have missed a move. How's that again?"

Anne's eyes came back into focus and she smiled disarmingly. Whatever she had been looking at was gone, sunk in the depths of the ocean, or her mind. "Nothing," she said easily. "I was just talking to myself." She stifled a yawn that could have been feigned. "I'm sorry," she said. "I'm very tired."

Douglas summoned the steward and signed his check, then escorted Anne out of the lounge. Zoltan and the yellow-eyed man had already left.

Anne chatted pleasantly on the way back to her cabin, but Douglas could sense that something in her had changed. She was distracted, and he had become nothing more than a shadow at her side that talked. This bothered him, and he tried unsuccessfully to break down the barrier that the mention of a man's name had erected.

Douglas' mind rapidly shifted to other things when he reached his own cabin. He was positive he had locked it before leaving, but the louvered door swung open at his touch.

114

He stepped inside and switched on the light, then froze. His berth had been torn apart, thoroughly and professionally. His suitcases had been opened and their linings torn out; his clothes and personal possessions were strewn over the floor.

In the air was the faint but unmistakable odor of the man with the yellow eyes.

Douglas sensed rather than heard a movement behind him. He had just started to turn when something hard and heavy smashed into the base of his skull. What started out as a terrible, rending pain ended as a warm wave sloshing back and forth inside his brain. He didn't even remember falling.

"Hello, Douglas," the girl said. "You look terrible."

"I had a rough night." Douglas gently touched the back of a head that felt like it was filled with broken glass. "I got mugged."

"Really?"

"Really. And the man who did it was the same man who was with Zoltan in the lounge last night."

Anne's eyes narrowed. "How do you know that?" She tried to adopt a casual tone, but her voice was tight and had a sharp edge to it.

"I smelled him," Douglas said evenly.

"Did you report it to the captain?"

"Sure. He was properly upset. Said he'd look into it."

"Was anything taken?"

"That's why I called you. You see, I don't have that much to begin with, and it was all there when I woke up. I double-checked. It wasn't until I took off my jacket that I realized what was missing. It was the score sheet you gave me. That's what the man was after."

115

Anne paled and quickly looked away. "You could have lost it." Her voice was strangely muffled, as though damped by some intense emotion held tightly under rein.

"I didn't lose it."

Anne quickly regained control of herself. The face that she now presented to Douglas was totally expressionless; the green eyes cold and distant.

Suddenly, without warning, she laughed. "Is *that* what you wanted to talk to me about?"

Douglas felt his face grow hot. He'd realized before he called Anne that he would risk sounding foolish, and she was not making things easier for him. Still, he felt sure that whoever had sapped him had known exactly what he wanted to find. If the score sheet had been taken, there was a reason.

"I know it sounds strange," Douglas said tightly. "That's the point. I thought you might have some idea why somebody would want to steal that particular score sheet."

"Please leave me alone," Anne said coldly. "I've heard some stupid lines before, but this tops all." Her eyes flashed. "Really, Douglas, you're such a child. Is this another game? Must you make everything into a game?"

"What is it, Anne? What's wrong?"

"Stick to your chess; that's obviously what you do best. You've already begun to bore me." She punctuated the last sentence by slamming the cabin door in his face.

Douglas stared at the closed door for a few moments, then turned and walked slowly back the way he had come. When he reached his cabin he found Armand Zoltan and the ship's doctor waiting for him. The room had been straightened; his clothes had been neatly folded and packed in two new, expensive-looking suitcases. There was a large basket of fruit and a bottle of Scotch on the table beside his bed.

116

The doctor, a thin, reedy man with a chronic case of dandruff, sat stiffly on a chair at the opposite end of the room, a huge, leather medical bag propped on his knees. He smiled nervously as Douglas entered.

Zoltan rose from his chair and gestured expansively around the room. 'Mr. Franklin!" Zoltan's smile did not touch his eyes. "I hope you will now find everything in order. I wished to take the liberty of coming personally to apologize for this terrible incident. The man you described to Captain Barker is under close surveillance." Zoltan took a check from his pocket, signed it with a flourish, and then held it out to Douglas. "I trust this will be sufficient compensation for the suffering and inconvenience you've been caused."

"Nothing was stolen," Douglas said evenly, but it suddenly struck him as odd that Zoltan should be on this particular ship. From various newspaper accounts Douglas knew that Zoltan was a multibillionaire, with a large fleet of ships trafficking on the oceans of the world. What was he doing on a five-day cruise from Spain to Scotland? It was unlikely that he had even had anything to do with the decision to book a boatload of chess players. That type of mundane business affair was usually taken care of by mundane business managers. Zoltan should be at his island hideaway, counting his money. What was he doing here?

"Please take the check anyway," Zoltan insisted. "You've proven yourself to be a most valuable part of this cruise, without a doubt underpaid. Accept this as a token of my appreciation."

Douglas took the check and shoved it into his pocket without looking at it.

"I've brought Dr. Macklin with me to examine you," Zoltan continued. "We want to make absolutely certain that you're all right."

117

"All I've got is a headache," Douglas said. "It'll pass." He suddenly wanted to escape from Zoltan, the cabin, and the questions. He glanced at his watch. "I have a class on chess openings in twenty minutes," he continued. "I want to make sure I earn my keep."

"As you wish, Mr. Franklin. The captain, the crew and myself are at your disposal. Please let me know if there's anything you require."

Douglas started for the door, then stopped and turned. "By the way," he said, watching Zoltan's face, "I'm going to be discussing the Four Knights Game. What do you think of that opening, Mr. Zoltan?"

Zoltan looked puzzled. Finally he shrugged. "I'm aware that it's a very old opening, and not particularly aggressive. But I'm certainly no expert by any means."

If the question meant anything else to Zoltan, he had managed to disguise it well. Once again Douglas felt foolish, a participant in a shadow game that might exist only in his mind. He excused himself and walked out of the cabin.

Douglas' class was well attended, his lecture and demonstration enthusiastically received. Still, he found his mind constantly returning to Anne Pickford, for reasons that he could not fully explain to himself. Probably it was pride; he was not used to having doors slammed in his face. Douglas finished with the class at one, and then went to the dining lounge. He had hoped to catch sight of Anne, perhaps try to speak to her again. She wasn't there.

After lunch he went to the girl's cabin, knocked repeatedly on the door, but got no answer. He tried the door and found it locked.

Douglas had no responsibilities for the afternoon so he set out to look for Anne. He started on the upper deck. It was a calm, clear day at sea and the European coastline could be seen far in the distance, off the starboard bow. A number of passengers were sunning themselves or playing chess. Douglas strolled casually among the players, greeting familiar faces, occasionally stopping to answer questions or give advice. All the while he kept looking for the girl. There was no sign of her.

Next, Douglas traversed the lower deck, swimming pool, cocktail lounges, and any other place he could think of where the girl might be. By five o'clock his head was splitting and he went back to his cabin to take a nap. He arose in an hour, showered and dressed for dinner. He ate and stayed in the dining lounge until it closed, nursing coffee, watching the doors. Anne did not appear. He went to her cabin; there was still no answer to his knock.

Douglas felt a cold chill pass through his body. Once again he searched through all the areas of the ship that were open to passengers. Then he headed for the ship's bridge.

"I think you're missing a passenger," he reported.

The deck officer stared at him. "I beg your pardon, sir?"

"I said I think one of your passengers may be in trouble. Her name is Anne Pickford. If she's on the ship, I can't find her."

The officer, a Greek of moderate build and deep-set, soulful eyes, shook his head. "It is possible that you simply missed this person, sir. The *Argo* is a large ship."

"It's also possible that she fell overboard. I think you'd better call the captain."

The officer hesitated a moment, then said, "As you wish, sir."

Captain Barker arrived a few minutes later, with Zoltan. There was no question as to who was in charge, and who would do the talking. Barker's face was flushed with interrupted sleep, and his coat was only half-buttoned. His

119

eyes darted nervously about the room and refused to meet Douglas' gaze.

Zoltan stepped forward and took Douglas' elbow solicitously. "Mr. Franklin, how are you feeling?"

Douglas eased himself out of the other man's grip. The expression on Zoltan's face was imponderable. "It's one of your passengers I'm worried about," Douglas said tightly. "Miss Pickford is not in her cabin. I've been—"

Zoltan made an impatient gesture with his hand. The folds of flesh on his face rearranged themselves into something that might have been a leer. "You have a taste for the finer things in life, Mr. Franklin—Douglas, if I may call you that—but you needn't concern yourself about Miss Pickford. She's in good hands."

"Is that right? Whose hands?"

"Miss Pickford took ill quite unexpectedly this morning. Dr. Macklin examined her in her cabin and diagnosed her illness as acute appendicitis. As you may know, appendicitis can often strike without warning. Dr. Macklin thought it best that she be hospitalized immediately. As luck would have it, there was a British patrol boat in the area. Our request for assistance was immediately granted. By now Miss Pickford is undoubtedly in an English hospital."

"I didn't see any patrol boat."

"Of course not. I believe you were giving a demonstration-lecture at the time. In fact, I hope none of the other passengers saw it. We try to keep these unpleasant matters as unobtrusive as possible. The sight of a woman being carried off on a stretcher would be, at best, unpleasant. Before you know it there would be rumors of food poisoning, or something like that. The cruise would be ruined for many passengers. Miss Pickford was transferred from the loading platform at the bow of the ship. Are there any other questions, Douglas?"

120

There were many other questions, but Douglas decided he would keep them to himself. If Zoltan were telling the truth, everything was fine; if he were lying, nothing could be gained by arousing his suspicious.

"No," Douglas said, fixing his gaze on Zoltan's chest, "I'm glad you acted quickly."

"You are a good person to have on board, Douglas," Zoltan said with a wide grin that could have meant anything. "Most people would not notice the absence of a casual acquaintance. Such concern is to your credit. Now I suggest we all go back to bed and leave the deck officer to his duties. Good night, Mr. Franklin."

There was a note of finality to Zoltan's voice, and Douglas knew he was being dismissed. He nodded curtly and left the bridge. As he stood near the rail in the moonlight, smoking a cigarette, he stared at the red lettering on the door leading to the lower levels of the ship: NO ADMITTANCE. AUTHORIZED PERSONNEL ONLY. If Zoltan had lied and Anne was still on the ship, that was where she must be. It was the only place he had not looked.

The thought that he was actually considering going through the door bothered Douglas—perhaps the blow on the head had transformed him into an idiot. At best, if he were caught below, he would have compromised himself and his job. At worst, assuming Zoltan was involved in some criminal activity, he might never reach Glasgow. The sea was the ultimate garbage dump, and a ship at sea was a world unto itself, with no place to run and no place to hide; and it was obvious that Zoltan was the final arbiter of the law on the *Argo*. An outside observer might be fascinated by Zoltan's story of how he disappeared, but Douglas had no interest in allowing such a situation to develop. Money was power and power was often more potent than truth. There was no doubt in Douglas' mind that Zoltan had a

121

number of high-voltage connections. One person had already disappeared, and that did evidently not distress Zoltan.

Had Anne actually disappeared? *Why* would Zoltan lie?

Douglas mentally reviewed the reasons for his uneasiness: a bump on the head during the course of a robbery that wasn't a robbery; Zoltan's acquaintance with the yellow-eyed man who had hit him; a vague reference to a chess opening that Zoltan hardly knew. Finally, there was the girl's strange behavior. Beneath Anne's cold exterior there had been fear— he was sure of it.

Douglas flipped the cigarette into the wet darkness beyond the railing. He glanced around to make sure he was unobserved, and then slipped through the hatchway, closing the steel door quietly behind him.

He found himself at the top of a steep, narrow stairway that was only faintly illuminated by a string of naked, low-wattage electric bulbs. The steps led down to a narrow corridor lined on both sides with cabins. The corridor was empty. Douglas removed his shoes and moved past the cabins, which he assumed held sleeping crewmembers. He reached the opposite end of the corridor and tried the door there. It was open. He passed through the door, closed it behind him, and then put on his shoes.

The corridor beyond the crew's quarters was wider, lined on the right with recessed steel doors on which the word *Cargo* had been stenciled. At the opposite end of the corridor, fifty yards away, was another door.

Douglas tried the first cargo hold. It was locked, as were all the others. Frustrated, he tried the door at the end of the corridor. It, too, was locked. He cursed softly to himself as he realized that he had maneuvered himself into a *cul de sac*.

122

He turned and started back the way he had come. He froze when he heard the footsteps. They were echoing off the metal floor beyond the closed door leading to the crew's quarters, and they were coming toward him.

Douglas was abreast of the second, recessed steel door. The recess wasn't very deep, but it was the only conceivable hiding place. He flattened himself against the steel plate, and heard the door at the end of the corridor open and close, and the footsteps resume. He peered around the edge of the recess.

The footsteps belonged to the man with the yellow eyes. He was in his shirtsleeves, and the shoulder holster he wore was stuffed with a large, ugly, blue-steel automatic.

Douglas braced, ready to kick out at the man's groin as he came abreast. Then the footsteps stopped. Douglas again looked around the corner of the recess in time to see the yellow-eyed man turn a key in the lock of the first door, open it and pass through. He left the door open behind him. Douglas waited thirty seconds, then slipped down the corridor and looked in the open door.

The cargo hold was large and brightly lit, with two doors at the opposite side. One of the doors was open, revealing a corridor, and Douglas assumed that was where the yellow-eyed man had gone. The right side of the hold was filled with large wooden crates stacked neatly in piles of four.

Douglas entered the hold, darting across the concrete floor and ducking behind one of the piles of crates. A few moments later he heard the sound of footsteps again. The yellow-eyed man emerged from one of the corridors, walked quickly across the cargo hold and exited through the steel door. The door closed behind him with an ominous click.

Douglas stepped out from his hiding place and examined the crates. There were no markings on them, and each was circled by a tight, metal band. There was a large pair of wire clippers hanging on the wall. He took down the clippers and cut through one of the bands. The band snapped with a loud, singing crack that reverberated throughout the closed confines of the hold. Douglas ducked behind the crates again, his heart hammering in his chest, but the silence returned. He waited a few more minutes to make sure no one was coming, then used the handle of the clippers to pry back four of the plywood slats.

The crate was filled with machine pistols; a protective coating of light oil glistened on the black metal. Douglas picked up one of the guns, wiped off the oil with his handkerchief and examined it. The serial number on the frame had been carefully filed off. The pistol felt heavy and alien in his hand. He searched through the crate for ammunition but couldn't find any. It was just as well—he wouldn't know what to do with a loaded gun.

He replaced the pistol in the crate, found a tarpaulin and threw it over the broken band and slats. Then he crossed the hold and moved down the passageway from where the yellow-eyed man had come. The corridor was about fifty feet long. At the end it branched off at right angles to form another corridor. There were small, glassed-in office cubicles on either side.

He found the girl in the last cubicle on the left. She was lying on a cracked leather couch, tightly bound. There was a wide strip of adhesive tape over her mouth. Her eyes widened when she saw him.

Douglas suddenly realized that he was trembling; his clothes were pasted to his body, and he could smell his own fear in his nostrils. He took a deep breath, and then went to the top of the T formed by the intersecting corridors and glanced around the corner. There was no one there. To the left and right were steel ladders leading up to hatch covers. Douglas quickly climbed one of the ladders and tested the wheel gear on the bottom of the cover. It turned easily. Douglas breathed a sigh of relief at the discovery that there was another way out from below decks without going back through the cargo hold and crew's quarters. If they could manage to get back to the passengers' section, Zoltan just might be forced into a sort of Mexican standoff. He climbed back down the ladder and slipped into the office.

Anne's breath exploded in an urgent whisper as Douglas stripped the tape from her mouth. "Douglas! Zoltan will kill you if he finds you here! Get out!"

Douglas laughed shortly. "That's a strange request. What's he going to do to you if I leave you here?"

The girl said nothing.

Douglas knelt beside her and examined the ropes. They were thin, and an expert had tied the knots. There was blood on the girl's wrists and ankles where the rope had cut into the flesh. He searched through the cubicle but could find nothing sharp to cut the ropes so he went to work on the knots with his fingers.

"Who are you?" Douglas asked quietly.

"I'm a British agent," Anne said after a pause.

Douglas smiled wryly. "That's your game?"

"That's my game.

"Well, it certainly isn't very ladylike."

Anne smiled. "Don't talk like a male chauvinist pig, Douglas."

"Chauvinist, hell. None of my opponents has ever tried to tie me up.

"It adds a different dimension," Anne said dryly.

"You like to play word games, too," Douglas said seriously. "The Four Knights Game you referred to: that's the Four Horsemen of the Apocalypse, right?"

Anne winced but did not cry out as Douglas pulled the ropes free from her wrists. Her hands and feet were

125

swollen and inflamed. "Death, war, pestilence and famine," she said through clenched teeth. "Zoltan deals in death: drugs, guns, adulterated medicine. If the price is right, he'll smuggle anything in or out of any country in the world."

"I've seen the guns. Where are they going?"

"Northern Ireland. Special delivery to the terrorists. My job was to notify my superiors when and where the drop was to be made. I had a portable transmitter, but they found it."

"I don't suppose you can explain to me how I got involved in all this."

"Somehow, Zoltan found out about my cover and mission, but he didn't dare move against me until he could be sure I was working alone. My playing in the exhibition aroused his suspicions. He became even more suspicious when he saw I was beating you, and that you wanted my score sheet. He thought you might be a contact, and the score sheet might contain some sort of code. That's why Hawkins—"

"Hawkins. He's the one who's allergic to soap?"

Anne nodded. "You might say Hawkins is the executive director of the seamier side of Zoltan's business enterprises. In any case, they realized they'd made a mistake when they examined the score sheet. They tried to cover up, but by then you'd already talked to me. They knew I'd make the connection, and that's when they moved in."

Douglas finished removing the ropes. Anne eased her legs over the side of the couch and tried to stand. The blood drained from her face.

"Can you walk?"

"Just give me a minute to get the circulation back."

She bent over and started to massage the muscles in her legs. "I acted toward you the way I did because I didn't want you involved," Anne said quietly, without looking at

126

Douglas. "I must say, I'm glad you're so persistent. It must be that Grandmaster egomania."

The odor hit Douglas' nostrils a split second before he heard the words.

"You should have minded your own business, sonny."

The voice and smell belonged to the man with the yellow eyes, the one Anne had called Hawkins. Douglas spun and crouched. Hawkins was standing in the doorway, his legs braced. His lips were drawn taut as a bowstring in a strange, cruel smile. The pistol in his hand was aimed at Douglas' head.

"Checkmate, sonny," Hawkins said, and pulled the trigger.

However Douglas was already moving, warned by his sensitivity to other people's moods. He knew that Hawkins intended summarily to execute him and that he had little to lose by trying to fight back. He ducked low and drove for the man's legs.

Douglas' speed saved him. The sudden movement caught Hawkins by surprise, throwing off his aim. The bullet smashed into Douglas' wrist, shattering the bone. Numbed by the effects of a massive surge of adrenaline, Douglas barely felt the pain as he hurled himself through the air and hit Hawkins at the knees. Douglas hit the floor hard. Hawkins crumpled over the top of him.

"Run, Anne!" Douglas heard himself shouting. "Get out of here! There's a hatch cover around the corner!"

"Douglas - !"

"Run!"

He was vaguely aware of a lithe body hurtling through the air over his head, then the sound of footsteps turning the corner. A few seconds later there was the sound of a steel hatch cover clanging shut.

He was not dead yet. Douglas interpreted that as meaning that Hawkins had lost control of his gun. The yellow-eyed man's breath was coming in short gasps, and he was moaning with pain.

Douglas started to wiggle out from beneath the other man's body. It was then that the pain hit him, exploding in his wrist and coursing through his body like bolts of electricity. He cried out and clutched at his wrist. The fingers of his right hand were immediately enveloped in a warm, sticky fluid.

Hawkins rolled off of him. Douglas lifted his head and almost vomited with terror as he saw the gun lying on the floor a few feet away. There was no way he could get to it before Hawkins.

Hawkins took a step toward the gun, and then screamed in pain, clutching his right knee as he slumped to the floor. He then began crawling across the floor toward the gun.

Douglas pushed himself to his feet with his good right arm. His head swam with pain, and for a moment he was afraid he would pass out. Then it cleared enough for him to see that Hawkins had the gun. Douglas wheeled and ran out through the door at the same time as a loud explosion thundered in his ears and a bullet smashed into the wood paneling beside his head.

Douglas sprinted around the corner, let go of his wrist and pulled himself up the ladder to the right. He managed to turn the wheel gear, then, bracing his legs on the rungs of the ladder, he pushed against the hatch cover with his shoulder. The steel cover was jammed.

He started to climb down, intending to try the other cover. He froze when he saw Hawkins suddenly emerge from around the corner. The man was staggering, clutching his ruined knee with one hand. His eyes were clouded with pain and hate.

128

For the second time Douglas pulled himself up the ladder and pushed against the hatch cover with his shoulder. His head was filled with a sound like crashing surf—the sound of terror.

Hawkins leaned against the wall, lifted his gun and fired, but the pressure on his shattered knee ruined his aim. The bullet bit into the metal inches from Douglas' left side, and then whined off down the corridor.

The hatch cover suddenly burst open. Douglas scrambled up through the opening as a second bullet whined through the air beneath him. He slammed the hatch cover shut, then lay on his back, gasping for air, drinking in the cold, wet sea breeze.

He would have given anything to be able to lie there, not moving, and wait for them to come and get him. There seemed no sense in resisting; Anne and he had not really gotten away, but had merely escaped into a larger pen. They were still trapped on a ship at sea.

The thought of the girl brought him to his feet. He was not ready to die yet, and he would not be a Grandmaster if he had not learned to play out some end games that were apparently lost. He looked around him and immediately saw that he had made a tactical error—he had come out the wrong hatch. He was on a narrow walkway, blocked off from the passenger section by a steel bulwark.

Hawkins' voice, fogged by pain and rage, came out of the darkness above him. "You should have taken the trouble to learn the layout of the ship, sonny. You came up the hard way—I took the freight elevator." There was a pause filled with hoarse, heavy breathing, then, "You're going to have a lot of company in a few minutes, sonny. But I'm going to take care of you personally."

Douglas pressed flat against the bulkhead. To his left, separated from him by twenty yards of moonlit walkway, were dark, undefined shapes in the open storage area at the stern of the ship. *Twenty yards.*

"Where's the girl?" Douglas asked.

"We'll find her," Hawkins said. The voice seemed closer, almost directly above Douglas.

Douglas tensed, clutching his injured wrist to his side. "You can't afford to do a lot of shooting, Hawkins. It'll wake the passengers."

The answer was a soft, spitting sound, like the cough of a cat. The wood on the walkway to Douglas' left splintered.

"End of the line, sonny".

Douglas pushed off the bulkhead and dashed toward the black shapes at the stern. Bullets whined in the air like angry steel bees. Finally he dove through the air, landed heavily on an oil drum and rolled off on the other side. His wrist felt as if it was bathed in molten metal, and he bit off the scream that formed at the back of his throat.

Finally, after what seemed an eternity, the pain subsided. Douglas lifted his head slightly and looked around him. He was on the edge of a forest of oil drums that had been loaded on pallets and lashed onto the deck. He lowered his head and crawled backward, deeper into the tangle of steel drums.

Somewhere in the darkness in front of him a door opened and closed. Then he heard the curious, shuffling footsteps of a man dragging one foot behind him. The drums could explode from the impact of a bullet, Douglas realized. Hawkins knew that too. The yellow-eyed man would be very careful, wait for a sure shot at close range.

Douglas turned as far as he could without making noise and desperately searched for something with which to defend himself. His knee brushed painfully against something—a chain. Douglas' mouth went dry. He reached down and caressed the thick, rusted links with his fingers.

The chain was heavy, perhaps too heavy for him to use in his weakened condition. Still, it was the only weapon he had. One end was anchored firmly beneath a wooden pallet, probably having become lodged, and then abandoned, during the course of loading. He estimated the loose end to be about eight feet long.

Douglas peered over the top of a barrel. Hawkins was about fifteen feet away, moving carefully, the gunmetal extension of his hand glinting in the moonlight. Douglas sank back down to the deck. It was only a matter of time before Hawkins or one of the other men moving out in the dark found him, and the longer he waited the weaker he would be. He would be executed, shot like a helpless, wounded animal. His left arm had begun to smolder with a white heat. He could wait no longer if he hoped to take Hawkins with him.

Douglas kicked at the nearest barrel. The drum produced a dull, thudding sound. The shuffling footsteps stopped, then started again, coming directly toward him: twelve paces, ten paces.

"Where the hell are you, you stinking—"

Douglas gripped the chain in the center with his right hand and sprang to his feet, shifting his weight and pulling on the chain with all his strength. The steel links clanged against the drums, skipped free and described a wide, whistling arc. The end of the chain caught Hawkins in the center of the forehead. There was a sound like the popping of a knuckle and the yellow-eyed man fell to his knees, and then crumpled onto the deck.

Douglas leaped from behind his barricade, intending to search for Hawkins' gun. Out of the corner of his eye he saw two crewmen, guns drawn, converging on his position. He ducked down, frantically groping in the dark for the gun.

"Douglas!"

131

Douglas glanced up at the sound of Anne's voice. He could see the girl standing at the railing on the upper deck, silhouetted by the moonlight. She was frantically waving her arms and could not see the man coming up behind her.

"Anne!" Douglas yelled. "Behind you!"

He didn't see what happened next. He ducked down behind a barrel as a bullet ricocheted off steel. He heard Anne call out his name again; he looked up in time to see her body hurtling down. The sound of her body hitting the water floated up to him through the darkness.

Douglas reacted instinctively, although he probably would have done the same thing if he'd had time to think about it—he would be no worse off in the water than he was on the ship. Bending low, using the barrels as a shield, Douglas raced for the side of the ship, and then leaped over the rail, aiming for the area where he had seen Anne fall.

His own fall seemed interminable, and when it finally ended he wished it hadn't. The water came up to meet him like a slab of concrete and once more pain shot through his wrist, blinding him, tearing the breath from his lungs. The icy cold of the water kept him conscious, but his strength was gone; the water was closing over his head and his lungs burned. In a moment, he knew, he would end it all, open his mouth and suck in the water.

Someone was yanking at his hair, pulling him up. Douglas kicked the last few inches to the surface, drinking in great drafts of air. Anne was supporting him in the water. "Hey," Douglas sputtered at last, "I was supposed to rescue *you.*"

Anne smiled. "I didn't want you to rescue me, I just wanted you to follow me."

Douglas shook his head. "I can't swim. My wrist is broken."

"Can you float?"

132

Douglas slowly lay on his back in the water, resting his left wrist on his chest. "Uh, I don't mean to sound pessimistic, but I'm not sure this is a solution. It's cold out here."

Anne glanced toward the east. The sun was just breaking over the horizon. "If you can hold out for an hour or so, we'll be eating breakfast on a British destroyer."

"How'd you manage that?"

"By being unladylike toward a. very surprised radio operator. That's why I had to leave you down there with Hawkins. Duty and all that. Besides, I thought you'd be able to handle him."

"Thanks a lot. What about Zoltan?"

"Well, I suspect he's going to have to take a big loss on this particular shipment. That ship will be a lot lighter by the time it pulls into Glasgow. By the way, did I thank you for saving my life?"

"I don't think you had time. Did I thank you for saving mine?"

"We can properly thank each other later."

Douglas smiled. "Are you any good at blindfold chess?"

"Pawn to king four."

Douglas thought for a moment, and then said, "Pawn to queen bishop four."

THE CLUB OF VENICE

JOHN PARVE watched the rat with mild interest, trying to decide whether it was real, or merely one more imaginary terror leached out of his subconscious by the alcohol in his system. The animal was nimbly stepping its way toward a hillock of garbage floating in the gutter next to Parve's head.

The rat paused and sniffed, then, sensing the presence of fresher meat, veered and headed toward Parve. The rat was the size of a terrier to begin with, and from Parve's angle of perspective on the sidewalk it looked big as a horse. Parve thought he should move, and couldn't. He blinked his eyes a few times, but the animal ignored the slight movement.

The rat sniffed at Parve's face, then bit deep into the soft flesh of his cheek. Blood, warm and salty, flowed down across Parve's lips. Parve still couldn't move, but he could feel.

Parve laughed soundlessly. The thought of being gnawed to death by a rat amused him. There were worse ways to die; he'd seen most of them.

Something metallic glittered out of the corner of Parve's eye. The rat saw it too and slid its teeth out of Parve's cheek. The silver tip of a cane flashed in an arc that ended in the rat's belly with a dull, hollow sound, like somebody beating a mattress. The rat squealed and rolled over into the gutter. It came up wet and mad, braced on its hind legs, its teeth bared. It was looking at something above

Parve's head. There was a soft sound, like a man spitting out a wad of gum. The bullet smashed into the rat's head, splattering its brains among the rest of the offal in the gutter. The animal's body skittered down the sidewalk, out of Parve's field of vision.

Now Parve heard a strange set of footsteps, like those of a man with three legs. The third leg was the cane that came to rest on a spot not far from Parve's nose. Two highly polished, black leather shoes flanked the tip of the cane. Conservative, banker's shoes, Parve thought; there were all types of animals down on the Bowery, and he was about to be rolled by one of the more bizarre types.

The tip of the cane came up and poked him on the shoulder. It wasn't hard enough to hurt, but the action caused something to stir inside Parve's brain; he decided he wasn't about to be poked around and rolled by some kinky dandy who might just decide to leave a bullet in his brain as soon as he was finished.

Suddenly Parve found his feet under him and he was lunging toward a dark shape, his rigid thumbs describing two deadly arcs aimed at the man's kidneys.

Then the shape wasn't there anymore. Something hard crashed down behind his right ear and Parve crumpled back to the sidewalk.

He woke naked between perfumed sheets. His body felt clean and there was a bandage on his face where the rat had bitten him.

The room was decorated in an odd combination of Victorian and Sanitarium, a white-walled hospital room with a Tiffany lamp and leather upholstered chairs. One of the chairs had a man in it. He was tall and wore tweeds. A silver-tipped cane rested in his lap, along with a black bowler hat. Parve again thought of a banker; only the man's eyes didn't fit the image.

136

Parve was an expert on eyes; for years they'd served as traffic signals for him: *Caution, Stop, Go.* Often his life had depended on noting the subtle shifting of gears and drawing of curtains that took place in the depths of men's eyes.

This man had eyes that revealed nothing, and that was an accomplishment that required years of training and practice. The man's hair was full and black, with streaks of silver that perfectly matched the tip of his cane. He had high cheekbones parenthesizing a narrow, aquiline nose.

The man spoke. "I see you are awake, John Parve."

"Jesus," Parve said. "A Limey with a Liverpool accent. Where the hell am I?"

"Does it matter, after where you've been?"

"Who are you?"

"My name is Sir James Roderick."

"How long have I been here?"

"Almost a week now. Your sleep has been drug-induced, and, naturally, you've been fed intravenously. Your body and mind needed the rest."

"What are you, the Salvation Army?"

"Hardly. Perhaps you would like some solid food now."

"No, Sir James Roderick, I don't want any solid food. As a matter of fact I want a drink."

"Perhaps later," Sir James said easily. "After we talk."

"You won't get me a drink, I'll go someplace else." Parve sat up. He felt surprisingly strong; he couldn't remember a time in recent years when it hadn't been difficult to move. "Where are my clothes?"

He'd expected some kind of resistance. Roderick simply pointed to a wardrobe set back against a wall. Parve got up and walked toward it. Roderick's voice followed him.

"A few days ago you displayed a short but remarkable burst of energy when you tried to maim me. Why didn't you use some of that energy on the rat that was eating your face?"

"I only get mad at human rats," Parve said without turning. "The furry kind doesn't know any better." He opened the wardrobe; it was filled with expensive clothes. He turned back to Sir James. "These aren't mine."

"They're yours."

Parve didn't argue. He turned back to the open wardrobe and dressed. The clothes fit perfectly, and were obviously hand-tailored. They made him feel strange, like a whole man again. It wasn't a feeling he desired because it was ephemeral. However much Sir James Roderick built him up, Parve knew it would take only a short time for the acid of his memories to wear him down again.

The door to the room was open. Parve had every intention of dressing and walking out of the room, perhaps killing anyone who tried to stop him. Now his legs wouldn't move. "You son-of-a-bitch," Parve said quietly. "You know I won't leave here until I find out what this is all about."

"I'd hoped that would be your attitude," Sir James said evenly. He didn't smile. "Why don't you sit down while I satisfy your curiosity?"

Parve sat. 'I'd still like a drink."

His host almost smiled. "Not yet," Sir James said. "When I have said what I have to say, you may have anything you like."

Parve wasn't used to having people tell him what he could or couldn't do. Still, he sat, watching the other man closely. He knew there was more substance to Sir James Roderick than the cane and bowler hat; there was steel in the man, and the honed, razor edge of it could be heard in the man's voice.

"So, talk," Parve said after a few moments.

"I will tell you about myself, John Parve, but first we will talk about you. Then we will both be on equal footing all the way."

"How do you know who I am?"

"That's irrelevant."

"I don't think so."

"What is relevant is that you are an ex-C.I.A. agent. Six years ago your assignment took you to Zobatu, an emerging African country. The government at that time was threatened by an imminent military coup. The generals who were planning the coup were being counseled by a rather unique, international Jack-of-all-trades who had taken the code name given him by the Allied intelligence services—Hannibal. Your job was to investigate him, not to determine his attitudes toward the Zobatu people, but to determine whether he and his people were sufficiently anti-communist to satisfy your State Department."

Parve didn't want to listen any more. He would have done anything to stop the voice, but once again he felt paralyzed, trapped and motionless on a hard concrete sidewalk of the mind. Around him were pieces of flying, bloody flesh, chunks of metal, the smell of burning hair, a stifled scream, a child's charred, rubber ball rolling past him...

"Hannibal didn't take kindly to your interference," Sir James continued, "so he blew up your family. In broad daylight."

He'd just gotten off the airplane. Elizabeth and their two children had been waiting for him in the car parked in the airport parking lot. It had all been over in two minutes. They'd shot him full of a paralyzing drug, and then laid him down on the pavement twenty yards from the car.

The doors of the car had been sealed with jamming devices before Elizabeth and the children had had time to react. His son had been looking at him, beating at the car window with his tiny fist, screaming for his father to get up and help them. The boy had still been screaming when the car went up. A few seconds later, amid the screams of police and ambulance sirens, a black rubber ball had fallen from the sky, bounced twice, then rolled up to Parve's paralyzed face.

"Naturally, you went quite out your mind from grief," Sir James continued. "But you were also a highly disciplined man. The answer to your grief, naturally, was to return to the assignment and kill Hannibal in the most horrible manner you could devise. Unfortunately, the coup had been accomplished by this time, and the attitude of your government had changed. The generals were in power, and Hannibal installed as one of their chief advisers.

"The State Department of your country had decided to compete with the Russians and Chinese for influence in Zobatu, and this meant the shipment of money and armaments. There wasn't much you could do about this turn of events, except blow your brains out. That, of course, was too obvious for a man like you. You are subtle—so you chose an appropriately subtle way to kill yourself, through alcohol."

John Parve practiced the words in his mind until he was sure he could say them in a voice that didn't quake. "I should kill you."

Sir James ignored the threat. "I represent an organization which calls itself The Club of Venice," he said. "COVE, if you like. Simply put, COVE is a highly secret organization of international figures dedicated to—doing good."

Parve felt sickness bubbling up in his throat. He threw back his head and released it as peals of manic

140

laughter. Sir James waited until the sound had trailed off into a series of tortured gasps.

"My employers are known only to each other," Sir James continued, ignoring Parve's outburst. "Their instructions are carried out by operatives like myself, on the basis of written instructions delivered at various postal drops throughout the world. They are all men of virtually unlimited financial resources. In effect, what they have done is to organize a private espionage network that is action-oriented.

"Quite frankly, many of the members are motivated by bad consciences. I'm quite positive that a number of COVE members are ex-Nazis and fascists who fashioned their fortunes from the blood and twisted lives of other men. However, I offer that opinion solely for your own information; it is irrelevant to the existence of COVE. The members' design now is to do what they can to eradicate injustice, whenever and wherever possible.

"COVE's constituency is that which the governments of the world largely ignore, the people of the world. However, COVE does not attempt to overthrow existing governments; its members are experienced enough in international politics to know that such activity, over the long run, is largely an exercise in futility. COVE does not subvert governments; it circumvents them."

"How long has this COVE been in existence?"

"I don't know."

"I'll bet about a week. That's how long a bunch of bleeding hearts would last out there in that jungle."

Sir James made a clucking noise in his throat. "You don't seem to understand. The members of COVE work for humanitarian reasons. The people they hire to work for them do not. They work for money. They are certainly not humanitarians, and the great majority could not even be described as liberal; such people tend, on the

141

whole, to be inefficient. Most of COVE's agents are professional killers—as you once were."

"You expect me to work for you?"

"No, Mr. Parve. I will not insult you by trying to flatter you. You are, as you well know, finished—'over the hill' is the expression your own people might use. No, I'm afraid you would be of no use as a COVE agent."

"Then what do you want with me?"

Sir James placed his cane across his lap and stared at Parve. "We are prepared to offer you an honorable way to die."

Parve watched the other man's eyes, but said nothing. The eyes remained clear and depthless, like the eyes in a very poor—or very great—painting.

"You are a dead man, John Parve," Sir James continued. "You are merely going through the motions. Your life is worth nothing to yourself or to others, which is why you're drinking yourself to death. On the other hand, you do possess something which is of value to us, your knowledge of Zobatu and the ways of its people."

"I also speak Bantu. What does Zobatu have to do with all this?"

"The military government of Zobatu has recently decided to eliminate its most persistent critics, which means just about every intellectual, teacher and academician in the country. If this execution is allowed to take place, the intellectual soul of the country will be destroyed, as well as any hope of a better life for the Zobatu people. At this moment the Zobatu government is holding ninety five people in a compound in a solitary military outpost on their southern coast."

"Mandringo?"

"Yes."

142

"I know the place. It's surrounded on three sides by jungle, and the sharks in that water are so thick you can just about walk on their backs."

"Yes, it is a rather remote and well protected region. Which is why COVE plans to use three military transport helicopters to airlift the prisoners out. They are scheduled to be executed in three days."

"You've got military transport helicopters?"

"COVE has unlimited financial resources. When I say unlimited, I mean unlimited." He spread his hands meaningfully.

"Well, you might as well try to use kites. They have a radar station at Mandringo."

"Yes. If the radar station is operating when we go in, we will be confronted by an unusual assortment of American Phantom jets and Russian MIG 21's. That's where you come in. It will be your job to knock out the radar station at exactly 1:21 A.M., our time, next Wednesday night. That is five and a half hours before the prisoners are scheduled to be shot."

"You're crazy."

"I think I indicated it was a suicide mission."

"I mean you're crazy to think I'd agree to do something like that. I'll choose my own way to check out."

"Alcohol and rats?"

"You're goddamn right! Why should I play cannon fodder for a bunch of rich bastards who are playing games with other peoples' lives?"

"At 3:00 Tuesday afternoon the military adviser to the Zobatu government will make an inspection of the Mandringo radar station. Arrangements have been made for him to spend the night, which means he'll be there when you make your raid. The man's name is Hannibal."

143

Parve jerked his head to one side; the sudden movement caused a ringing in his ears. He focused on a vase of
flowers in a corner of the room. They were roses, and they
looked like they'd been dipped in blood.

"Now, Parve, would you care for a drink or some
food?"

"What?"

"I asked if you'd like a drink or some food."

Parve's voice came at him, as if shouted from a great
distance. "I like my steak rare. Bloody."

John Parve dove into the blackness. At 2,000 feet, the air
over the African jungle was cold. He waited a few seconds,
and then pulled the ripcord on his parachute. There was a
whooshing sound, then a wrench as the straps tore into his
armpits and groin. It was the only way Parve could tell the
chute had opened. Above him, the dyed silk was virtually
invisible against the dark slate of the moonless night.

He drank in the night air, imagined he could feel it
swirling in his lungs. The air was intoxicating, and Parve
wished to enjoy this reprieve to the fullest, before he blew
himself up with the radar station. That was assuming he
didn't break apart in the jungle below him.

Then things started to go wrong.

There was a soft, pinging sound under his left
armpit, and then something heavy slipped down his side,
bounced off his foot and was gone.

That would be the sack containing his satchel
charges. Parve groped until he found the leather strap that
had bound the charges to his side. He followed the strap to
its end. His fingers came away moist and burning.

Acid.

Parve quickly wiped his fingers on his jump suit. In
a few moments the stinging sensation went away. His rage
didn't. The pilot of the plane that had run the drop had

144

been anonymous; Parve had never even seen his face. It didn't really make any difference, because it could just as easily have been the people, whomever they were, who had packed his chute. It could be any one of thousands of faceless men he had never seen, someone who didn't want the mission to succeed. COVE had a traitor.

But then why not just kill him? It would have been just as easy to pour acid on one of the straps binding him to his parachute and then he'd be plummeting down along with the satchel charges. It seemed a hell of a way to abort a mission.

The charges hadn't been designed to survive the impact of a thirty-two feet per second acceleration. They hit and exploded in the jungle below him, sending up a single, brilliant burst of light, like the blink of a Cyclops's eye. The sound came to him a few seconds later, muffled by the surrounding jungle but still loud enough to attract some unwelcome attention from the radar station a mile or two away.

Parve cursed loudly; as if he didn't have enough problems already, there were going to be a few dozen Zobatu soldiers strolling through the night jungle soon after he landed.

He got lucky, hitting the edge of a small clearing. He absorbed the force of the landing shock with flexed legs and rolled, taking care to keep clear of the harness. Something growled a few feet away in the jungle, and then crashed off through the underbrush.

Parve dragged in his chute, quickly dug a hole in the ground with his knife and buried the silk and harness. Then he sat down to catch his breath. He glanced at the illuminated dial of the calibrated watch-compass he wore on his wrist. The radar station would be almost due east, about forty-five minutes of hard walking away. He had four hours.

Parve tensed at a sound in the jungle, behind him and to his left. Lights moved through the trees, the interposing brush lending them a strobe effect. That would be the soldiers come to investigate the explosion, Parve thought.

Parve considered it for a few moments, then decided that the explosion had not been that loud; the soldiers would poke around for a half hour or so, then decide that the noise had been thunder and go away. In the meantime, they offered him the opportunity to re-arm himself.

Parve went into a crouch and slipped off into the jungle. Twenty-two minutes later he clapped his arm around the man's neck, slipped his elbow under the chin, positioned his hip in the small of the man's back and yanked. The soldier died without a sound. Parve quickly covered the man's body with some brush, and then scooped up the man's flashlight and automatic rifle. Then he melted back into the jungle to wait.

A half hour later the soldiers began to regroup. It didn't take them long to discover that one of their members was missing. They searched for a few more minutes, and then disappeared back down a trail in a babble of excited voices.

That made one more strike against him, Parve thought; their missing comrade would make the soldiers at the station that much more uneasy. Of course, there was always the chance they would write him off as a leopard dinner, but that wasn't something he could count on. And then there was the blast; finally, if the missing soldier and blast didn't tip off the soldiers to his presence, the person who had treated his harness with acid would. Hannibal would be on his toes; Hannibal was a great many things, but he wasn't stupid.

The thought of Hannibal made Parve physically ill; he doubled over as his stomach knotted with hate.

146

Hannibal, the man who had blown up his family was about to blow away close to a hundred more lives, and it was up to him to stop him.

But the hate had its positive effects also; it stiffened Parve's muscles and kept him from trembling; it temporarily cancelled out the ravages of the six years of suicidal neglect Parve had subjected his body to. Finally, the hate gave Parve a steely resolve. That was what Roderick had been counting on, Parve thought, and he'd been right. He would get through this night feeding on his hate.

With the satchel charges gone, knocking out the radar station was going to be a little more difficult than he'd first imagined. Of course, the automatic rifle would help some, and with it he'd make sure he got one shot at Hannibal, even if he was carrying a pound of lead in his belly when he did it. But he would need more than an automatic rifle to get into the radar station. He needed an edge.

He checked his watch. He had three hours left. The existence of the trail the soldiers had used would cut down his traveling time considerably. It hadn't taken the soldiers more than fifteen minutes to reach his position. It would be risky to use the trail, but it would give him valuable time, time that he needed. He would give himself an hour to reach the station and get in. That left him two hours to look for his edge. He decided he would spend the time hunting.

He'd spent a great deal of time in the jungle during his C.I.A. assignment in Zobatu, and he'd seen what the natives could do with two candles and a knife. Two hours wasn't very much time to find what he wanted, but if he could get it he would have the edge he needed. In any case, it was worth a try.

Parve made his way back to the clearing and dug up his parachute. He cut out a large square, then used his knife to jab small holes along the perimeter of the nylon through which he threaded a length of harness cord. When he had finished he had a usable sack with a drawstring. Next he fashioned a small masque for the flashlight and cut two small holes in its face. He put the materials under his arm and headed back into the jungle.

Parve found the site he wanted, then turned on the flashlight and propped it in the roots of a tree a few inches off the ground. The light shining through the two pin pricks in the masque resembled eyes, which was exactly the effect he had intended. He rubbed his body down with dirt, which he hoped would kill, or at least deaden, his own scent, and then moved back ten yards and climbed up into the protective crook formed by the boughs of a large tree. There he crouched and waited, staring intently at the area illuminated by the light.

The nocturnal visitors began to arrive a few minutes later. Parve crouched and waited. The first three inquisitors were big cats, a leopard and two lionesses. They sniffed around the flashlight for a few moments, growled softly, and then went away in search of more warm-blooded prey. The fourth visitor was the one Parve had been waiting for. The creature emerged from the night, first its triangular head, then slowly, foot by foot, the rest of it. Its forked tongue flicked out, touching the masque over the light. It tensed, waited a few moments, and then began to crawl away along a route that took it directly beneath the tree in which Parve was waiting.

Parve counted slowly to ten, then leaped to the ground and threw the large square of silk toward the animal's head. The silk billowed in the air, and then settled down over the python's body. The animal immediately coiled around itself in a protective reaction. Parve pulled on the drawstring and the sack tightened around the animal's body. He ran forward, stuffed the

148

remaining length of the snake's body into the sack, and then pulled the top closed. He waited a few minutes until the animal's thrashing stopped. Then he heaved the sack over his shoulder and set off for the trail.

The radar station was fairly modern, a concrete, rectangular building with a geodesic dome on top surrounded by a walkway for guards. Parve calculated from the building's size that it could probably accommodate a garrison of up to fifty men.

Hannibal was somewhere inside that building.

Parve's mouth was dry and his legs hurt from their cramped position in the crouch he had assumed. The smell of the sea came to him from beyond the building. In the darkness, somewhere to the north, ninety-five men were waiting to be slaughtered.

Parve glanced once more at his watch; he had a little over a half hour before the raid was scheduled to begin. He had already decided that he must take a considerable risk beforehand. He must find a way to sneak inside the building and then hide. That was the only way he could be sure of knocking out the radar equipment.

An area of about ten yards had been cleared around the perimeter of the building. Parve stayed just inside the edge of the jungle and slipped around that perimeter until he found the entrance to the building.

There was a burly guard standing in front of the door. Parve had no way of knowing exactly how many men were inside, or the layout of the interior itself. It would be all over before it began if he should manage to slip inside only to find himself nakedly exposed in the middle of a large open area. But that was a chance he would have to take.

If it came to that, he would simply open fire on the men and equipment, hoping that he could knock out the radar before they knocked him out. He'd keep shooting at anything that moved, trying to stay alive just long enough for Hannibal to stick his head out from wherever he was hiding.

He couldn't kill the first guard himself; that would only run the risk of bringing the entire garrison down on his head prematurely. The snake would have to do his killing for him.

Parve, taking care to hold the drawstring tight, turned to the sack on the ground beside him and used a sharp stick to poke at the steely coils. The sack began to writhe. Parve poked the animal again, and the writhing increased. There was an angry hiss. Finally, Parve snapped the stick between his hands.

The guard stiffened, his rifle held at the ready. Parve waited a few more moments, and then snapped another stick. The guard looked over his shoulder and called to someone inside. Two more men came running around the side of the building and came to a stop beside the first guard. They exchanged a few words, and then the first guard started forward.

Parve carefully opened the top of the sack, gave its occupant another jab, then moved off to the side, walking softly on the balls of his feet. He moved ten yards, and then braced his back against a tree near the perimeter around the building. He waited.

A moment later the first guard screamed. Parve glanced around the tree in time to see the man stumble out of the jungle, a hundred pounds of python wrapped around his body.

The other two men began to yell and move back. The snake's coils tightened around the first man's legs and he tumbled to the ground. His two companions started forward again, circling warily. The first guard's face was turning gray and his eyes were glazing. The swollen tongue protruding from his open mouth was black.

One of the other guards stepped close, put the muzzle of his rifle next to the snake's head and squeezed off a shot. That wasn't going to do the first guard much good; even in death, the snake's coils would remain locked around its prey. But it did bring a number of soldiers from inside running, and that was what Parve had wanted.

He watched as the soldiers gathered in a knot in the center of the cleared area. They were Hannibal's men, Parve thought, and he would dearly have loved to step out from behind the tree and open fire with the automatic rifle. But that would only serve to warn Hannibal and the other soldiers inside. Instead, Parve gripped his rifle and, crouching low, raced across the cleared area and into the building.

He almost collided with Hannibal.

Hannibal grunted with surprise and staggered back a few steps, his eyes wide, still reddened with sleep. Parve felt frozen in time, inundated by a wave of hate that welled up from the deepest part of him.

In that instant their eyes met and held. Hannibal seemed smaller, weaker than Parve remembered, or perhaps it was only what Hannibal had done that had made him seem so gargantuan in Parve's memory. Now, eyes glazed, clad only in shorts and a T shirt, Hannibal seemed more like a beekeeper than a man capable of cold-bloodedly killing a woman and two children.

Yet that was precisely what the man in front of him had done. And now there was one more thing that added to Parve's horror. Hannibal didn't even recognize him; the man who had ordered his family killed didn't even know who he was. The realization reached into his stomach and pulled like a steel hand at his intestines.

Hannibal might not know who he was, but he knew what the business end of an automatic rifle could do. He

151

stared with his small, green eyes at the single, black eye that was staring at his midsection. Then Hannibal began to retch.

Parve's finger tightened on the trigger. In his mind's eye he could see the man in front of him cut in half by a hail of bullets from the gun he held, and then he himself cut down from behind. He saw the radar scanner picking up the tiny blips of the transport helicopters, heard the call go out for the jets.

At the last moment Parve eased the pressure on the trigger and swung the stock hard, smashing it into the side of Hannibal's head. Hannibal crumpled to the concrete floor of the station. Parve grabbed him by the shirt and dragged him to the closest cover, a pile of wooden boxes stacked off to his right. Parve eased Hannibal behind the boxes, then sat down on his chest. In the few brief moments of the confrontation, Parve had surveyed his surroundings.

The main bank of radar equipment was across the room and to his left, about twenty yards away. There were a few smaller machines, but the main power source had to be in the main bank. Knock out that machinery and the radar was gone.

A catwalk with guard posts circled above his head, broken at various intervals by hatchways that looked as though they led to the roof. To his right, across the room, was a corridor that Parve guessed must lead to the station's living quarters.

The floor plan clear in his mind, Parve sat and waited.

Once, Hannibal started to moan. Quickly, expertly, Parve clipped him on the jaw with the butt of his rifle.

It was 1:20.

The guards and radar operators had taken their positions once again. For the past fifteen minutes a contingent of soldiers had been scurrying around; Parve had heard Hannibal's name mentioned. He waited until the sweep

152

hand of his watch had gone around one more time, then stood up and told them where Hannibal was.

"He's here, you bastards!" Parve screamed. "Come and get him!"

His first burst of fire raked the bank of machines to his left. The bullets tore into the metal, ripping the guts out of the electronic sensors; the screens went dead, and then disintegrated under the hail of bullets. The three operators flew out of their seats, slammed against the equipment, and then fell to the floor, their bodies shredded.

A single glance told Parve that the equipment was out. That accomplished, Parve swung the rifle in an arc, mowing down the first group of soldiers, and then continuing on across the back-up equipment to his right.

Soldiers appeared in the mouth of the corridor; and there were still the guards on the catwalk above. Parve dropped to one knee and had begun to rake the catwalk when the first slug hit him, tearing into his thigh and passing on through.

The force of the bullet spun him around, bringing him up hard against the rough surface of the wooden crates. He gritted his teeth, waiting for the deadly shower of steel to wash over him.

There was the sound of a machine gun above him; Parve dug his fingers into the wood and grimaced. But the bullets didn't come. He glanced up at the catwalk.

Sir James Roderick stood on the walkway, near an open hatchway. He had one polished black shoe braced against the metal railing and his bowler hat slung down low over his forehead, like some movie cowboy who had wandered into the wrong costume. His suit jacket was buttoned properly, but the silver-tipped cane had been replaced by a British Sten gun. Roderick knew how to use it; his touch was light, and he played the gun like some musical instrument. The tune he played was death.

Then it was over. The entire garrison of soldiers lay dead or dying on the cold floor, amidst the rubble of the machinery.

Sir James laid the gun down on the catwalk, rose and carefully straightened his bowler hat.

"Can you walk, John?"

"What the hell are you doing here?"

"I've been here for some time, watching from the roof."

"Then the station was covered, regardless of what happened to me?"

"You might say that."

Sir James' words echoed faintly, spoken as they were from his position on the catwalk, competing with the lingering reverberations of gunfire. The room smelled of cordite, blood and death.

"The prisoners?"

"They're safely out."

"You were the one who put the acid on the tether strap."

"Well, not personally."

"But you had it done."

"Yes."

"Why, you bastard?"

"In our opinion, it wouldn't have done for you to blow yourself up."

Parve looked down at his leg. It was gushing blood. He was beginning to feel light-headed. He took off his belt and wrapped it around the leg, pulling the leather tight and knotting it. The bleeding stopped.

Sir James waited silently.

"I don't understand," Parve said when he was finished.

"The man Hannibal took your life away from you. You had a right to try to get it back, to exorcise your

154

hatred. Since this mission was planned anyway, it seemed a fine way to afford you that opportunity."

"How did you know about me?"

"COVE has many contacts, keeps many files. You see, COVE is not above helping one man. One life, many lives; it's all the same, isn't it?" He gestured toward the bodies on the floor. "Unfortunately, our actions may appear contradictory. Indeed, they often are contradictory. But that's the way the game is played. Incidentally, you handled your assignment with considerable initiative and efficiency. You have a job with COVE, if you want it."

"I'll give it some thought."

Sir James nodded in the direction of Hannibal, who was just regaining consciousness. "I see you've caught your prize."

"Yeah."

"Kill him," Sir James said evenly. "There's a helicopter waiting for us outside."

Parve picked up his rifle and swung it on Hannibal. Hannibal's eyes were crossed; they slowly uncrossed and came into focus. Then he jackknifed forward and vomited down his front.

"Meet me outside on the beach," Parve said quietly.

"Ten minutes. No longer. There'll be planes when they discover the radar isn't working."

Sir James disappeared through the hatchway, closing it after him. Parve reached down and yanked Hannibal to his feet, shoving him towards the door. Bracing himself with the gun, Parve walked after him.

"Who are you?" Hannibal said. The words barely made it out through his broken jaw.

"Keep walking, you son-of-a-bitch. To the beach. Sneeze, and I blow you in half."

Hannibal walked, Parve hobbling along behind him. A crescent moon had broken through the cloud cover enough to reflect its image a thousand times in the gentle swells of the sea beyond the beach. Parve waited until they were a few feet from the water's edge, then stopped and fired a burst into the sand by Hannibal's feet.

Hannibal danced, then stopped and stood rigid. Parve walked around in front of him. He stood close so as to be heard above the sound of the helicopter above them. "My name is John Parve," he said, watching the other man. "You blew up my wife and children. Or you ordered it done."

Hannibal's eyes filled with terror and rolled, but there was still no recognition. Parve felt dizzy; apparently, Hannibal didn't even remember the incident. But, Parve thought, perhaps it was fitting: one day a brother of one of the soldiers he had killed in the radar station might come after him, and Parve wouldn't even know why. He hadn't even seen the faces of the men he'd killed. He hadn't even looked.

Parve loosened the belt around his thigh, waited for the blood to ooze, then slowly began to back into the water. Even from that distance Parve could see Hannibal's eyes begin to glow. Parve raised his gun and continued to back away. The water numbed his leg, but the blood was flowing faster now, a warm, red signal to the sleek black killing machines that infested the waters.

Hannibal stiffened, saliva dribbling from the corner of his misshapen mouth. His hands were clenched tightly together, like those of a child barely able to contain his excitement at the prospect of an unexpected gift.

Parve kept backing until the water lapped at his armpits. He held the gun above the water, his finger tight on the trigger; at the first sensation of teeth cutting into him he would blow Hannibal away. Or try to.

Something hard and rough brushed across his mid-section; Parve's finger tensed, then relaxed. There were no teeth. The first shark had been on a scouting mission.

Parve moved forward. In a few moments he was back on the beach. He tightened the belt-tourniquet again, and then pointed the gun at Hannibal's chest. Hannibal's eyes were black, like charred holes in paper.

"Now it's your turn," Parve said. "Go on in. The water's fine."

"Sharks!" Hannibal said. The sound was something between a muffled shriek and a hysterical hiccup.

Parve pointed toward a small island a hundred and fifty yards off shore; it was dark, foreboding, like a mole on the skin of the sea. "You make it out there and you live," Parve said. "My guess is that that's more of a chance than you ever gave any of your victims. It's certainly more than you ever gave my wife and children. If you prefer, I'll cut you down where you stand."

Hannibal had begun to tremble. He dropped to his knees and clasped his hands in front of him in an attitude of prayer. That made Parve nervous. He stepped back and fired off a burst into the sand in front of Hannibal. Hannibal screwed his eyes shut and continued praying. Parve brought the spray of bullets even closer.

Hannibal suddenly leaped to his feet and began running to his right. Parve fired over his head, herding him toward the foam at the edge of the sand. Hannibal ran to the water's edge and plunged into the sea. His arms spun like pinwheels as he struggled toward the island in the distance.

Parve dropped the gun at his feet and watched. Hannibal had made it almost to the halfway point before the sharks hit him. There was no time for him to scream; one moment he was flailing the surface, and the next he was gone, leaving nothing behind nothing but a red froth staining the surface of the sea.

Parve turned and grabbed for the rope ladder dangling from the helicopter above. He locked his fingers around the bottom rung and swung off into the darkness.

TOURIST TRAP

AUGIE MANSON wiped the thick lenses of his glasses, and then returned them to his eyes. The thick blur of colors swimming around his head immediately resolved into the vast expanse of Madrid Airport. By now, the surroundings had become quite familiar to him; Augie, along with the other members of The Horizon Travel Club, had been waiting seven hours for the charter flight that would return them to the United States.

Augie had heard jokes about the Spanish airlines, but this example of inefficiency exceeded even his cynical expectations. There was a rumor someone had called the embassy.

The rest of the group was strung out around the huge waiting room. Olga Helmut, the physical education instructor, was keeping a sharp eye on her gaggle of young, tittering, female colleagues. Four or five of the older, more experienced travelers were talking quietly out on the observation platform. The rest were at the bar.

Augie thumbed through an old issue of a magazine and let his mind wander back over his experiences of the past ten days. He supposed it was appropriate that he should now be waiting alone for the return trip, for he had been alone throughout their stay, separated from the others by an insurmountable wall of sensibilities and taste. This sense of

159

isolation was not, in itself, the cause of Augie's disappointment. He was used to loneliness, and he had never expected that any of the flighty, young single women on the trip would be attracted to a small, slight, hopelessly myopic bank clerk.

No, the trip itself had been a major disappointment. He earned very little money, and it had not been easy to save enough for even a charter flight. He'd been so tired of New York City, tired of the sour air, plastic people, and culture reserved, for the most part, only for those who could afford it. He had looked forward desperately to this trip to La Costa Del Sol, the "Sun Coast" of Spain. It had sounded so beautiful, so fresh and clean.

He had ended by finding himself sequestered, along with the others, in a *Deluxe* hotel in Torremelinos, an almost perfect Spanish imitation of Miami Beach.

He had signed up for all the excursions, and found each one just as dreary as another, principally because he was always in the company of others who seemed to delight in behaving like cardboard characters plucked from the pages of *The Ugly American;* and the Spaniards endeavored to do everything possible to surround the *turistos* with all the "comforts" and "atmosphere" of the United States. This included, in the homeland of Andres Segovia and Manitos Del Plata, piping into every hotel suite the music of Lawrence Welk.

He had gone to a bullfight, and vomited at the sight of people waving white handkerchiefs while the bull coughed up its lungs.

Finally, he had, against his better judgment, hired a four-cylinder *Seat* and started out across the Mountains De Malaga toward Granada, only to break down and wait eleven hours for some kind of help.

The last three days in Torremelinos had been spent in his room fighting the dysentery brought on by drinking unbottled water.

Now, it was back to New York and a job he hated. There was nothing to show for this trip, no experiences, nothing to feed his mind.

An innate, sense of dignity, Augie thought, *is a fragile foundation on which to live a life.* Yet, that was all he had; it was all he had ever had. Dignity. A man becomes tired, and he must float on whatever raft is available to him.

"Flight eighty-three to New York, now boarding!"

Augie rose from his chair and fumbled in his pocket for his boarding pass. He looked up to find a large man in a gabardine coat blocking his way. Augie moved to his left. The man moved with him.

"Excuse me, sir," Augie said, throwing back his shoulders and flaunting his small stature like a weapon. "I have to board my plane."

"Please, mister," the man said, "I've got to talk to you."

For the first time, Augie noticed that the man was grimacing as if in pain, and held his left arm in close to his body. As Augie watched, the man reached across with his right arm and opened his coat. A red stain had grown on his shirt and coat like an obscene flower.

"You're hurt!" Augie said, grabbing the man's arm. "I'll get you to somebody who can help you."

"No," the man said, pulling out of Augie's grip with a strength that was surprising in a wounded man. "There isn't time. They're after me."

"Flight eighty-three to New York, now boarding. Flight eighty-three"

"I don't understand," Augie said, glancing back and forth between the man and the rest of the group now lining up on the boarding platform. "You need a doctor."

"No time," the man repeated, shaking his head. "There are men after me. I need your help."

"Well, I don't really see how I can—"

"C.I.A.," the man said. "I have to talk to you privately. I think the men's room would be best."

Augie suddenly felt a ringing in his ears, numbness, as if someone had attached electrodes to opposite sides of his skull. The man was already shuffling toward the men's room. Augie hurried after him.

The moment the door swung shut behind them, the man once again reached under his coat and withdrew a large, steel, quart Thermos. He shoved it into Augie's hands.

"You must get this back to the United States," the man said. "It contains microfilm that is vital to our nation's security."

"But I, ah—"

"Don't open it, and don't let anybody else open it. Never let it out of your sight. There's no reason anyone should question your carrying a Thermos. Remember, you're carrying many lives in your hands."

Augie swallowed hard. "Whom will I give it to?"

"It will be picked up at Kennedy Airport. Someone will be there waiting for you."

"But how will they know me?"

"By this," the man said thickly, pinning a small, metal American flag into Augie's lapel. "Remember, your country's counting on you."

"But you need a—"

The man had already turned and headed back toward the door, leaving Augie standing alone clutching the Thermos bottle.

Suddenly the door swung open and an equally large man, wearing a black leather topcoat and black beret, blocked the second man's way. The man who had spoken to

162

Augie reacted first, lifting his knee up into the other man's stomach and, as black beret doubled over, driving his fist into the side of the man's head.

Black beret staggered against a long row of sinks, and the other man pushed out the door and was gone.

Black beret's eyes rolled in his head, but he didn't go down. He gripped a sink with one hand and reached out for Augie with the other.

There are men after me. Your country is depending on you.

"Flight eighty-three to New York, now boarded."

The voice with the thick Spanish accent hesitated, and Augie imagined someone handing the announcer a slip of paper. *"Would Mister August Manson please report to the Information Desk? Mister August Man-son."*

Black beret was staggering toward him now, blocking his escape.

Augie made an instant decision. He brought the end of the steel Thermos crashing down on top of black beret's head. The man's knees buckled, and he sank to the floor.

Time seemed suspended as Augie stared down at the still figure on the shiny tiles, then at the Thermos he held in his hand like a club. He shook his head in an attempt to clear it, and then glanced in the direction of the door. He knew that door could swing open at any moment. Then it would be all over. Or black beret might have a partner waiting for him outside. Even now he might be glancing at his watch, wondering.

Augie set the Thermos on the floor, then bent down and grasped black beret under the armpits. He strained; the body did not move. Augie sucked in his breath, planted his feet under him, and pulled with all his might. It seemed to Augie that he could feel the muscles popping in his stomach and back, but black beret was moving. Pulling, resting, and then pulling again, Augie finally managed to

163

move black beret into one of the stalls. He quickly shut the door behind him.

He could not tell whether black beret was alive or dead, but he knew he could take no chances. If the man should gain consciousness before the plane was aloft, there was always the possibility that he, and the microfilm, would be captured. Perhaps the plane had taken off already.

Augie fought against the panic that arose in him when he imagined himself trapped alone in Spain with a Thermos full of microfilm, and nobody he could trust.

Augie ripped off his necktie and stuffed it into black beret's mouth. Next, he removed the belt from black beret's coat and used it to strap the man's hands to the plumbing pipes.

Augie rose to his feet, and his eyes traveled down to where black beret's coat had fallen open; the thick, black butt of a pistol showed above the waistband of black beret's trousers. Augie wiped his sweating palms on the side of his jacket, and then impulsively bent down and grabbed the pistol, stuffing it into the front of his own pants.

He pushed out of the stall at the same time as another man entered the room. Augie stood very still, gnawing at his lower lip. The other man gave Augie a cursory glance, and then went to one of the washbasins. Augie grabbed the Thermos and hurried out through the door.

Clutching his coat over the gun, Augie scurried across the vast expanse of marble floor toward the loading platform—and was halted.

"Just a moment, sir!"

Augie glanced up to find a determined-looking stewardess blocking his way. He resisted the impulse to try to hide the Thermos behind his back.

"My name is Manson," Augie said, holding the Thermos in front of him, knowing he must not do anything to arouse suspicion.

"Oh, Mister *Manson*" the stewardess said, making no attempt to hide the irritation in her voice. "We have people looking all over the airport for you. Your plane is ready to leave."

"I'm sorry," Augie said evenly. "I'm afraid I fell asleep."

"Please hurry."

Augie hurried down the ramp, then paused for a moment at the entrance to the plane. He took a deep breath, and then walked slowly and deliberately into the interior. He almost bumped into a livid Olga Helmut standing in the center of the aisle, her thick hands on her hips.

"Well," Olga Helmut said, her outrage distorting her voice, giving it a high, nasal quality, "look who's decided to join us! Of all the nerve!"

"I had business," Augie said, raising himself up to his full height. "I apologize to all of you."

Augie blinked rapidly, remembering too late that he had told the stewardess he had fallen asleep.

"I suppose it was absolutely necessary for you to hold up the entire plane just so you could buy a Thermos bottle you could have bought in your own country!"

Augie felt as if someone had hit him in the stomach. He looked around at the staring faces, then down at Olga's trembling finger, which was pointing at the Thermos.

"I'm sorry, but I don't know what you're talking about," Augie said quietly. It took all of his energy just to keep his voice from trembling. Already, he was exhausted. "You're not very observant. I've had this Thermos with me throughout the trip. I was alone, and I didn't hear the announcement."

"I thought you said you had business."

"I *did* have business. I—"

"And you can't tell me you've had that Thermos all along. I *see* what's going on around me!"

"Now *look,*" Augie said, astonished to find that the rage in his voice was real, "I'm not one of your giggling teacher friends. You have no right to question me! Get out of my way!"

The physical education teacher's mouth dropped open, and Augie brushed past her and dropped down into an empty seat near the middle of the plane. He sat very straight, looking straight ahead. He heard Olga mumble something, and then the plane was quiet. Augie felt his stomach churn. He looked for the airsickness bag, but the spell passed. Augie smiled and sat up even straighter as he felt a twinge of pride race through him, stiffening his muscles.

It seemed an eternity before the loading ramp was finally pulled back, and the engines started. Finally the plane began to taxi down the runway.

Augie fixed his eyes on the telephone in the stewardess' alcove, half expecting it to ring at any moment; *they had found black beret, and were stopping the plane so as to question and search the passengers. Black beret had friends; it was the Spanish government itself from which the secrets had been stolen. They would catch him and execute him.*

There was a sudden surge of power, a slight bump, and the airplane leapt into the air. Augie laid his head back and quietly passed out.

The unrelieved tension caused Augie to doze frequently throughout the trip. Each time he felt the drowsiness coming on, he would curl up around the gun and Thermos and wait for the nervous, restless sleep to put him out again.

The seconds ticked away in his head. *How much longer? How much longer?* Tick. Tick.

Finally he was aware of people whispering, far away, as at the end of a long tunnel. The whispering grew louder as he strained upward to consciousness. He could feel the pressure building in his ears, and he barely managed to muffle a small cry of delight as he realized that the plane was descending; they were over New York, the end of the journey. His fingers were numb and bloodless where they gripped the Thermos.

The whispering was growing even louder.

Augie turned his head sideways and found himself looking into the faces of two of Olga Helmut's teachers. They were staring at his midsection. Augie glanced down and his stomach leaped as he saw that his own coat had fallen open, exposing the butt of the pistol.

Augie flung his coat across the gun and looked up at the women; they stopped talking, and avoided his eyes.

The seconds were ticking in Augie's head again, their sound mingling with the pounding of the blood in his ears. *Would the women ring for the stewardess? And what would I do if they did? Pull my gun? Force them to land? And then what, Manson . . . ?*

"Please fasten your seat belt, sir."

The stewardess was leaning over him, handing him one of the straps. Augie slowly buckled his belt and held his breath, not daring to look across the aisle.

The women remained silent, and the stewardess walked away. Augie suddenly realized that the two women were *afraid* of him. It was an odd sensation, having someone actually afraid of *him.*

Augie gripped the Thermos even tighter. The plane bumped to a landing and taxied down the runway. Augie unbuckled his seat belt and stood up. The whoosh of the reversing engines almost knocked him off his feet.

"Please remain in your seats until the plane has come to a complete stop. Please remain in your—"

Augie sat back down, but leaned forward in his seat, waiting for the plane to come to a stop. He suddenly realized that, for the first time in his life, he felt truly *alive,* every nerve ending taut, every sense tingling. He imagined he could smell the upholstery and see every pore in the faces of the passengers. Their expressions were so *dull.* What did they know of living in the shadow of danger? What did they know of how this could make a man come alive? It was as if the Thermos he was holding was a battery pack, filling him with energy for living life as he had always wanted to live it.

The plane rolled to a stop. Augie felt supremely confident now. He slowly rose and headed for the forward exit. The two women headed for the rear. Augie smiled and squeezed the Thermos as he headed down the ramp; the New York air had never smelled so good. He turned and headed for the baggage area.

"Would you open your suitcases, please?"

Augie reached over and unlocked his twin pieces of luggage. The customs inspector riffled through his clothing, then closed the cases and marked the sides with chalk.

"What's in there?"

"Where?"

"The Thermos bottle. What do you have in it?"

"Uh, tea."

"Open it, please."

"Really, sir!" Augie said, dancing at the edge of desperation. "I don't see how—"

"Give it to me!"

Augie handed the Thermos to the customs agent. At the same time, he began going over his story in his mind.

The customs agent unscrewed the red plastic top and passed the mouth of the Thermos under his nose. Augie tensed.

"This is coffee," the agent said, glancing up at Augie.

Augie looked down at his feet, concentrating on keeping every muscle in his face frozen. "Of course," he mumbled. "Coffee, yes. I'm afraid I'm a little absent-minded."

The customs inspector stared at him for a few moments then screwed the top back on the Thermos and handed it to him.

"May I go now?"

The customs inspector nodded. Augie turned and walked off.

"Sir, your suitcases!"

Augie summoned up as much dignity as was possible, and then turned around and went back for his suitcases. He tucked the Thermos securely under his arm and picked up the suitcases. Walking very slowly, virtually defying the customs inspector to call him back a second time, Augie finally made his way to the main visitors' lobby. He paused and looked straight ahead. At the same time he pushed his chest forward so that the tiny medallion in his lapel would be visible to whoever it was that was supposed to meet him. He vaguely wondered if he would receive some kind of recognition for the job he had done; perhaps even a letter from the President. He hoped so. It was worth all of that.

He was conscious of movement to his left and turned to find a red-capped porter staring at him. The man's eyes were dark and murky.

"Take your luggage, sir?"

"No," Augie said tersely, clamping his arm down on the Thermos. He could feel the hairs rising on the back of his neck; there was something about this man that was just not right.

The porter glanced quickly over his shoulder, and then made a grab for the Thermos, but Augie was ready for him. He dropped the suitcases and spun around, ripping the Thermos from the man's uncertain grasp.

"Hold it right there!"

The voice came from behind him. So there was more than one, and they certainly didn't represent the people who were supposed to meet him. They had merely to come up and identify themselves.

Augie closed his eyes, lowered his shoulder and rammed it into the wild-eyed porter. The man went down. Augie made a futile grab for his glasses, then stepped over the man and raced toward an empty corridor leading back toward the planes. Colors swam in a blur around him.

"Hold it!"

It was too far, Augie realized. He would never make it to the door at the end. Already, he could hear the footsteps of two men closing in on him. He groped in his waistband for the pistol grip, found it, and took the gun into his hand. It felt cold and heavy in his palm.

Augie braced his feet and slid to a stop. At the same time, he whirled and pointed the gun at the two figures now almost upon him. He had hardly touched the trigger, and yet he felt the gun explode in his hand, jerking his shoulder and wrist painfully, spinning him around.

There was a sharp crack behind him, then a sharp, needle-pain in his right knee. Pieces of Augie's kneecap were suddenly strewn out on the floor around

170

him. He fell, squeezing the trigger again and again. There was the sound of breaking glass, then two more explosions, very close to him.

Augie was only vaguely conscious of the white-hot pieces of metal tearing into and through his chest. His fingers clutched at the empty air, searching for the Thermos. A sob formed deep in his throat, then he was still.

"He dead?"

"Stone dead," the second man said, staring down at the bloody carnage that had once been Augie Manson's chest. "You wouldn't think a guy like that could drop Blanchard. He looks like a bank clerk."

"You've been watching too many movies. Where's Peters ?"

"Back on the phone talking to Blanchard. Where'd Blanchard say the stuff was hidden?"

"In the Thermos."

The second man reached down and picked up the Thermos from beside Augie's body. He unscrewed the top and poured two or three ounces of coffee out on the floor. Then he stuck a pencil down through the false bottom; the tip of the pencil came up white and the second man touched the powder to his tongue.

"Heroin, all right. About a half million's worth."

A fat man with red veins running through his nose and cheeks pushed his way through the police lines at the opposite end of the corridor and shuffled hurriedly toward them. He stopped a few paces away from the men and stared down at Augie's lifeless body.

"Why the hell did you have to kill him?"

"He had a thirty-eight Police Special that he somehow managed to sneak past the metal detector in Spain. There were a lot of people behind us."

"He was a lousy tourist," Peters said, half-swallowing the words. "A lousy tourist."

"A *tourist?*"

"Right," Peters said, not looking up. "Blanchard says they finally found the other one, the guy that gave the Thermos to this guy. Turns out the Syndicate has a new gimmick; they smear some guy up with fake blood, then pick out some nobody on a charter flight. Tell him the Thermos contains microfilm, tell him it has to be brought back here. Give him an American flag medallion and get him all hopped up. Secret agent stuff, you know. Really appeals to them. Then when they get here, the Syndicate snatches it away from them. Simple. Really cuts down on the risks of smuggling the stuff in."

"This one was tougher than they figured."

Peters nodded slowly, unconsciously touching Augie's body with the toe of his shoe. "It's just a damn shame."

FIREFIGHT OF THE MIND

THEY'RE all yours, Eddy," Brokaw said, stepping out into the hallway and closing the classroom door behind him. "Did you get your business with the draft board taken care of?"

"Yes, sir," Eddy said to the principal of the Marsten Elementary School. "I'm sorry to have to be late on the first day of school, but—"

"Listen," Brokaw said, touching Eddy's arm solicitously, "you just let me know if the draft board gives you any more trouble; I'll call them personally." Brokaw winked broadly. "We need all the men we can get in the elementary schools. This war keeps up much longer, and we'll have them."

Eddy jammed his hands into his pockets and looked away to hide his anger. He knew he could not really blame Brokaw for assuming he had entered the teaching profession because it was a deferred occupation, the easiest way to beat the draft—it was a widespread practice—but he wished Brokaw and the others would keep their opinions to themselves and stop acting like smug, self-satisfied collaborators.

"Well, your class looks like a bright bunch," Brokaw said hurriedly, sensing Eddy's embarrassment. "Believe it or not, there's even an apple on your desk."

"Thanks for covering them for me," Eddy said evenly. "I don't think my board will have any more questions now that I've actually started on a job."

173

"Well, good luck," Brokaw said. "Don't hesitate to call me if you have any problems."

"Thank you. I won't have any trouble."

Brokaw smiled nervously and hurried off down the hall.

Eddy waited until Brokaw had turned a corner, then he turned to go into his classroom. He hesitated with his hand on the knob. A month before it would have been inconceivable to him that he would be made nervous by the prospect of facing a roomful of fifth graders; now he recalled his own elementary years and he imagined himself being greeted by a large spitball in the middle of the forehead, or a fleet of attacking paper airplanes.

Eddy laughed aloud, and stepped into the room.

"Good morning, Mister Reese!"

It's going to be all right, Eddy thought. He could feel his anxiety melting in the vibrant glow of the children's eagerness and warmth. He walked up to a blond-headed boy with braces on his teeth and rumpled the child's hair.

"I see you know *my* name," Eddy said, laughter tugging at the corners of his mouth. "It shouldn't take me more than six or seven months to learn all of yours."

The children giggled. Eddy strolled to his desk and picked up the large, gleaming apple someone had placed there. He juggled it in his hand. The long, thin streaks of brown discoloration on the skin of the fruit registered somewhere just below the surface of his consciousness.

"I want to thank whoever brought me this apple," Eddy intoned with mock seriousness. "We're all going to get along fine as long as you keep me well fed."

There were more excited giggles as Eddy lifted the apple to his mouth. The muscles in his jaw tensed, but not before his teeth had broken through into the crisp meat of

174

the fruit. Now the memory of the brown slashes in the fruit surfaced, tripping a warning signal in his mind.

The warning came too late.

The sound of metal scraping against bone echoed inside his skull as the acid tartness of the apple was blurred by the warm, salty taste of his own blood in his mouth. The ribbon of steel screeched down between his teeth and sliced into his gum and upper lip. The front of his tie and white shirt were suddenly spotted with red.

Eddy jerked the apple from his mouth and stared at it; his blood, diluted with the juice of the apple, was beading on the exposed edge of the razor blade. He threw the apple to the floor and wadded his handkerchief into his mouth to stanch the bleeding. He glanced up at the faces of the startled children.

Which one? Which child was so sick that he or she would try to destroy a man's mouth? And *why?*

The faces of the children were white. Two girls in the back of the room had begun to cry, and others soon joined them. The aura of excitement and anticipation that had greeted Eddy when he first entered the room had now hardened into the sour smell of fear.

Which one?

Eddy walked over to the intercom. It seemed an eternity before Brokaw's secretary finally came on the line.

"I'd like to speak to Mister Brokaw."

"Mister Brokaw is in conference now."

"Get him!"

There was a moment of shocked silence, then the sound of another phone buzzing. Eddy continued to stare at the faces of the children. The children stared back. At last there was the sound of Brokaw's voice crackling over the line.

175

"This is Mister Reese," Eddy said around the edge of his handkerchief. "I need you right away."

"Eddy, what's the matter with your voice?"

"Right away," Eddy repeated, and then replaced the intercom on the wall. He glanced up to find the children turned around in their desks, staring at something in the back of the room. Eddy followed the direction of their gaze, and froze.

A tall man with lean, hard features was standing at the back of the room in front of an open closet door. Both his hands were buried in the pockets of a worn, checked jacket. Intense, pale green eyes searched for and locked onto Eddy's.

"I see my booby trap was not entirely successful," the man said. His voice was soft, but his words carried clearly, like the distant sounds of rifle shots on a cold day.

Eddy continued to stand very still, holding the man's gaze. He was too far away to rush. Too many children. The man had made no move toward any of the children, but Eddy knew that was no guarantee that the man wouldn't if there were any sudden move on his part. There were four girls sitting directly in front of the man; a single swipe with a razor could kill or at least disfigure all of them.

Eddy struggled against his own panic. He knew there was a small fire-alarm box just outside his room in the hallway. One blow on the glass would set off a cacophony of bells, which would in turn summon scores of police and firemen to the school; but the alarm was out in the hall, and he had closed the door to the classroom.

"Who are you?" Eddy asked quietly. "What do you want?"

The man walked slowly and deliberately toward Eddy. Eddy pressed his lips tightly around the cloth in his mouth and tensed, ready to leap. The man stopped directly

176

in the center of the room; he was now completely surrounded by children.

"You're very fortunate," the man said, still looking directly into Eddy's eyes. "I can see the bleeding's almost stopped. By rights, that apple should have been a land mine; I'd like to see you try to stuff your handkerchief into a hole where your leg used to be."

The man was not drunk. He spoke very clearly, every word distinct, but the blood was draining from his face, and his voice was steadily rising in pitch. Eddy thought he could hear Brokaw's steps in the hallway.

"On the way to school this morning," the man continued, "you should have fallen into a pit lined with bamboo stakes. They say it takes four strong men to pull a man off one of those things."

"I don't even know you."

"My name is Plakker," the man said. "Ernest Plakker."

"I still don't know you. What reason do you have to want to hurt me or the children?"

Something clicked far down in the green depths of Plakker's eyes. "Your father didn't know my son either. Not really."

Eddy blinked at the mention of his father. He tried hard to find some association. None came.

"My father's a major general in the Army," Eddy said tightly. "He's in Vietnam."

"I know where your father is." The man's voice was like silk pulled over the edge of a knife.

The door clicked open and Brokaw burst into the room, then stopped when he saw the blood on Eddy's face and clothes. His startled gaze swept down to the apple with its deadly seed, then up to the man standing a few paces away.

"What the—!"

177

"This man's name is Plakker," Eddy said hurriedly, half turning in Brokaw's direction, but keeping his eyes firmly locked on Plakker. He spoke softly, with a perfectly even cadence. "It seems like he's after me. I'm sure he wouldn't want to harm the children, but I think it would be a good idea if you pressed the fire alarm out in the hall."

Brokaw did not hesitate; he wheeled and darted out into the hall, swinging his fist through the air and smashing it into the tiny glass box. Immediately, the air was alive with the sound of clanging bells.

Plakker stood impassively, as if the sounds—and the results they would bring—held no meaning for him.

Brokaw raced back into the room and went directly for Plakker. Plakker calmly lifted his hands out of his pockets. Brokaw jumped backward, smashing into a desk and falling to the floor. He pulled himself to his feet and slowly backed away.

Plakker was standing with both his arms extended in front of him, a hand grenade clenched tightly in each fist.

"I don't know whether either of you is familiar with this type of grenade," Plakker said. "As you can see, the pins have already been pulled. They will explode six seconds after I release the levers on the side."

Someone had shut off the alarm bells. A horn was blowing a few blocks away, and there was the distant, ghostly wail of fire engines.

"Get out," Brokaw whispered fiercely to Eddy. "I'll handle this."

"No," Plakker said, raising both his arms. "I'm here because of Reese. He's not going anywhere. Not until I want him to."

"Let the children leave, man!"

Plakker shook his head. "In war, there is

178

always the danger that innocent bystanders will be hurt. This is no different."

"This isn't a war!"

"Yes it is," Plakker said. "It is because I say it is."

"You're crazy," Brokaw said through clenched teeth. Muscles in his jaw rippled and danced. "In a few minutes this whole building will be surrounded by police and firemen. You can't possibly get away with whatever it is you're trying to do."

Plakker smiled thinly and motioned Brokaw toward the door. "You get out there," Plakker said, holding one grenade over the head of a boy who whimpered and crouched down behind his desk. "It will be your responsibility to make sure no one comes into this room. If anyone does try to come in, I explode the grenades."

"And kill yourself?"

Plakker's answer was in his eyes. Brokaw continued backing away until finally he was out the door. At the same time there came the sounds of booted feet running in the corridor. Brokaw shouted, and the running stopped. Then there was nothing but silence.

I am alone, Eddy thought. *Completely responsible for the lives of twenty-six children. Alone with a madman where all our lives could depend on what I say, or how I say it. Or maybe, after all, it really makes no difference; Plakker will release the grenades anyway.* Eddy shivered. *I am adrift on an ice floe, freezing under a blue, frigid sun.*

Plakker settled himself down on top of one of the desks. The child at the desk got up and ran to the back of the room. Plakker seemed to take no notice. He seemed to be studying Eddy.

Eddy could feel his legs begin to tremble. Occasionally, a dark spot would well up and swim before his eyes.

179

"You know," Plakker said in a tone that was more conversational than threatening, "your father thinks you're a coward. He's said so."

Plakker seemed to be waiting for Eddy to say something. Afraid that he would say the wrong thing, Eddy remained silent.

"Your father was my son's commanding officer," Plakker continued. "Your father used to tell his men how ashamed he was of you. Did you know that? He told them you were one of the people trying to tear this country down. Does it surprise you that your father would say these things about you ? "

"No," Eddy said flatly, "it doesn't surprise me."

"Frank used to write me about the things your father told his men. Your father thinks you're a rotten coward, Reese. So do I."

Eddy breathed deeply in an attempt to clear his head. The dark spot in front of his eyes was growing larger, furrier. His voice sounded thick and muffled as he forced his words through lips he dared not move.

Plakker's arms remained extended out in front of his body, and it seemed to Eddy that the arms must be suspended from invisible wires; they never wavered or trembled despite the steel bundles of death they supported.

"Frank is your son, isn't he?" Eddy murmured. "That's what this is all about, isn't it?"

Eddy glimpsed a movement out of the corner of his eye and he glanced out of the window in time to see two policemen duck behind trees about fifty yards away, at the very edge of the school yard. Both men carried rifles with telescopic sights.

Eddy felt his mouth go dry. He could imagine policemen moving toward them on the outside, hugging the side of the building. *Hadn't Brokaw explained?* Even

180

if they could be sure of killing Plakker without harming any of the children, the grenades would almost certainly go off when Plakker fell.

Don't let them shoot, Eddy thought. *Don't let them be stupid enough to shoot.*

"They'd been out in the field for three weeks," Plakker said. His voice was unsteady now, and he continually glanced around the room as though he were speaking to the children as well as to Eddy. "All that time they'd been sleeping in the water and the mud. They'd take off their clothes and find chunks of their skin inside. And all the time the VC were taking pot-shots at them, picking them off one at a time."

Plakker heaved a great sigh. He was standing at the window now, his hands at his sides. Eddy studied the man, feverishly trying to explore any possibilities open to him. He could still try to rush Plakker, but that would mean he must somehow find a way to grab the grenades *before* Plakker released the levers. Eddy suspected that once the levers were released, there was no way of stopping the explosion. *Six seconds.*

There was no way. Eddy stood still.

"The word came down that a battalion of North Vietnamese Regulars would be sweeping down through their area," Plakker continued. "The men were told to stand and fight." Plakker looked up at Eddy, and for the first time Eddy felt pity for the older man. "Those men were in no condition to fight. They were hungry. They were exhausted."

"Your son was killed," Eddy said softly.

Plakker shook his head. He closed his eyes and grimaced as though he were trying to erase the memory his words conjured up.

181

"Frank ran. He turned tail and ran. When they found him, Frank was sprawled in a ditch, crying his eyes out."

"That's nothing to be ashamed of," Eddy said carefully, watching Plakker's face. "Your son's not the first person to suffer from battle fatigue."

Sunlight glinted off metal somewhere out in the yard. Eddy braced himself, half expecting to hear a shot.

"Your father decided to bring Frank up on charges of cowardice in the face of the enemy," Plakker continued "He said it was necessary to preserve the morale of his men."

"My father was wrong," Eddy said with genuine anger. "My father's wrong about a lot of things."

"But *you* have no right to say that!" Plakker snapped. He clicked the two grenades together and the sound crashed around inside Eddy's skull. "My son *hanged* himself three days before his court martial was scheduled to begin! Frank *killed* himself rather than live branded as a coward! You! You *revel* in your cowardice!"

"You've already said that I'm a coward," Eddy said, afraid now to stop speaking, afraid that Plakker was working himself up to a pitch where he would release the grenades. "My father has said it, and I admit it. You've made your point."

"It's not enough!" Plakker's voice was approaching a shrill scream. His hands had begun to tremble. "You don't suffer, and your father won't suffer until *everyone* knows that you're a coward! I want that fact plastered across the pages of the newspapers! I want to hear it on radio and television! I want people to whisper behind your father's back! I want *him* to suffer like *I've* suffered!"

Outside the window, three firemen were constructing a bunker from a pile of sandbags. Occasionally they glanced nervously in the direction of the classroom. Two policemen with drawn revolvers stood guard.

So that was the plan, Eddy decided. He was supposed to ask Plakker to go outside and drop the grenades in the bunker. Eddy shivered.

"It won't do any good to harm the children," Eddy said. "I'll admit anything you want. By now, there are plenty of reporters here. They'd have monitored the police calls. I'll hold a press conference. I'll say anything you want me to say."

Plakker's eyes glittered. The flesh around his eyes and mouth had taken on a greenish cast.

"That will do for a start," he said. "You can start right now. You can walk out that door and start talking to the people out there."

"Where will you be?"

"Right here. That way we'll both be certain that you put on a good performance. You'll have to keep your promise. I want you to make it real good."

"No. You come out with me. I'll keep my promise."

Plakker raised his arms. Eddy sucked in his breath and shook his head feverishly. The scab on his lip cracked open, splashing blood on his wrist. He knew he should have known better than to try to bargain with a madman.

"All right," Eddy said. "For God's sake, all right." He paused to catch his breath and press his jacket sleeve against his lip. "If I go out there and say the right things, you'll follow me out and drop the grenades behind those sandbags?"

"Of course. All I want is your public announcement. I want your father to read about it."

"How do I know *you'll* keep your promise?"

"You don't know, but you're in no position to bargain. I think you know I'm not afraid to die. I'll drop these grenades if you *don't* go out. You have no choice, you see."

Eddy hesitated. He could feel the sweat pouring from his body, pasting his clothes to his skin. How could he leave a classroom full of children alone with a maniac? Yet, if he didn't, they would be killed anyway.

"I'll do everything you say," Eddy said evenly. "I'm going. You just keep a tight hold on those grenades."

"I'm waiting!"

Eddy dropped his eyes and found himself looking directly into the face of the blond-headed boy with the braces. The boy stared back at him, his child eyes wide and trusting.

Strange, Eddy thought as he turned and headed toward the door, *I hadn't even had a chance to ask the boy his name.*

"*Run,* Reese! I want to see you *running* out of here! *Run!*"

Eddy froze; something tore at the fabric of his senses, paralyzing his muscles. His reflection on the glass panel of the door stared back at him. Something was wrong, and he could feel twenty-seven pairs of eyes boring into his back as he struggled to discover what it was.

Run, Reese, run! Run, Reese! Run!

Plakker was obviously mad, but he was not stupid. He had said that he did not care about dying, and Eddy believed him; the only thing keeping Plakker alive was the hope of vengeance for the death of his son and his own humiliation. Why, then, should Plakker accept a lifetime in prison—or a mental hospital, where he would have nothing to do but dwell on the very thoughts that had driven him mad—for a statement that Plakker could not even be sure he, Eddy, would not qualify and explain away the moment the children were out of danger?

Run, Reese! Run, Reese! Run, Reese!

184

Then it came to him, and the enormity of the realization rose up and choked him. Eddy then slowly turned to face Plakker.

Plakker looked stunned, unable to comprehend the change in the other man. Eddy walked across the room and stopped a few paces away from Plakker.

"What's the matter with you, Reese?" Plakker's face was livid as he danced up and down on the balls of his feet, clicking the grenades together. "Get out of here! Run! I'm going to drop these grenades and blow this whole room to hell!"

"No, you're not," Eddy said, wrenching each word from deep inside himself, digging his nails into the palms of his hands.

"Please leave, Mister Reese." It was the blond-headed boy. His voice shook uncontrollably and his face was wet with tears *"Please,* Mister Reese! The man will hurt us if you don't leave!"

"You won't drop those grenades as long as I'm in the room," Eddy said, wrenching his eyes away from the boy's. "You see, I know that the only way you can be sure of getting the kind of publicity you want is by blowing up the room *after* I leave. You want me to *live* while you and the children are killed. That's the only way it would work." Eddy paused. Plakker's mouth was working rapidly, but no sound emerged. "I'm staying. The only thing you'll get by killing me is a martyr."

"Get out!" Plakker screamed, pushing Eddy with one hand-grenade fist. "I'm going to drop them!"

"Give them to me," Eddy said, holding out his hands. "It's all over now. We want to *help* you. Please give me the grenades."

Plakker's eyes opened wide and he made sounds deep in his throat as though he were gasping for air. The saucer-wide eyes and the bunching of the muscles in Plak-

185

ker's neck and arms were warnings that cascaded over Eddy just long enough to show him that he had been wrong. Time stopped. Children sobbed. Please leave, Mister Reese. Please, please . . .

Plakker's hands came together, then flew apart. The grenades flew through the air in opposite directions. There were two sharp, obscene clicks as the levers were released.

ONE:

Click, click. The first grenade hit the blackboard at the front of the room, then fell onto a bookcase and off onto the floor. The second landed in the rear of the room, caroming off the wall and coming to rest against the leg of a chair.

TWO:

Eddy leaped to the front of the room, skidding across the floor on his belly. He reached out and grasped one of the grenades in his hand.

THREE:

Eddy rolled over on his side and came up on his feet. He brought back his arm to fire the grenade through the window and found himself staring into the confused, terrified faces of a group of police and firemen. Eddy knew that could serve no purpose anyway; there was still the second grenade.

FOUR:

Eddy's fall had smeared blood from his lips into his eyes, and Eddy saw everything through a hazy red curtain. He tucked the grenade firmly into his side and raced toward the rear of the room, knocking Plakker and the children in his path to one side.

FIVE:

Eddy was afraid for a moment that he would not be able to find it. Then it was there in front of him, ugly and bloated, resting on the shining tile. He had always said that one day the war would come home. Eddy tucked the first grenade into his belly and fell on the second.

SIX:

"Don't be a fool, Reese! Get up and run! Save your life! Run, damn it, run!"

SIX:

It was the waiting. The waiting. He wondered if he would scream when the jagged slivers of metal tore through his body, and he wondered how long he would feel the pain. He could hear himself making grunting sounds, and he supposed he was choking on his own blood.

SIX:

Somewhere, a thousand miles away, glass was breaking and men were running.

SIX:

Flapping on the ground, like a shattered bird.

SIX

SIX

SIX

SIX.

"Eddy, can you hear me? Get up, Eddy! It's all right now!"

Someone was daubing at his face with a wet cloth that reeked of antiseptic. Eddy writhed on the floor and pressed his fists into his belly.

The grenades were gone.

He slowly rolled over on his back and found himself looking up into Brokaw's sweating face. Brokaw was holding the grenades.

"Deactivated," Brokaw said, juggling the pieces of metal in his hands. "Plugged up with cement. He must have picked them up in a war-surplus store."

187

Eddy blinked and looked around him. A policeman came into the room and walked over to Eddy.

"That was really something you did there, pal," the policeman said, apparently embarrassed by his own emotion. "You had no way of knowing they were no good."

Eddy nodded dumbly. The policeman walked away.

"Plakker?" Eddy asked Brokaw.

"They took him away ten minutes ago," Brokaw said. "We got the grenades away from you, but we couldn't get you to open your eyes."

"The children?"

"Out playing on the fire trucks. 1 heard one of the girls say she thought you were 'real cool'. How does it feel to be called 'real cool' by a fifth grader, Eddy?"

Eddy sat up, and his head spun. Brokaw pushed him back.

"They're sending an ambulance for you," Brokaw said. "Do you think you'll be ready to come back in two weeks? I don't think your students will let me keep you out much longer than that."

"I don't have that much sick time," Eddy said stupidly.

"It's on the school board. When you come back, you'll have to tell me what this was all about."

Eddy nodded, and almost passed out from the exertion, but he had seen the look of awe and respect on Brokaw's face.

"Eddy," Brokaw said, "welcome to the teaching profession."

THE TOWER

Pam's scars burned. Although the wounds had been inflicted more than two decades before, the stripes of puckered flesh on her back and belly still stung when she was stressed, which was certainly the case now as she looked down from the window of her fourth-floor office on the scene below her. On the grass quadrangle in front of the Pinnacle of Prayer, where Horace Cassady had been in seclusion for almost exactly a week, the plastic wreaths and black bunting marking off the site for the proposed monument to Joseph, the savagely murdered son of the former mining engineer and televangelist up in the tower, had been trampled by a throng of reporters and camera crews. The media had been milling about for almost two hours, hoping for an interview with, or at least a glimpse of, the mysterious businessman who had pledged one million dollars to help keep Horace Cassady's Creation Park going up, and his college for fundamentalist, Charismatic Christian youth from going under.

   Now it seemed their patience was to be rewarded, for a long, gray limousine suddenly appeared around a bend in the driveway, pulled over to the curb at the walk leading to the tower's entrance. The door on the passenger's side opened, and a tall, rangy man got out. Although it had not rained for weeks, and was quite warm, the man wore a raincoat with a large, floppy collar he had drawn up around his face to hide his features. He pushed his way through the crowd of reporters, hurried toward the door to the Pinnacle of Prayer, which was being held open for him by two fresh-

189

faced students. When he was a few steps away from the entrance the man stopped and, as if sensing Pam's gaze on him, turned and looked up at her.

Pam gasped when she looked down into the familiar face with its firm jaw, high cheekbones, piercing dark eyes, and thick black hair. The man, the collar of his raincoat still hiding his face from the people on the ground, grinned at her and winked, then abruptly stepped into the marble tower.

"Damn him," Pam murmured, clenching her fists in frustration and rage as she quickly turned away from the window. "He has no right. *Damn* him."

She strode stiffly back to her desk and began returning the complex questionnaires she had been working on back into her briefcase. It wasn't working anyway, she thought, and winced as pain flashed along the network of scars on her body. The conditions that had enabled her to carry on her research were threatened by the emotional chaos pervading the campus. The ritualistic murder of Joseph Cassady in the desert north of Creation Park, combined with the dramatic ascent of the college's aged founder to his Pinnacle of Prayer to await dollars or death, had plunged virtually the entire student body into a state of religious hysteria, altering the Charismatic Christians' body chemistry as well as their perceptions, hopelessly skewing Pam's data. She had not yet gathered sufficient data to satisfy her research design, and if she did not complete her project on time, it was unlikely that she would receive any more of the meager grants that had kept her going this long. She would be rejected for tenure in the fall, her academic visa would be revoked, and she would have to return to South Africa.

She would rather die than be forced back to a homeland, where there were no uses at all for a cultural anthropologist, and life itself was a wound.

190

She started and wheeled about at the sound of a single, sharp knock on her office door. Before she could say anything, the door swung open. The Reverend Richard Cassady and his wife, Rita, strode into the room. They stopped just inside the entrance and stared at her with the mixture of hostility and suspicion to which Pam had grown all too familiar during her one-month stay on the campus of Cassady College. Now she thought she detected something else in their eyes, and in the set of their pinched features: triumph. It made Pam decidedly uneasy.

"Hello," Pam said, and smiled tentatively. The Cassadys had always seemed to Pam more like twins than husband and wife. They dressed alike, always in stark combinations of somber colors and white; they had the same thin, almost gaunt, bodies, the same tension in their faces, and the same kinds of pale eyes she had never seen reflect either warmth or humor.

Unlike his father, Pam thought, Richard Cassady displayed almost a total lack of charisma, which probably explained why the son had failed so miserably at carrying on the televangelism and fund raising for the college when Horace Cassady had retired to devote all his time and energies to the construction of Creation Park, a planned educational and entertainment complex, that now lay sprawled, incomplete, across 15 acres of desert to the north, reminding Pam of nothing so much as fossil bones of the great dinosaurs these people denied could be more than a few thousand years old.

"You needn't bother packing up your briefcase, Dr. Marishee," Rita Cassady said coldly, arching her neck slightly. "You've already harmed our students enough, abusing them with your blasphemous questions, and even asking them for blood and urine samples. Your work is disgusting and obscene, and it stops now. You came here under false pretenses; you fooled my father-in-law, but you can't fool us.

191

You'll be leaving now, and you may not take any of the fruits of your exploitation with you."

"False pretenses?" Pam asked quietly.

It was the man, in Pam's estimation the weaker of the two, who answered. "Dr. Felikan was supposed to be welcomed at your university. That was the agreement you made with my father. Dr. Felikan was rejected from your campus, so now we have to ask you to leave ours."

Pam slowly shook her head, willing herself to continue speaking in a soft, deliberate tone, fearful that her normal speaking voice could quickly soar out of control into shouting. "I did not come here under false pretenses. I asked your father if I could come here to continue my studies, and he granted his permission. The exchange was his idea, not mine; he appealed to the chancellor of my university, and the chancellor agreed to accept Dr. Felikan on campus for the semester. I was here as a kind of academic experiment. He thought it might be interesting to have a 'Creationist scientist' on campus for a semester. I thought from the beginning that it was a bad idea, and I said so."

"He was thrown off the campus!" the woman snapped.

"No, Mrs. Cassady. I've been in touch with my colleagues, and I know what happened. Dr. Felikan agreed to accept a post as a visiting lecturer in the philosophy department. His courses in Creation Science were listed in the catalog, but nobody signed up. You can't force students to take courses they don't want to take, and which aren't required."

"Their minds were poisoned!"

"No, ma'am. My university accepts only top students, and those students' days are filled preparing for careers in medicine, engineering, and the sciences. Some might have taken his courses if they thought they had time for fun and games, but they didn't. I predicted that would happen."

"That's blasphemous!"

"It's the truth. You can't just declare something to be scientific because you want it to be, Mrs. Cassady. Creation Science isn't about science at all; it's about faith."

"You're prejudiced," Richard Cassady said.

"No, Reverend. The simple fact of the matter is that Dr. Felikan couldn't attract students to his courses because they don't share his faith in Creation Science."

The man raised a trembling index finger, pointed it at her. "You're a humanist!"

"I'm an anthropologist. My religious faith—or lack of it—has nothing whatsoever to do with my purposes here, which involve studying fundamentalist Christians as a group."

The woman raised her eyebrows slightly. "That's what you told my father-in-law, Dr. Marishee, and he believed you. But you lied when you said you were neutral in your feelings toward religion in general, and our faith in particular."

Pam felt the anger rising in her, threatening her control. She balled her hands into fists and pressed them in hard against her stomach, resisted glancing over her shoulder at the papers that were so important to her. "I'm a respected authority in my field, Mrs. Cassady, and that field is comparative religion. I've traveled all over the world, studied more fundamentalist groups than you can name—the Dakwah Islamic movement, Sikhs, Hasidic Jews, movement Catholics. I've asked the same kinds of questions of all these people, taken blood and urine samples when it was permitted. I haven't always been successful in gaining access to the groups I've wanted to study, but my good faith has never been questioned."

"Perhaps those people weren't aware of some of the things you've written," the woman said, her mild tone belied by the hard glint in her eyes. She withdrew a sheet of paper from her purse, unfolded it and held it out for Pam to see. "Do you deny that you wrote this, Dr. Marishee?"

From where she was standing, Pam could not read the text of the photocopied newspaper article, but she could make

193

out the distinctive masthead *of The Guardian.* It was enough. She knew she was lost, knew she would be leaving Cassady College that afternoon with her field work incomplete. She lowered her gaze, backed away a step. "No," she said quietly, "I don't deny it. But that was written a long time ago."

"Do you deny that you wrote that all religion is super- stition that may have served a useful purpose in ordering primitive societies, but that is now an evil and murderous and outmoded thing responsible for more death, cruelty, and wasted lives than any other facet of human existence? Did you not describe God as a 'kind of Santa Claus for grown-ups'?"

Only when she was certain that she could speak without a sob in her voice did Pam look up. "Yes," she said in the same soft, even tone. "But I wrote those things 15 years ago, and I believe I manage to be more objective now. The anger you detect in that article could have to do with the fact that the white tribe that once ruled my country used its own brand of religion to justify its every outrage and cruelty, including the brutal whipping of a little black girl who became separated from her servant mother and got lost in a Whites Only area. If you deny me the fruits of my research, I may have to return to a place that only holds bad memories for me."

"Then you'd best pray for God's help, dear."

Pam felt her rage rising within her until she could taste it like bile at the back of her throat. "I know who gave you that article, Mrs. Cassady!" she snapped.

"Who?" Richard Cassady said in a puzzled tone as he turned to look at his wife, who had stiffened slightly.

"The same man who's talking to your father up in his tower right now, Reverend," Pam said quickly. "The same man who brought your father the money. I don't know what he's told all of you, but he's not who he says is."

Rita Cassady flushed with anger, while her husband simply stared at Pam, the same puzzled expression on his face. "You know Mr. Denkler?" the man asked.

Pam smiled thinly. "Mr. Denkler?"

"William Denkler."

"And what is it that Mr. Denkler claims he does for a living, Reverend?"

Rita Cassady said quickly, "That's none of you business."

Richard Cassady said, "He owns a factory that makes ladies' undergarments."

"I love it," Pam said with a short, bitter laugh. "Your mysterious Mr. Denkler's real name is Perry Parker, and he works for the Department of Defense in their research and development division. He gave that letter to Mrs. Cassady to discredit me. I don't know why, but I can assure you that it bodes no good for your father, or for Cassady College."

"That's ridiculous," the woman said curtly. "This article was sent to me anonymously by someone who obviously wanted us to know that you're against religion, and against us."

Richard Cassady glanced at his wife, then back at Pam. He shook his head slightly. "What would someone from the Defense Department want with my father, Dr. Marishee? For that matter, what did he want with you? How do you know him?"

"You'll have to ask him what he wants with your father, Reverend. As for me, he's been trying for the past three years to get me to accept DOD funding for my research into common patterns of thought in fundamentalist religious groups; they seem to think my work could be important to what they call 'defense planning strategy.' That could mean anything. I'm more than a little suspicious of government-sponsored research and development. I

195

refused, because acceptance of their money would mean they could control my research and its publication. Perry Parker and I are old . . . acquaintances. I don't know what he's up to now, but he's no philanthropist, and the interests of the Department of Defense aren't necessarily yours. I just wanted to study you; he wants to use you for some purpose."

"Enough of this nonsense!" Rita Cassady snapped as she abruptly walked forward into the room, brushing past Pam. She went to the desk, snatched the questionnaires from Pam's briefcase, collected the others from the desktop, then strode stiffly back to where her husband was standing. "We'd like you to leave the campus today, Dr. Marishee," she continued as she took her husband's arm and turned him forcefully toward the door. "Goodbye."

Richard and Rita Cassady really had no right to abort her program or order her off campus, Pam thought as she listened to the couple's footsteps receding in the hallway outside her office. It was Horace Cassady who had invited her. Still, under the circumstances, she knew it was useless to argue or fight against the combined wills of Richard and Rita Cassady, and the deviousness of Perry Parker. There was nothing to do but go home—which might not be home for much longer.

She felt better by the time she'd showered, dressed in casual clothes, packed, and taken a taxi to the airport. In fact, she had not realized how oppressive she had found the atmosphere surrounding Cassady College until now, when she was away from it. She had mailed copies of earlier questionnaires back to her off-campus office; she certainly didn't have anywhere near all the data she would have liked, but she might still be able to construct a valid statistical profile of the Cassady College student body, and there were the early biosamples she had obtained that could be matched against this profile.

196

If she had any regrets, it was that she was leaving with personal unfinished business. As far as she was concerned, Richard and Rita Cassady and Perry Parker deserved each other. But Horace Cassady was another matter. The old man might be hopelessly dotty, Pam thought, but he had welcomed her to his home and college, and given her free rein to do her research. He deserved to be warned that the DOD was manipulating him, even if he didn't believe it.

Pam changed her reservation to a later flight, put her baggage into a storage locker, and went out of the airline terminal to hail a cab to take her back to Cassady College.

She had the driver let her off at the edge of the campus, so as not to attract attention, then walked through the chill, dry, desert night air to the quadrangle. She had assumed that Horace Cassady would have returned to his living quarters, and might even be asleep. Thus, she was surprised to see that lights remained on in the dome of the tower, and that upwards of 50 students, many holding candles, were gathered around the base of the tower in what appeared to be a prayer vigil.

It meant that Horace Cassady was still in his tower, and Pam did not understand why; nor did she understand why she experienced a sudden, unmistakable sense of foreboding. The structure had always reminded her of Key 16, the tower in the tarot deck designed by Smith and Waite, and she wondered if anyone else at Cassady College was aware of the resemblance.

Her scars burned.

The old man had shown her an alternate route to get into the tower, and she used that underground passageway now. She paused at the bottom of the spiral staircase that was at the core of the tower and listened, but she heard no sounds from above. Thinking that Horace Cassady might be asleep, and not wanting to startle him, Pam ascended the staircase slowly, her sneakers making no sounds on the concrete steps. She came to the top, stood in the open doorway of the largest room in the dome and smiled grimly.

In the center of the dimly lighted room, Perry Parker sat at a small table, his face and hands brightly illuminated in a cone of light cast by a red gooseneck lamp set up on the far edge of the table. He appeared to be totally absorbed as he slowly leafed through what looked to Pam like a lengthy legal document. Suddenly, apparently sensing her presence, he stiffened, thrust the document into a thin leather portfolio, which he snapped shut, and then looked toward the doorway.

"Pam!"

Pam crossed her arms over her chest, stepped into the room. "Hello, Perry."

The man's lips drew back into a taut smile that reflected no warmth or humor, and that did nothing to mask his shock at seeing her. "I'd heard you'd left Cuckooland."

"An agent who works for the R and D arm of DOD should be very careful what he describes as Cuckooland, Perry. Why aren't you pestering some virologist to build you a new disease, or accidentally killing a herd of sheep? What the hell are you up to here, and why did you have to torpedo my research project?"

"You came up here to try and warn Cassady about me, didn't you?"

"Where is he?"

The dark-eyed, dark-haired man jerked his thumb in the direction of a closed door behind him. "He's in there on a cot sleeping off a snootful."

"What?"

"The man's a closet alcoholic, lady. With that red nose of his, I'm surprised you never guessed. The man comes up here to drink. I think maybe that's the real reason he built this tower in the first place; he wanted a hideout where he

198

could booze it up without anybody bothering him. Naturally, he thinks he has God's personal approval."

Pam shook her head in disbelief. "How do you know all this?"

Parker laughed softly. "You have your means of research, I have mine. As a matter of fact, the Reverend Cassady and I have been rather close for some months now."

"And Rita Cassady put you next to him, didn't she?" Pam asked in an even tone, watching the man's face. "She may be a bitch, but she's no actress. She damn well knows who you are; I could see it in her eyes when I challenged her about that old Guardian article you slipped to her. Whatever's going on, you two are in it together. Are you sleeping with her, Perry? Is that how you set this up?"

Suddenly the smile vanished from Perry Parker's lips, and a hard light glinted in his black eyes. "Easy, Pam, easy," he said softly. "Let's keep this friendly." He paused, glanced at his watch. "You should be leaving; it's for your own good. Old Horace isn't going to believe anything you have to say. You may be a pretty face, but I'm the one who supplies him with his Scotch malt whiskey."

"Perry, it's very hard to be friendly toward you when what you've done is likely to get me shipped back to South Africa. I need my data from here to round out my statistical profile."

Parker abruptly rose from his chair. He put the leather portfolio under his arm, went to the closed door and listened for a few moments, then walked over to Pam. "You've got only yourself to blame," he said with quiet intensity. "You kept turning down our requests to have first access to your raw data. If you'd listened to me, you'd never have had any problems with funding, and you'd have had your green card by now."

"But *why,* Perry? You've always known how I feel about DOD-sponsored research; it's what comes from being born the wrong color in a country that insisted on keeping live smallpox virus in stock just in case we ever got *too* uppity. Since when have you people been interested in anything but the hard sciences anyway? Why pick on me? I'm not the only one studying fundamentalist sects. You can pick up dozens of sociological journals and read about people like this until you go blind."

Again, the tall man with the cold, dark eyes smiled thinly. "Ah, yes, but the DOD isn't interested in reading speculations on a 'fundamentalist temperament,' or being told that zealots tend to link religious ideology to national identity, or that they use sacred scripture to justify violence. And we certainly know how effective these movements are at organizing popular anger. We know all about that. So do you. You've been less than truthful with us, Pam. You've always been after bigger game. You've been hunting in Nobel Prize territory, trying to establish that there's an actual genetic basis, a kind of disease model, for religious faith. You want to demonstrate that some people – fundamentalist types, in particular – come down with religious fervor like others come down with Huntington's chorea, or Tay-Sachs disease. You intend to demonstrate that religious faith is actually the result of a kind of physical affliction. That would be most useful information, particularly if an actual genetic marker could be found."

Somehow he knew, Pam thought, and she felt the blood drain from her face. "You bastard," she breathed.

Parker shook his head. "The tragedy—or farce—of you refusing to accept our funding is that it was actually cheaper for us to bribe the laboratory technicians who are doing your blood work and urinalysis to keep us clued in on exactly what kinds of tests you were ordering up. Then, of course, we put some of our own people to work on the same kinds of tests. By the way, it seems your disease model is correct. Building on your work, and using a Cray computer you'd have had access to if you hadn't been so stubborn, we've found what we think is the genetic marker for religious faith; we think it's somewhere on chromosome four, very close to the marker for schizophrenia."

"It's my work, Perry," Pam whispered, hoping the defeat she felt in her heart couldn't be heard in her voice. "I won't let you get away with just stealing it."

"I'm afraid you have no choice. You'll be returning to South Africa eventually, and when you get back to your university you'll find that much of the data you've collected over the past few years is now classified; you can't get at it."

Pam bit the inside of her cheek to keep from shout-ing—or screaming. "God, Perry, what are you going to *do* with the information?"

"Now that's a question that might better be answered by a medical researcher, a virologist or biologist, no?"

"Are you going to kill more sheep, Perry?"

"A lot of these sheep are killers themselves, Pam, as you're well aware. They blow up airplanes, march their kids across minefields, use poison gas, and think it's all just dandy because they have a special dispensation from God. They take hostages and torture them. It might not be a bad idea at all for someone to try and come up with a biochemical agent—a vaccine, if you will—that would enable us to herd these killer sheep in a different direction."

"You mean manipulate them; killer and non-killer alike."

"As you like. You know R and D's motto: Do unto others just in case they're trying to do unto you."

"And you intend to use the students and faculty of Cassady College as laboratory animals to help DOD search for the religious gene marker and develop means of exploiting it. Just how long do you think you're going to be able to fool that old man in—" She suddenly stopped speaking as a chill went through her. She pointed to the leather portfolio under the man's arm. "That's a will you've got in there, isn't it? You've sold him some kind of story, and now you're waiting for him to come around so that he'll sign it. It's his death warrant. Oh, my God."

"Leave now, Pam." Perry Parker said in a low voice.

"Did you kill Joseph Cassady so that his brother—and, most important, his wife—could inherit this whole operation, Perry? Is that how you plan to turn this college into a DOD research facility?"

"We're not assassins, Pam."

"Spare me."

Parker smiled, shrugged. "I'm not an assassin."

"Then don't kill the old man, and don't let anybody else—."

She stopped speaking when she saw the distressed look on Perry Parker's face as he stared at something behind her. She turned, and was startled to see a thoroughly bewildered-looking Richard Cassady standing in the doorway. He glanced back and forth between the two of them, then down at the pistol in his hand.

"I, uh . . . I thought I heard voices up here. I'm sorry about the gun. After what . . . happened to Joseph." He paused, looked up again. Now suspicion glinted in his pale eyes. "What are you two doing up here? Where's my father?" Pam glanced at Parker, who gave a brief shake of his head—a clear warning, which Pam intended to heed; suddenly she was very much afraid of this man.

The click of a woman's high heels on the concrete staircase was faint at first, growing louder as the footsteps came closer. A few moments later Rita Cassady, head down and apparently deep in thought, entered the room. She stopped, looked up, gasped and clutched the small beaded purse she carried to her chest.

"Perry?" she said in a hollow voice. "What's happened? What's going on?"

202

"Jesus H. Christ," Parker said, and turned his head away in disgust.

"Perry?" Richard Cassady said, slowly turning to his wife. "Why did you call this man 'Perry'?"

Rita Cassady swallowed hard repeatedly, and then looked at Perry Parker. For the first time, Pam could clearly see the madness in the woman's eyes, marbled with panic.

"You have to do something, Perry," Rita Cassady said in a hoarse whisper.

The agent from the Department of Defense merely shook his head.

"Give me that!" The woman shouted, and abruptly grabbed for the gun in her husband's hand.

And then Pam realized the truth. "No!" she shouted at the gaunt man in the dark suit. "If you give her the gun, she'll kill your father and me! That's why she's here! If you look in that purse she's carrying, I think you'll find the same knife she used to kill your brother! She wants you to inherit your father's operation, because she's sure she'll be able to control it! She and this man planned it together! If you don't believe me, ask her to show you what's in the purse!"

Richard Cassady stared wide-eyed at Pam, clearly shocked; but he held the gun away from his wife when she grabbed for it again.

"You fool!" Rita Cassady screamed, starting to beat at her husband's head and shoulders with her frail fists. "There are tens of millions of dollars at stake here! If you let your father keep pissing it away in that hole in the ground—!" She abruptly bit off the sentence, and her face, when she turned back, reminded Pam of the expression on a child's face when the child has been discovered in a particularly shameful act. "Help me, Perry," she whispered in a voice that was barely audible.

Parker grunted, and started walking toward the door. "I don't know what you're talking about, lady. I'm gone."

"Wait!"

Pam wheeled around, and was startled to see the disheveled, haggard figure of Horace Cassady standing in the open doorway of the room where he had been resting. In his right hand, he held a thick, heavy cross that was the color of gunmetal. After her initial shock, Pam's reaction was to wonder how much the man had overheard; the haunted look on his face was her answer.

The old man walked unsteadily across the room, pushing aside both Perry Parker and Rita Cassady. He gripped Pam's arm and led her to the doorway, then used his other arm to draw his son close to him.

"Did you help kill your brother, Richard?" Horace Cassady said, leaning so close to the other man that their foreheads were virtually touching.

Richard Cassady's mouth opened and closed. He swallowed hard, managed to say, "Father, I don't understand any of this."

"I believe you," the old man said after a pause. "Give this woman back all her papers, Richard, and help her bear witness to what's happened here. Cooperate with her in any way she wants. It's God's will. Goodbye."

And then, displaying surprising strength and quickness, he pushed them both out through the doorway. The last thing Pam saw before the steel panel that had been hidden in the wall slammed shut across the entranceway was Horace Cassady holding up the heavy cross he carried and pressing what appeared to be a button embedded in its handle.

Suddenly the entire tower seemed to be filled with clicking sounds—electric relays being activated, closing. And suddenly Pam understood why the former mining engineer who had exercised such close control and personal supervision over the construction of his Creation Park had been so certain he was going to die if his wishes were not fulfilled.

Richard Cassady was pounding with his fists at the steel panel, shouting his father's name.

Pam wrapped her arms around the man's waist, pulled him away from the panel and toward the staircase. "Come on! We have to get out of here! He's wired the whole place with dynamite!"

Together, they raced down the stairs, out the front entrance. Shouting, pushing and pulling, they struggled to move the students outside away from the base of the tower to safety.

Creation Park was the first to go, multiple explosions lighting the night sky and raining debris down over the campus of Cassady College moments before the dome of the tower disappeared in a thunderous flash of fire and smoke.

DREAMS

"EVER DREAM?"

The old man finished his move and glanced up from the checkerboard. "Everyone dreams, Johnson."

The pale brown eyes were watery, the tired eyes of a man who has parlayed acceptance into a kind of wisdom and lost a chunk of his soul in the process. The eyes peered at him from a head without a body, a wizened face that swam on the edge of the ragged pool of light carved out of the darkness by the flickering candle at his elbow.

"Have you ever dreamed of dying?"

"I'm not afraid of death, Johnson. You shouldn't be either. Are you tired of the game?"

"No," Johnson said quietly. He moved a checker, then pressed down very hard on the surface of the red wooden circle. His fingernail snapped back and he felt a stab of pain in the soft quick. Johnson frowned. "I'm not afraid of death," he continued, taking his finger away and cradling it in his other hand. "Everybody dies sometime, and that's enough comfort for me. Dying of old age, or cancer, or even sticking your own head in the oven; that's one thing. But having other men *take* your life; that's something else again. A man's life is something special, an infinite collection of memories and hopes, loves and hates, fears; wonderful, secret, hidden places that even he may not

207

know about. It isn't right. A man's life shouldn't be like a lamp just anybody can pull the plug on."

"Men kill other men, Johnson. Sometimes they kill in passion, or stupidity, or rage, and sometimes they just kill out of meanness. What is a society to do with these killers?"

"If they're soldiers you promote them or give them medals. Usually both."

"You're not being serious."

"Judge them, I guess," Johnson said quietly.

"Yes." There were three sharp clicks. A palsied hand mottled with liver spots emerged from the darkness and removed three of his men. "Now I think you're in trouble, Johnson. That was a triple jump."

"I dreamt once that I killed somebody," Johnson went on, advancing one of his checkers. If he could get a king he might still stand a chance. "I couldn't even remember what the man looked like, or why I'd killed him. It was like a dream within a dream; maybe I was stoned, or drunk out of my mind. Anyway, I'd killed him and a court had sentenced me to hang. The next morning.

"I didn't even know that until a few hours later when a priest told me. I'm not even Catholic but they sent a priest because he was the only one in the village who could speak English. It was a real small town, really just a patch of dust with some shacks on it, somewhere in Guatemala. At least I think it was Guatemala. At first I laughed. I mean, the thought that they were going to *execute me* was ridiculous. I'd get hold of somebody; somebody who'd explain for me, somebody who'd at least get me another trial in a language I could understand.

"Then I realized there *wasn't* anybody. I'd been drifting for two, three years. Country to country, living off the land and the women. And even if there'd been somebody to get, there was no way to contact them. No phones, and no time to write a letter to the embassy because they were going to snap my neck the next morning. Like a chicken."

The withered hand hovered over the pieces, almost made the wrong move, and then made the right one.

"In the evening, they asked me if I wanted anything. I asked for a glass of orange juice. Years before, I'd always had a glass of orange juice before I went to bed. I'd sit on the edge of the bed and drink the orange juice and smoke a cigarette and think of the day. That day. The next day. Anyway, they found some oranges somewhere, squeezed them up and made me my orange juice. They were very decent about that. It was pulpy and warm, but it was good, and it helped me remember better times. Then I realized that was the last glass of orange juice I would ever have. There would still be oranges growing; there would still be people picking them and selling them and buying them and eating them. There would still be people . . . *washing dishes,* or sending their children off to school, or beating up their children, or scratching themselves, or looking up at the sky, or making love, or going for walks. But that was the last glass of orange juice I would ever have. Because in the morning people who couldn't even speak my language were going to take me out to a gallows and put a rope around my neck and drop me through the air. I'd dance and crap in my pants and be dead. I wouldn't even know if . . . I wouldn't even know *anything."*

"It's your move, Johnson."

The promise of dawn was bleaching the fabric of night and Johnson could see that the old man was

209

huddled against a cold he himself could not feel. He moved and lost two of his remaining three men. He moved the last man into a corner.

"Of course I woke up," Johnson continued. His own voice sounded strange in his ears, as if the sound track of his words was out of synch with the film of his thoughts. "I sang in my car on the way to work that morning, sang at the top of my lungs. It was spring, and I ran over every pothole I could find. During the day I drank a lot of water, sipping it slowly and sloshing it around my teeth. I looked into people's faces and smiled; when they spoke, I listened very closely. One person had a lisp and I asked him to repeat something just so I could listen to that lisp. Later that day I walked around a block in the city. I found a brick on the sidewalk and I stopped and stared at it for a long time. I picked it up and dropped it. I picked it up and threw it just so I could see what it looked like sailing across the sky. Do you know why I did all those things?"

"No."

"I was celebrating my dream. Love and hate and pleasure and pain, depression, *excitement;* in the end, they're all illusions. Sometimes they are grand, and men write symphonies, or write stories, or they dance. But these things are still insignificant. They're not *life*. Life is little things."

"It's your move, Johnson."

The light was stronger now, muscling its way across the floor, bumping up against a sweating clay wall. Johnson rose and walked to the single window. He wrapped his fingers around the rusted bars and stared at the gallows in the dusty courtyard below. The rope had been used before. Many times. It dangled limp, like a dead worm. Somewhere a door opened and

210

closed and children ran to play in the shadow of the scaffold. They shouted in a language Johnson could not understand. He turned to the old man.

"I'm afraid, Father."

"I think it may be good to pray now, Johnson," the priest said, drawing his hands into the folds of his dark tunic and bowing his head.

Beside the priest was a bench. On top of the bench was a checkerboard. Beside the checkerboard was a candle. And a glass. Flies buzzed on the rim and at the bottom of the glass, poking their hairy needle snouts into the orange, pulpy residue that had dried there.

A key bumped in the heavy iron door at the opposite end of the room. Two men in ragged uniforms entered, walked to him and grabbed his arms. One man yawned without covering his mouth. Johnson's feet would not move, so they dragged him.

"Father, the game's not over!"

"It's over, Johnson," the priest said, rising and resting the gossamer weight of his hand on Johnson's shoulder. "The game is finished."

Johnson lifted the finger he had pressed against the wooden checker and examined it. It still hurt. A tiny blossom of blood had sprouted beneath his cracked nail. "Why don't I wake up, Father?" He was crying now. The warm tears rolled down over his lips, salting his mouth. *"Why don't I wake up, Father?!"*

"Because it's time to rest now, my son," the priest said softly. "It's time to sleep. Try to think of all this as a dream."

THE DRAGON VARIATION

Morning on the Gornergrat was cold, dry, space-clear. Ringed by the Alps, the glacier was a ribbon of ice flowing down the side of the mountain to drip waterfalls and rivers into the July valley below. In the distance the east wall of the Matterhorn spewed clouds into a china blue sky; the jagged peak thrust up into the sky like an angry, jealous god guarding the village of Zermatt at its feet. It was all in Technicolor and totally unreal.

Zermatt was where Douglas Franklin came when he had played in one chess tournament too many, when tension had stretched his nerves and shriveled his emotions to a point where the most beautiful cities became no more than squares on a playing board and he no longer cared to distinguish between people and chess pieces.

Douglas eased his backpack onto the ice, and then sat down on it. He threw back his head, opened his mouth wide and sucked in the icy breath of the mountains. With the terrible tension gone he could begin to relax and think about the good things, the first-place trophy and $30,000 check back in his hotel room. He had won an Inter-zonal, and the victory would launch him into the elimination finals for the world championship. It was something to think on, to savor, and Douglas intended to do just that.

He removed a bottle from his pack, uncorked it and sipped at the thick, clear liquid. The liquor hit his stomach and exploded in a warm glow that left a pleasant ringing in his ears. He waited for the echoes to die away before rising, shouldering his backpack and resuming his trek down the face of the glacier. Fifteen minutes later he found the dog.

The small black poodle was still alive— barely. Its eyes were closed, its breathing labored and shallow. An irregular, speckled trail of blood in the snow ended in a large stain surrounding the dog's hindquarters. The cold had stopped the bleeding, but was killing the exhausted dog. Threads of torn muscle were interwoven with black, kinky fur along a single, deep groove cut in the animal's left flank. It was the kind of wound that might be left by a bullet.

Douglas quickly removed his fur-lined   parka and   wrapped it around the animal. Then he picked up the bundle and cradled it in his lap. He was rewarded with a weak whimper. A stubby abbreviation of a tail worked its way out through a fold in the parka and began to wag feebly.

"You just hang in there, pal," Douglas heard himself saying. "I'm going to fix you up." He'd always thought it silly in the past when he'd seen people talking to animals; now he found himself crying.

He picked up a handful of snow, let it melt, then pressed his hand over the dog's muzzle; he could feel a small tongue licking the palm of his hand. He repeated this procedure until the tail wagging became stronger and the eyes opened. The dog's eyes were large, very black and soulful. They had the gleam of intelligence, like those of a precocious child. He poured a mug of coffee from his thermos, let it cool, then laced it generously with the liquor. He held the mug in front of the dog's muzzle and the animal lapped it up. The dog coughed, barked, and licked Douglas' hand.

"There, dog," Douglas said affectionately, "what'd I tell you?" The dog barked. Douglas produced a sandwich from his pack and the dog wolfed it down.

There was a license and a leather pouch hanging from a collar around the dog's neck. Douglas opened the leather pouch. Inside was a note announcing that the dog's name was "Dragon," and giving the name, address and telephone number of the dog's owner. The address was an apartment building in Zermatt. The name of the dog's owner was Victor Rensky.

It occurred to Douglas that he'd heard the name before. He thought for a few moments, and then placed it; Rensky—if it was the same one—was a former OSS officer turned journalist after the war. His books on little-known aspects of covert Nazi operations in Europe had made him famous, not to mention rich.

"All right, Dragon," Douglas said, rising to his feet and cradling the dog in his arms, "let's get you home."

Dragon barked his assent, and then promptly fell asleep.

It was past noon by the time Douglas emerged from the network of hiking trails into the town of Zermatt. He walked to the river flowing through the center of town and turned right, heading for the cluster of apartment buildings jutting up from a steeply rising slope to the west. Two hundred yards to his left a red jet helicopter rose from a large heliport cut into the side of the mountain. That particular sound was a familiar one in Zermatt; usually it meant that someone was dangling—or dead—on the Matterhorn.

The main entrance to the Helvetia apartment house was open. Dragon was awake now, trembling with the excitement of being back in a familiar place. The apartment directory indicated that Victor Rensky

215

lived in 3C. Douglas entered the lift and got off on the third floor.

There was no answer from 3C. Douglas rang the bell a third time, gave a perfunctory knock, then turned to go. Dragon was not willing to give up so easily. Showing an unexpected surge of strength, the dog leaped from Douglas' arms, yelped with pain when he hit the floor, but remained on his feet. He scampered back and used his paw to push aside the mat in front of the door, revealing a key that had been hidden there. Dragon picked up the key in his mouth and trotted triumphantly back to Douglas. The key dropped with a minor clatter at Douglas' feet.

Douglas laughed. "Is this an invitation? I know your master will be glad to see you, but I'm not so sure he'll appreciate your bringing any two-legged friends into the house."

But why not? Douglas thought. Perhaps Rensky would be back in a few minutes. Dragon, after being shot and almost freezing to death, deserved a taste of home before being locked up in some doctor's office. Douglas decided he would wait a half hour. If Rensky wasn't back by then he would leave a note and drop Dragon off with a veterinarian, as he'd originally intended. He scratched Dragon behind the ears, picked up the key and went into the apartment.

The interior was tastefully decorated in dark browns and gold, lightened by a series of framed blowups of the Zermatt valley and the Matterhorn. It reflected a journalist's mind, the constant, not-quite-successful struggle to create order out of chaos. There were magazines on every conceivable subject strewn about the room. One wall was book stacks, filled with five or six hundred well-worn volumes. A workbench extended the length of another wall; on the bench were

216

two typewriters—one portable and one electric—and a stack of manuscript paper surrounded by more books. There were a dozen chess sets around the room. Beside each was a small pile of postcards, identifying Rensky as a postal chess player. There was one set on the workbench, along with another pile of postcards.

Douglas went to the bookcases. The collection was a potpourri of books and subjects, with the emphasis on Nazi Germany; many of the books were Rensky's own. One shelf was devoted to chess, and the first book that caught Douglas' attention was *his* own, a small but popular monograph on The Dragon Variation of the Sicilian Defense. "Good taste," he grunted. He turned to Dragon and said, "I wonder if you know that you're named after a chess opening?"

Dragon's bark indicated that he certainly did. The dog lay down on a well-worn throw rug, licked his injured hindquarters, then promptly fell asleep. Douglas went to the workbench.

The books that Rensky was using all seemed to be on the same subject. The one that was open bore the title, *The Nazi Fifth Column In Switzerland: The Hidden Traitors;* and it appeared that Rensky was writing a book of his own. The pile of typescript was heavily annotated in what Douglas assumed was Rensky's handwriting.

He moved on to the chess set and picked up the postcards, intending to go through the moves in his mind. He riffled through the cards, stopped when he was halfway through the pile and started again, this time more slowly. They didn't make sense.

Douglas was thoroughly familiar with the rules and method of playing postal chess; he usually had a dozen games going at one time, using postal chess as a painless means of analyzing new opening ideas in a painless, non-tournament situation. He knew that in Europe they would use the algebraic method of chess notation in order to send moves. That would mean that the eight squares on the first rank of the chessboard would be assigned the letters A to H; the squares on the files, counting from White's side of the board, would be numbered from 1 to 8. The cards, datelined from a number of different cities in both Germany and Switzerland, bore just about every letter of the alphabet, and the numbers were frequently higher than 8; and there was something else that was odd: all of the postcards had been written by the same person who had annotated the typescript.

Douglas dropped the cards back onto the bench and shrugged; if Rensky wanted to play postal chess with himself using a system that didn't exist, that was certainly his business.

The phone rang. Dragon's head jerked up from the rug and his tail began to wag. Douglas hesitated, and then picked up the phone. "Hello?"

The person on the other end of the line grunted in surprise. There was a long silence filled with tense, heavy breathing, then: *"Wer ist das?"* It was an old voice, old but tough, a voice clearly accustomed to giving orders. It carried clearly from the receiver into the room. Dragon pulled back his lips from his fangs and growled.

Douglas looked at Dragon and frowned.

"Wer ist das?"

Dragon's growl became a snarl, then a series of short, savage barks that, coming from a small poodle, might have seemed comical were it not for the fact that that same poodle had been shot a few hours before. Douglas didn't laugh.

"Uh, I don't speak German," he said carefully. "How's your English?"

"Who is this?"

218

"My name is Douglas Franklin. Am I speaking to Mr. Rensky?"

Another pause, then: "This is a friend of Mr. Rensky's. I hear a dog barking. Do you have a dog with you?"

"That's Dragon. I found him up on the glacier. He was hurt. I was bringing him back to Rensky."

"May I ask what you are doing in Mr. Rensky's apartment?"

The tone of the question was harsh and strained. Douglas felt anger rise within him but he contained it. After all, he *had* walked into a stranger's apartment. "The dog showed me where the key was. I thought I'd wait for Rensky."

"Mr. Rensky is away for a few days." Now the words were carefully measured. "I will take care of Dragon. Perhaps you would be kind enough to bring him to me. I am an old man, and I do not climb steps well."

"All right," Douglas said shortly. "Who are you and where do you want me to meet you?"

"I am Hans Vorteg. I will meet you in front of the Tourist Office by the athletic field. Do you know where it is?"

"I do. I'll be there in a few minutes."

Douglas hung up the phone and looked at Dragon, who had been snarling throughout the conversation. Now Dragon coughed and lay still. Douglas was aware of a pain in his stomach where the muscles had knotted. He walked across the room and picked up the dog.

If Vorteg knew Rensky would be away for a few days, why was he calling? *Who* was he calling? "I don't like it either, Dragon," he said, petting the dog. "I think we'll pass on Mr. Vorteg. You know where we can find a vet around here?" Dragon barked and wagged his tail.

Douglas smiled and shook his head. "I know that's an answer, but I don't understand Dog as well as you understand English. C'mon, let's get out of here."

He started toward the door, and then froze when he heard the sound of metal scraping in the lock. Rensky? He backed up and pulled his face into the kind of smile he thought he'd want to see on a stranger standing in *his* apartment.

It wasn't Rensky. The thin blond man was in his early thirties, about Douglas' age. He was still holding the strip of metal he'd used to pick the lock in a right hand that was missing the ring and little fingers. He was limping badly, favoring his left foot. His left trouser leg was torn and dirty, as though he had recently fallen. The man looked up, startled, as Dragon snarled. The blood drained from his face, leaving splotches of red on paper-white flesh.

Douglas had to yell to be heard above Dragon's frenzied barking. "Looking for somebody?"

The man recovered, wheeled and limped out as fast as he could. Douglas heard him stumbling down the stairs. He considered going after the man, then decided against it. In a village the size of Zermatt there couldn't be that many thin blonds missing two fingers and walking with a limp.

"Another friend of yours?" Douglas said, scratching under Dragon's ears. The dog nuzzled Douglas' hand. "I know some Swiss law," Douglas said after a thoughtful pause. "Let's you and me go find him."

He found Karl Henning on the tennis courts of the hotel owned by Henning's father. Henning was a well-built, ruddy-complexioned man who was pushing forty and looked thirty. Henning approached his job as local constable as a kind of civic duty; his father was a member of the Zermatt "commune", a group of old fam-

220

ilies who literally owned everything of value in Zermatt, ran the enterprises jointly and shared all profits. Henning took no pay for his work because there wasn't that much work; Douglas didn't consider him much of a policeman, but then Zermatt wasn't exactly the crime capital of the Western world. Douglas had met him on a previous visit, and liked him. He was a terror on a tennis court and Douglas admired competitiveness. Henning recognized him as he came into the fenced-off playing area. The constable waved off his partner and came over to Douglas.

"Douglas!" Henning had a deep, natural bass voice, pleasant to listen to for five or ten minutes, numbing after that.

Douglas shifted Dragon to his left side and shook the hand that was extended to him. "Hello, Karl," he said. "It's good to see you. You look fine."

"So do you. How are the chess wars?"

"A little frantic. That's why I'm in Zermatt."

"And you're not staying with us? You know we would have insisted that you take a room without charge!"

Douglas smiled thinly. "I know. That's why I'm not staying with you."

"How many famous Grandmasters do we get in Zermatt?" Henning looked hurt. It passed. He nodded in Dragon's direction. "A traveling companion?"

Douglas shook his head. "I found him up on the Gornergrat. He was hurt. I think somebody took a shot at him."

Henning rolled his brown eyes; it was the reaction of a man who didn't want to talk about hurt dogs and gunshots. "What were you doing up on the Gornergrat? It's dangerous up there; the ice is shifting. There are crevasses. We lost three Italians yesterday. The slopes have been closed."

221

"I just got here last night. I'd planned to do some summer skiing. When I found out the slopes were closed I decided to hike down. The funicular was still running." He cleared his throat. "Why do you think somebody would want to take a shot at a dog?"

Henning rolled his eyes again. Douglas had found it amusing the first time; now it was annoying.

"Who knows?" Henning said. "A crazy man; some hunter with bad eyesight. Where was his master?"

"That's what I want to talk to you about, Karl." Henning cast a glance in the direction of his tennis partner, who was swinging his racquet impatiently. Douglas moved around in front of him. "The dog belongs to a man by the name of Rensky. I got that from a message in a pouch around the dog's neck. I also got his address. He lives in the Helvetia. The dog showed me where the key was and I went in to wait. While I was there I had a strange telephone conversation with a man by the name of Hans Vorteg." The name brought a reaction from Henning. Douglas talked through it. "A few minutes after the call a man tried to break in. He'd fallen and hurt himself. Now, I think the call was meant for that man. The fact that he fell slowed him down; he wasn't in the apartment when he was supposed to be. To my mind, that brings up a few questions. For example, where's Rensky?"

Henning was staring at his sneakers. "The man who tried to break in—what did he look like?"

Douglas told him. That got another reaction. For a moment Douglas was afraid that Henning was going to faint. The blood had drained from the big man's face.

"You know who it is?" Douglas asked.

"Jan Vorteg, the son of the man who talked to you on the phone. He lost the two fingers on the north

222

wall of the Matterhorn two years ago." Henning sounded as if he were going to choke.

"Vorteg is a big name around here?"

Henning nodded. He looked totally distracted. "Mr. Vorteg is a commune member."

"Well, what the hell was his son doing in Rensky's apartment?"

Henning glanced over Douglas' shoulder and swallowed hard. "Perhaps you should ask Mr. Vorteg yourself."

Douglas turned. The man coming across the courts toward them was over six feet. Age had withered his frame somewhat, but not much. His hands, swinging militantly at his sides, were large and heavily veined. He had an almost square face framed by a mane of silver hair; his eyes were a deep blue and burned with a cold fire. As he came up and stopped in front of them, Douglas could see that his lips were compressed with anger, giving his mouth the appearance of a tiny, blue-white slash in his face.

Dragon had begun to growl. Douglas put a hand over his muzzle, quieting him.

Vorteg glanced at the dog, then pointed a thick finger at a spot between Douglas' eyes. "You are Douglas Franklin," he said in English layered with a thick German accent. "Why did you not meet me as you said you would?"

"I met your son along the way. He convinced me I should look for a cop."

Vorteg turned to Henning for the first time. "You are very free with information about my family, *Herr* Henning." Henning started to mutter a protest, but Vorteg continued: "There is a simple explanation for the questions I'm sure Mr. Franklin has raised in your mind. First of all, I have been caring for this dog since yesterday, at the request of Victor Rensky. As you can see, it is a thankless task; the animal is a spoiled, impossible beast."

Dragon squirmed, but Douglas held him tightly, stroking his throat, quieting him.

"Rensky was suddenly called out of town on business," Vorteg continued. "It was his custom to take Dragon for a walk each morning on the Gornergrat. This morning it was my son who took on this chore. The beast ran away from him. We have spent most of the day looking for him."

Karl Henning swallowed hard. His bass crept up to a tenor as he said, "Douglas tells me the dog was shot."

Vorteg's hands flew out from his sides and froze in the air. "Karl! Do you think Jan would shoot a dog?"

"Uh, did Jan hear a shot?"

Vorteg's eyes became slits, almost matching his mouth. The hands slowly descended to his sides. "As a matter of fact I think he mentioned that he did. Am I being questioned, *Herr Constable?"* He made constable sound like a dirty word.

Karl Henning was drowning in embarrassed silence. Douglas rescued him. "What was your son doing, coming into Rensky's apartment Mr. Vorteg?"

"He was there at my express wish, *Mr.* Franklin. First, to see if the dog had come back to the Helvetia. Second, to check the apartment to make sure everything was in order."

"He picked the lock."

Vorteg's eyebrows arched in triumph. "Because *you* had the key!"

"He ran away."

Vorteg snorted. "My son is not a coward; neither is he a fool. He had hurt himself—the reason he was not there to take my telephone call. When he saw you he naturally assumed you were a burglar. Knowing that he was in no shape to fight you, he did the wise thing. He ran for help. *You* were the one there without permission, Mr. Franklin, not Jan."

Henning looked immensely relieved, as though a doubles partner had just served an ace for match point. "Douglas was just trying to be helpful, Mr. Vorteg. I'm sure Mr. Rensky would not wish to press charges."

"That's your business," Vorteg said. He held out his hands. "I will take the dog now."

Dragon snapped at the hand. Vorteg's hand came back to cuff the furry head. Douglas quickly turned to the side, shielding Dragon with his body. "The dog is hurt," he said evenly. "I was taking him to a veterinarian. I still am. After that, you can make whatever arrangements you want." He was not about to have to look Dragon in the eyes while he handed him over to Vorteg.

Vorteg hesitated, then backed away. "Perhaps that is best. Dr. Jenck can tranquilize the beast."

Karl Henning nodded enthusiastically. "Dr. Jenck's office is across from the church. You know where that is."

Vorteg's large hand dipped into his pocket and came out with a wallet. "Something for your trouble, Mr. Franklin."

Douglas could feel a white-hot flush spreading up his neck, squeezing his eyes. He turned and walked away before it could blind him.

On the crest of a hill above the tennis courts he stopped and looked back. Something had been said to shake Henning out of his deference; the two men were arguing heatedly.

If Hans Vorteg was lying through his teeth, that was Karl Henning's problem, not his, Douglas decided, and there was no doubt in his mind that

225

Vorteg *had* lied. The story the old man had told might be barely plausible, if not for Dragon. Dragon simply was *not* an "impossible beast," but a highly intelligent and naturally affectionate dog, the product of a lot of love and training by the kind of owner who wouldn't leave Dragon with somebody he didn't like or trust. If Dragon didn't like the Vortegs, it was for a reason, something the dog knew.

He wasn't a cop, Douglas reflected, and he wasn't a hero. He wasn't even a dog owner. He was an exhausted chess Grandmaster badly in need of a vacation. Dragon and the Vortegs were none of his concern.

Then why couldn't he sleep?

Douglas dragged on his cigarette and stared down into the swiftly flowing waters of the river. Beneath a full moon the hissing water with its load of dissolved calcium glowed white; the Swiss called such water "glacier milk." In his mind's eye, Douglas could see Dragon staring up at him with trusting eyes as the dog was locked into his kennel.

The veterinarian's report had been a good one. Douglas had found the dog in time, soon after the shooting had occurred. There was no infection and no signs of pneumonia. A few shots and a few days of rest and Dragon would be as good as new.

But for how long? Douglas wondered. Somebody *had* tried to kill Dragon. Perhaps they would try again.

In the empty stillness of the Zermatt night the footsteps echoed clearly; they belonged to a man with a limp.

Douglas threw his cigarette into the water, then quickly stepped out of the light. A few minutes later Jan Vorteg passed beneath the street lamp directly in front of Douglas. In his right hand Vorteg carried a faded flight bag. The bag was bulky and, judging from the way Vorteg was listing to one side, heavy. He crossed the bridge over the river, then turned right at the first intersection. Douglas felt the muscles in his stomach begin to flutter; Vorteg's route would take him past the church— and the veterinarian's office. Douglas waited a few moments, then started after the other man.

Not wishing to advertise his own presence, Douglas kept a good distance between himself and the man ahead. As a result, Vorteg was already in the vast, grassy courtyard in front of the veterinarian's office a full minute before Douglas arrived there.

Douglas braced against the side of a building and peered around the corner. The courtyard was in total darkness, the moonlight cut off by three huge trees with upper branches that formed a virtual canopy over the yard. He strained, trying to peer into the darkness, undecided on what action he should take. He was concerned about Dragon, and at the same time not anxious to present himself as a target, in the event that Vorteg was armed.

The pungent smell of gasoline wafted to him a split second before the side of the east wing of the building erupted in a sudden flash of orange-white flame.

Douglas groaned and sprinted away from the protective cover of the building, across the lawn. Vorteg, gimping along as fast as he could, emerged from the darkness, saw Douglas, tried to cut to the left and fell to the ground. The man's eyes were wide with fright as Douglas sprinted past him; it was the second time in twenty-four hours Douglas had allowed Vorteg to escape from the scene of a crime; he'd be most curious to hear the elder Vorteg's explanation for this one.

He hit the office door at full tilt—and bounced back three feet. His shoulder went numb. The door was solid. From inside the building came the high-pitched yelps of frightened, panicky animals.

There was a window a few feet away from the rapidly advancing flames. He quickly removed his jacket and used it to shield his fist as he broke the glass, then to shield his face from the flames as he picked the jagged pieces of glass from the frame. This done, he braced his hands on the frame and vaulted headfirst through the window.

He landed on his shoulder, tucked into a ball and rolled, came up on his feet. First he unbolted the door, then he raced back along the corridor and through another door into the area where the animals were kept. The room was filled with black, acrid smoke. He could hear the hiss of flames above the din created by the animals. Dragon was to his left, standing on his hindquarters, his front paws braced against the wire of his cage. Across the aisle were three other dogs and a goat. He released the goat first, grabbing it by the fold of skin under its chin and leading it out to the door. Then he released the three other dogs. Finally, he opened Dragon's cage. Dragon wagged his tail, then leaped into Douglas' arms.

"Lazy dog!" Douglas whispered as he carried/ Dragon out into the cool night air.

He sat down hard on the moist ground beneath a tree and coughed, struggling to catch his breath. From the opposite end of town came the wail of fire engines.

Dragon licked Douglas' face, then leaped out of his arms, ran off a few paces and began to bark excitedly.

Douglas shook his head. "What's the matter with you, dog?" he said. "This isn't playtime." He was distracted by the thought of what would happen next, and he was convinced the sequence of events would be fairly simple: the Vortegs would simply lie. Hans Vorteg would claim that his son had not been out of his bed all night, and no one in Zermatt, least of all Karl Henning, would be prepared to call a member of the all-powerful commune a liar, not without the kind of evidence that Douglas didn't have. So, if members of the commune didn't lie, who was responsible for the fire, and the empty gasoline can on the lawn? An itinerant chess Grandmaster?

Douglas didn't like the scenario; it contained just enough paranoia to give it the ring of truth.

Dragon ran back to him and gently pulled on Douglas' jacket with his teeth. Then he again ran off a few paces, turned and barked.

"Dragon, what the hell-?" The rest of the sentence caught in his throat. Dragon was trying to get him to follow. He had been running in the direction of the mountain to the west; high up on that mountain was the Gornergrat. Douglas slowly rose to his feet. "You know . . . something," Douglas whispered. "And you can show me. That's why they had to kill you." He nodded his head and clapped his hands. "All right," he said to the dog, "we'll do it your way; we'll play the Dragon variation."

Douglas walked toward Dragon and clapped his hands. This time Dragon seemed to understand. He gave a small, high-pitched bark and leaped into Douglas' arms. Douglas skirted around the trees to avoid the fire trucks and official cars, and then started walking directly toward the mountain in the distance.

Dragon lay at the edge of the crevasse, whimpering. Douglas, standing above him, shivered in the freezing, glacier dawn. Fifty feet below them, wedged between two blocks of ice, was the body of a man who could only be Victor Rensky.

It was a perfect grave, an almost perfect murder, Douglas realized. The ice was closing up. In a few days, or perhaps only a few hours, this section of the glacier would be a seamless stretch of ice, and Victor Rensky's body would begin a slow, inch-by-inch journey that would take a thousand years.

Douglas reached down and touched the dog. "C'mon, Dragon," he said quietly. "You've done your job. Let's get out of here before we freeze."

The helicopter came at them from the east, out of the sun. Douglas heard it before he saw it, and it sounded too close. He dropped flat onto the ice, grabbing Dragon and holding him close as the helicopter passed a few feet overhead. Had he remained standing he would have been smashed and hurled into the crevasse.

The craft made a sharp turn and started back. It was a small helicopter, private, and piloted by Jan Vorteg. His father was sitting beside him. Sunlight glinted off metal inside the cockpit. A second later there was a gunshot and the ice next to Douglas exploded in a shower of sparkling slivers of frozen sunlight.

Douglas picked up Dragon and sprinted as best he could across the ice, keeping low, zigzagging on the treacherous surface. Again the helicopter zoomed overhead, and Douglas dropped to the ice as bullets whizzed through the air.

There was no place to run. Douglas knew he was too large a target. He pushed Dragon away from him. "Go, Dragon!" he shouted. "Get out of here!" The thought crossed his mind that now Dragon would have to start all over again, coaxing someone up onto the Gornergrat to find two bodies. He choked off a hysterical

230

laugh. *"Run,* you damn dog! You got away once! Let's see you do it again!"

Dragon stood his ground, growling and barking at the closing helicopter. Douglas cursed, jumped to his feet and started running again.

There was a roar of sound to his left, a flash of red, and then there were two helicopters overhead. The shooting stopped, and the two helicopters began a strange, aerial duet orchestrated by hand signals from Karl Henning. There was a double-barreled shotgun sticking out from the open window of his cockpit. Both helicopters banked and set down on the other side of an ice ridge that blocked Douglas' view.

Douglas rose and, with Dragon limping at his side, began walking toward the ridge. He felt dizzy, almost overwhelmed by the realization that he was still alive. He picked up a handful of snow and rubbed it vigorously against his face, savoring the clean, biting cold. The double shotgun blast was totally unexpected, an ugly mushroom cloud of sound billowing up from the spot beyond the ice ridge where the helicopters had landed. Douglas stopped and waited. His elation was gone.

A few moments later Karl Henning emerged from the other side of the ridge. He walked slowly, his head bowed. He carried the shotgun in the crook of his left arm. The big man walked to the edge of the crevasse and stared down at the body of Victor Rensky. Douglas joined him. Dragon lay down by the tear in the ice and began to whimper again.

"I couldn't help it," Henning said softly into the silence. "They both had guns. I guess they didn't take me too seriously. They just didn't leave me any choice."

Douglas touched the other man's arm. "Thanks for bailing me out, Karl. How'd you know I was up here?"

"It was a guess. Somebody saw Jan Vorteg running away from the fire. He also saw you walking with the dog toward the mountain. Later, when I saw that Vorteg's helicopter was missing from the pad, I thought I'd better check up here." He paused, then nodded in the direction of Rensky's body. "What do you suppose this was all about? Personal feud?"

Douglas shook his head. "I don't think so. Do you know anything about a Nazi fifth column in Switzerland during the war?"

A muscle twitched in Henning's jaw. He took a long time to answer. "There have always been a lot of rumors about prominent German-Swiss collaborating with the Nazis. The story goes that they wanted to turn Switzerland, at least the German-speaking part of it, over to the Germans. I don't know how much truth there is in it."

"Well, Rensky was writing a book about it. I saw the manuscript and the research materials in his apartment. My guess is that he had a list of the names of some of those traitors. Hans Vorteg's name was on the list. Somehow Vorteg found out about it. He couldn't face the disgrace of being branded a traitor, so he got his son to help him kill Rensky. If you check with Rensky's friends you'll probably find that he was in the habit of walking with Dragon early every morning on the Gornergrat. The Vortegs knew that. When the slopes were closed to skiers, the Vortegs saw their opportunity. They knew Rensky was up on the glacier before anyone else, so they went up in their helicopter and ambushed him, then pushed his body into the crevasse, but they missed Dragon, and they worried about that for good reason. They knew the dog might be able to lead somebody back to the spot where his master was shot. They spent the

232

whole morning looking for him, just as Vorteg said. That's why they didn't get down much before I did, Karl."

Henning thought about it for a few moments, then slowly nodded. "Jan Vorteg broke into the apartment to get the manuscript and the list of names."

"Right. When he saw me there, with Dragon, he knew they had problems."

Henning's face creased in a half-smile. "How right they were," he said quietly. He turned suddenly and slapped Douglas on the back. "Well, my friend, thanks to you it looks like I'll miss my tennis game this afternoon. I've got work to do. We'll have to get that body up. Then I think I'll go over to Rensky's apartment and see what names turn up in that manuscript." He grinned broadly. "But first I'm dropping you off at our hotel. You'll stay there as the guest of the Swiss government. It's the least a humble public servant like myself can do to repay you for what you've done. And I think our chef can find a steak for Dragon."

Douglas was staring down at the body. "I may be able to do one more thing for you," he said distantly.

"What's that?"

Douglas turned to face Henning. "I think the list of names is in the apartment—but not in the manuscript."

Henning frowned. "Then where?"

"There," Douglas said, walking across the room to Rensky's workbench and placing his hand on the single pile of postcards there.

"On postcards?" Henning sounded incredulous. He was standing by the door. The shotgun he still carried seemed ugly and out of place in Rensky's world of photos, books and chess sets.

"Rensky was a chess fanatic. Maybe he was also eccentric—or security conscious. In any case, the other postcards are properly notated, and they're from other people with whom he played postal chess. This deck is a ringer and, if I'm right, they're in a simple code, alternating letters and numbers corresponding to letters to spell out names, dates and any other information he might want to record."

Henning's voice seemed strangely hoarse.

"Why the hell would he want to do that? Assuming that he wasn't simply eccentric."

Douglas shrugged. "I can guess. First, he was dealing with highly sensitive information. But he was also doing a lot of research in East Germany. He risked search every time he went in or out. If routine written notes on the subject of Nazi collaborators in Switzerland were uncovered it might not be taken too kindly by any of the parties involved. Also, there was the danger of leaks if the Germans found his notes; they might warn the subjects of his investigation. So he coded all the important information and mailed it to himself as a postal chess card. He never underestimated the inherent risk in the project; he would be a target right up to the day the book was published. Vorteg somehow found out anyway, and what happened proved Rensky was right in taking the precautions he did. He should have taken more." Douglas reached across the workbench for a pencil and piece of paper. "It will be easy enough to see if I'm right. Let's try decoding some of the cards."

"No, Douglas," Henning said. His voice was flat, drained of emotion. "Leave the cards alone."

Douglas glanced up and found himself looking into the large, black, owl-eyes of the shotgun. He slowly let the pencil drop to the bench, then turned to face Henning squarely. Dragon lifted his head from the

234

worn carpet where he lay and began to growl. Henning moved closer.

"What is it, Henning?" Douglas asked softly. The shotgun had dropped to a point on his chest just above his heart.

The large man nodded curtly toward the stack of postcards. "My father," he said in a voice that was barely above a whisper.

"Karl, I'm sorry." Douglas shook his head. "I'm sorry."

"Shut up, Douglas! He doesn't need your pity, and neither do I! My father made a mistake . . . a long time ago. And he's always regretted it. He told me about it ten years ago. For decades no man in Switzerland has been more patriotic than my father. To have this . . . . *thing* . . . come out now would kill him. The cards must be destroyed."

"Karl, I don't give a *damn* what you do with the cards," Douglas said with feeling. The gun didn't waver. "You can't even be sure your father's name is in there. Maybe Rensky overlooked a few."

"It's there," Henning said flatly. "Vorteg told me. On the tennis court yesterday."

Douglas' breath whistled out through his teeth.

"Oh, yeah," he said. "Did he also tell you that he killed Rensky?"

It seemed to take Henning a long time to get the word out. Finally, he said, "Yes."

"You killed them, didn't you? Vorteg and his son. You didn't want to take a chance on their talking. That's plain enough now."

Henning's eyes flashed. "I don't have to explain myself to you,!" he said with some of the fiery pride that had first attracted Douglas to him, a pride that had

235

seemed sorely lacking the previous afternoon. "You can think what you want!"

"Yours was the only shot I heard."

"Maybe we fired at the same time. You wouldn't have heard a rifle over a shotgun blast. Isn't that beside the point? The important thing is that I didn't kill *you*, Douglas. And I didn't let the Vortegs kill you. Think about that."

"What the hell did you expect would happen?"

"I was hoping . . . everything would work itself out."

Dragon had been silent a long time. As a result, his single, sharp bark startled Henning, causing him to turn his eyes away for just a moment. Disarming Henning was almost ridiculously easy. Douglas reached out and pushed the barrel of the gun with one hand and hit Henning on the jaw with the other. Douglas felt something snap in his hand, but the one blow was enough. Henning dropped the gun and sat down hard on the floor. His eyes were glazed. By the time they cleared again Douglas had the gun trained on him. Henning didn't move.

"Why *didn't* you kill me, Karl?"

Henning didn't answer. Instead, he slowly pulled his jacket away from his body. There was a bullet hole in the material a fraction of an inch from where Henning's ribs would be.

Douglas swallowed hard. "So you did kill them in self-defense. You're still the law around here. You had—have a responsibility. You were going to let two men get away with a murder."

"To save my father. The only thing I was going to do with you was to threaten; I wanted your promise to keep silent." He added as an afterthought, "I don't suppose it would have worked anyway."

236

"It's wrong, Karl. It's all wrong." He felt—and sounded—defensive, and he wasn't sure why.

"What're you, Douglas? A cop?"

Dragon came across the room and lay down at Douglas' feet. Douglas reached down and touched the dog's head. He was surprised to find that his hand was trembling.

Karl Henning pointed to a telephone on a stand at the opposite end of the room. "There's the phone. Call Interpol, if you want. But you just remember that I saved your life. Now it's up to you to decide what to do with my life—and my father's." He paused, then added, "What are you going to do, Douglas?"

Douglas stared at the phone for a long time. Then he picked up Dragon and walked slowly out of the room.

Printed in the United States
26488LVS00004B/90